AUNT
VIOLET'S
LOCKET

BOOKS BY KRISTIN HARPER

AUNT VIOLET'S LOCKET

KRISTIN HARPER

Bookouture

Published by Bookouture in 2024

An imprint of Storyfire Ltd.
Carmelite House
50 Victoria Embankment
London EC4Y 0DZ

www.bookouture.com

ISBN: 978-1-83525-233-8
eBook ISBN: 978-1-83525-232-1

For my mother,
who taught me to be a risk-taker

PROLOGUE

EARLY AUGUST, 1943

The moon cast a silvery path across the dark water and highlighted the waves as they crested and spilled onto the distant sandbars in frothy white pools.

Leaning against the wide trunk of the beech tree, the young woman felt as if she could hardly remember a time when she'd gazed at the seascape simply for the pleasure of admiring its beauty. A time when she wasn't also scanning the water for what might be lurking beneath the surface.

During the past two years, several German U-boats had been detected perilously close to Dune Island, as well as off the coasts of Martha's Vineyard and Nantucket. Residents were instructed to report any unusual sights and sounds to the authorities, a responsibility the locals took very seriously, especially if their property overlooked the ocean, like her family's did.

When will this dreadful war end? She closed her eyes and mouthed a silent prayer for the Allies to prevail, but her petition was interrupted when a twig snapped nearby. Her eyelids flew open and she caught her breath—not from fear, but from anticipation.

"I'm sorry I'm late," the man said in a hushed voice. "I had trouble sneaking away."

She smiled as the tall, slender figure approached. "I was beginning to think you'd stood me up," she teased.

Drawing nearer, he solemnly replied, "I'd never do that to you."

"Not deliberately, no, but you might have had something more important going on."

"As far as I'm concerned, nothing could be more important than giving you this." He cupped her cheek and gently kissed her lips before confessing, "Actually, I was worried that *you* might have grown tired of waiting for me and left."

"I would have waited until sunrise if I'd had to," she assured him. "Although then my father would have sent my brother to look for me, and they'd have found out that I wasn't really out here stargazing."

"Maybe it's time they found out anyway," he suggested. "I've been giving this a lot of thought. I think we should tell our families about us. We can't keep our love a secret forever, especially not if I'm going to ask your father for your hand in marriage."

For the last few months, he'd often expressed his longing for them to become husband and wife, and it was her deepest desire to marry him, too. But this was the first time they'd spoken about marriage in practical terms and there were significant obstacles to consider.

Her tone was laden with regret. "There's nothing I'd love more than to be married to you, but how can I? My father's health and eyesight are getting worse. Pretty soon he won't be able to manage on his own. I can't count on my little brother being around to care for him—Frankie's almost old enough to enlist. My father needs me, and he'd never agree to move off the island."

"That's exactly why I plan to move here. *Permanently.*" He

squeezed her arm for emphasis. "We can live in a little house in town, so you can look in on your father every day and cook his meals, if necessary. Or he can join us for supper at ours."

"You'd really be willing to live in Hope Haven for good?" She'd assumed if they got married they'd have to move, since he wasn't well-suited for employment as a fisherman, shipbuilder or any of the other jobs held by most men on Dune Island. "What would you do for work?"

"I could get a job as a clerk for the steamship authority in Port Newcomb. Or I could work at the bank or in the post office. Or maybe I'll write for the local newspaper."

It sounded as if he'd given their future together a lot of consideration, but she had to be sure he truly understood what he'd be sacrificing to marry her. "Your life is so... so foreign from mine. Sometimes I feel like we come from completely different worlds. You'd be leaving behind everything you know. Your friends, your family..."

He smiled and touched her arm. "None of that matters! My parents could see us during the summer if they wanted to."

"But what about the rest of the year? You might get home-sick for city life. I love how quiet the island is during winter, but if you're not used to it, the seclusion can seem very bleak," she told him. "How can you be sure you'd be content living in a little house on Dune Island year-round?"

"Because Dune Island is where *you* are. So I know I'd never be content living anywhere else." The intensity of his tone melted away the last of her reservations. He added, "It'll be agonizing enough to be separated when I leave Hope Haven for a few months in September."

"I feel that way, too," she murmured, knowing she'd have to rely on memories of their summer together to keep her company until he returned.

"Then it's okay if I tell my parents about us when I get the chance?"

"Yes, if you think it's a good idea. I just hope they won't object to you marrying someone like me—"

He cut her off. "Don't be silly! You're lovely and clever and kind. Of course, they won't object."

She wished she could say her father wouldn't object, either, but he was so protective that she hadn't even told him she had a boyfriend. How was she going to persuade him to agree to their marriage? "If it's all right with you, I'd like to wait until you come back before you talk to my father about our plans. I need time to ease him into the idea."

"I understand." He cleared his throat. "I, erm, I'll have an engagement ring to give you when I propose properly. For now, there's something else I'd like you to have."

He slid his hand into his pocket and withdrew a small object. Even in the moonlight, she could tell that the heart-shaped pendant was made of sterling silver. It was one of the few metals that wasn't rationed during the war, but it was very costly. Handing it to her, he seemed embarrassed to admit, "I'm so sorry, there's no chain but—"

"That's okay," she said quickly. "A separate chain would draw attention and then someone might ask where I got it. I'll add this heart to the one I'm already wearing."

Ever since she was twelve years old, she'd worn a gold chain and cross that she'd inherited from her late mother tucked inside her modest, high-collar shirts. The young woman unfastened the necklace and deftly threaded the chain through the loop of the pendant. Then she held it up, dangling it at eye level. "It's beautiful. Thank you."

"It opens, like a locket," he informed her. "The inside is engraved. I'll light a match so you can read it."

"No, we'd better not take the risk." Although mandatory nighttime blackouts were no longer deemed necessary on the island the way they were the year the US first entered the war, many residents continued to exercise precautions along the shoreline. And she didn't want her family or someone up the hill to spot them. Besides, whatever was inscribed in the locket, she wanted to hear it from his lips while she still could. "I'd like you to tell me what it says, please."

She gave the necklace to him, turned her back and gathered her hair from the nape of her neck. He was all thumbs as he struggled to fasten the ends of the chain together and his bumbling touch made her shiver. After he'd softly recited the inscription into her ear, she turned to look him in the eye.

"Yes, I will," she answered, nodding. "I promise."

ONE

"*I've* inherited my great-aunt's cottage?" Paige Taylor repeated incredulously, pressing the phone against her ear. "Are you sure?"

"Yes. You're the sole beneficiary of Violet Atkins' entire estate," the attorney, Steve Reagan, confirmed. His voice was level and soft but it did little to calm Paige's reaction.

"How can that be? I've never even met her. I've never been to Dune Island, either."

Frankly, Paige had never *wanted* to visit the popular summer destination. Located off the Massachusetts coast, the island may have been renowned for its stunning views, pristine beaches, and picturesque historic charm. But she'd grown up hearing stories about what a sad, secluded life her great-aunt had lived there. So Paige felt conflicted about inheriting the cottage and property, and she couldn't quite believe the attorney had the facts straight.

"My grandfather and my mother are deceased, which means my aunt Sherry is Violet's closest surviving relative," she informed him. "I also have a brother, as well as three cousins on that side of my family. So why would Violet name *me* as the sole beneficiary?"

"She *didn't* name you, specifically, as her sole beneficiary," Steve pointedly corrected her error. "She bequeathed the property to her *eldest single female descendant who isn't married or engaged to be married*. In your family, that happens to be you."

Even though he was simply making a statement, Paige's cheeks burned. She'd been stigmatized for being single by her relatives so often that she felt self-conscious to hear him emphasize she was the *eldest single female* in the family. "I don't see what my marital status has to do with inheriting the estate."

"I can't be sure of Violet's intentions, since I've never spoken directly to her. I'm only managing this case because her attorney retired," Steve explained. "But my guess is that when she created the terms of her living trust, she was copying what her father had done for her."

"What do you mean?"

"He probably left the house and property solely to her because Violet didn't have a husband to provide for her financially. It was a way of guaranteeing she'd always have a place to live."

"That's kind of chauvinistic," Paige muttered, aware she sounded ungrateful, but she was annoyed at the notion that women couldn't support themselves.

"It may sound old-fashioned now, but that's sometimes how things were done, with good reason. On a small island like this, it would've been difficult for a single woman to earn a livable income," Steve said. "Anyway, I think you'll love her place. It's a quintessential Hope Haven cottage."

"Meaning what, that it's cute and cozy? Because I had the idea it was sort of tumble-down and weather-beaten."

Steve chuckled at her frankness. "Well, obviously, the cottage is habitable, otherwise the property management company wouldn't have been able to attract tenants for the past decade. But it might need a new roof and windows. The interior could benefit from some updating, too. Not that the utility workers who lived there during the off-season cared—they've always been young bachelors who were more interested in surfing than in the décor. And considering the property includes incredible ocean views and a private beach, the summer tenants knew what a great deal they were getting, so they never complained about the rustic accommodations. But if you're going to live in it year-round, you'll probably want to make the place more comfortable."

"Year-round? I'm not going to live in in it year-round!" Paige had just moved nearer to the hospital in Chicago where she worked as an in-patient nurse, and she still had a mountain of unpacked boxes in her living room. "I'm so busy that I'm not sure when I'd even make it to Hope Haven for vacation."

"Ah, well." Steve's voice fell flat. "I'm sorry if I haven't been clear about the terms of your inheritance, but there's a stipulation requiring you to live in the cottage year-round in order to retain ownership. Renting it out isn't permitted. And if you decide to sell the estate at any time, you must split the proceeds equally with the rest of Violet's great-nieces and great-nephews, regardless of whether they're married or not."

"What an odd requirement," Paige remarked. "Why would she try to force me to live in Hope Haven?" *Especially since she was so lonely and isolated there.*

"I doubt Violet was trying to *force* anyone to live in the cottage. I think she may have wanted to ensure the family home was available permanently to the relative who might need it — instead of giving it to someone who'd just use it as their family vacation house or rent it out during the summer months to turn a profit."

"But *she* rented it out during the summer months. During the winter, too."

"Yes, but that was for the purpose of offsetting the expenses of her off-island nursing home care. From what I understand, she was hopeful it was only a temporary arrangement and that eventually she'd return to Hope Haven and live independently again... Sadly, that didn't happen."

"No, it didn't," Paige acknowledged somberly.

After a respectful pause, Steve suggested, "It might be wise to take some time to really think this over. There's a tenant at the cottage whose lease runs until early June, so your hands are tied for the next three months anyway. But once he's gone, I'd strongly advise you to come see the estate in person, so you know what you'll be losing if you decide to give it up."

"There's no *if* about it," Paige emphatically replied. "I'm not relocating, so that means my only option is to sell."

"Even more reason to visit Hope Haven," he insisted. "You can inspect the cottage, make repairs, and hire a real estate agent. I think you'll find a trip out here will be worth your time and effort."

Paige hesitated. It was only March, but work had been so hectic that she'd already begun counting the days until summer. She had accrued over three weeks of vacation time and she intended to spend most of it at Lake Tahoe with friends she'd made on the West Coast when she'd worked as a traveling ER nurse. But she supposed preparing to put the cottage on the market was more important than relaxing with friends. After all, selling Violet's place would allow her to pay off a big chunk of her exorbitant mortgage—and reducing her debt would significantly decrease her stress levels.

"You're probably right," she reluctantly conceded. "I'll rearrange my travel plans for June."

Out of a sense of respect, Paige wanted to speak to her aunt Sherry before telling her brother, Dustin, or any of her cousins about the inheritance. Steve had already informed Sherry that

Violet had died, but he hadn't discussed the inheritance with her.

So Paige called Sherry and explained the terms of Violet's living trust. She told her aunt she'd already made up her mind to sell the cottage and share the money with her brother and cousins, but she still felt a little guilty about it.

"It seems unfair that Violet didn't leave the estate to you, Aunt Sherry. You're more closely related to her than I am," Paige said, because Violet's brother, Frank, Paige's grandfather, had been Sherry's father.

"I'm truly glad she didn't leave it to me. I wouldn't have wanted the headache of selling another home," asserted Sherry. "Besides, when your grandpa Frank died, I was the sole beneficiary of *his* property, since your mother had already passed away. So now it's your turn to receive an inheritance... But are you certain you want to sell it?"

"Absolutely. I just moved, so I'm staying put for at least five years. And the next time I relocate, it won't be to live in a dinky little hut in an island town where I don't know anyone."

Paige's position at work was so demanding that she'd recently bought a condo closer to the hospital, so she could at least eliminate the stress of a long commute. As it was, city living came with a different set of stressors, but Paige had no intention of leaving Chicago, where she was earning the highest salary of her career. Before taking her current position, she'd only been working part-time because she'd moved back to her hometown in the suburbs to provide end-of-life care for her grandmother. So now she had some financial catching-up to do.

She added, "I'll be able to use the money from selling Violet's cottage to make bigger payments on my mortgage, which will be a huge relief." She smiled at the thought.

"I can only imagine what the boys will buy with their shares of the profit." Sherry still referred to Dustin, Christopher, and Rick as "the boys," even though they were in their late thirties and early forties. "You haven't told any of them about the inheritance yet?"

"Nope. I haven't told Tara, either. I'm going to schedule a video call with everyone as soon as possible so I can tell all of them about the inheritance at the same time."

"I wonder how they'll react. Can I join the call, too?"

"Absolutely!" said Paige. Her aunt Sherry had been more of a mother figure to Paige and her brother, Dustin, than their stepmother ever had been. Paige wouldn't have dreamed of excluding her from such an important family announcement. "Please remember to keep the reason for the call a secret, though. I want them to be surprised."

The next day, Paige sat at her small, round kitchen table, smiling at her family's faces as they peered back at her from her laptop screen. She was pleased that her brother and three cousins were able to join her and Sherry on a video call at such short notice. It had probably helped that Paige had hinted they'd be extremely happy when they heard her urgent news.

After brief greetings, she introduced the topic of the inheritance. "As you're all aware, our great-aunt Violet died in February," she began.

"Hold on," Dustin immediately interrupted. "I wasn't aware of that."

"You *should* be aware of it," Sherry declared. "I got the news while you three boys were at the cabin, ice fishing. I called and told Rick."

"Well, he never told me."

Rick argued, "I did, too. You must have forgotten."

"Um, I think I'd remember if you told me a family member had died." Dustin sounded insulted, yet in the next breath he asked, "Which one was Violet again?"

Tara snickered. "She was our great-aunt. Grandpa Frank's sister. My mother's father—your mother's father, too."

"I know *that*, Tara. I'm not stupid. I meant I don't have any context for who she is. Like, where she lived and who her husband was. Or why we've never heard about her until she's dead."

"Seriously, Dustin, do you ever listen to anything anyone tells you?" scoffed Paige. "I can't believe you don't remember the stories Aunt Sherry told us about her when we were young."

Trying to jog his cousin's memory, Christopher interjected, "Violet was the eccentric spinster who lived on an island in the middle of the Atlantic."

"Aha. No wonder you remember stories about her and I don't, Paige—you two have so much in common," Dustin ribbed her.

"Hey, you shouldn't imply that your sister's an old maid," Christopher chided him, much to Paige's surprise. But then he added, "Paige has been married forever... to her *job*."

His zinger made Dustin and Rick crack up. Despite their ages, the three guys still found it amusing to push Paige's buttons and to her chagrin, she still had a knee-jerk reaction to their teasing.

"I have *nothing* in common with Violet," she replied hotly. "And for your information, Dustin, the reason I scheduled this call was to tell you something very important, so it would be helpful if you'd quit goofing off."

"Who's goofing off? I asked a legitimate question about our great-aunt Violet. I'm expressing an interest—isn't that part of being a good listener?"

Once again, Dustin's comeback made Christopher and Rick guffaw, but Paige was losing her patience. Fortunately, Sherry cut in.

"If you're sincerely interested in hearing about Violet's life, I'll tell you what my father told me, Dustin. But I don't want any interruptions until I'm finished. No wisecracks, either."

When Sherry used that tone, everyone knew she meant business. They were completely silent as she recounted their great-aunt's story...

"Violet was my father Frank's older sister and only sibling. As you know, their last name was Atkins. They lived in a little cottage in Highland Hills, which is the remotest of the five villages in Hope Haven, on Dune Island. Their mother died when they were children, so their father raised them on his own. He worked in the shipyard, but by the time Violet and Frank were teenagers, he had to quit for health reasons—he had diabetes and eventually he lost most of his vision to glaucoma.

"As I said, their home was very small. They didn't live in poverty, but money was always tight. A very wealthy family, the Hathaways, owned a mansion up the hill from them and they'd visit the island every summer. Your grandpa Frank claimed they were as arrogant as they were rich, and he resented the way they looked down their noses—literally—at his family's house.

"He especially disliked the youngest Hathaway son, Edward, an arrogant college student who went to Harvard. Supposedly Edward had a heart condition so he was exempted from the draft—this was during World War Two, of course—but there were rumors that his family had bribed a doctor to claim Edward was unfit to serve. Most people, including your grandpa Frank, believed the gossip. Not Violet. She always stood up for him. To Frank's embarrassment, she'd lecture her brother about how no one truly knows the condition of someone else's heart, inside or out, so they shouldn't judge.

"During the summer of 1943, the Hathaways hired Violet to babysit Edward's little nephew. Or was it his cousin? Either way, that's how Violet and Edward crossed paths on a regular basis. They'd chat when Edward came by to drop the boy off at the cottage, or when Violet walked the child back to the mansion in the evening. Somewhere along the line, she must have developed a crush on Edward and mistakened his politeness toward her for romantic attraction.

"It was utterly preposterous to think a guy like him would have been interested in a girl like her. Not that Edward was such a catch, but his family was extremely wealthy—they came from old money—and hers was working-class poor. Also, Violet was a little socially awkward around the opposite gender and her father was so protective of her that she'd never been on a date or had a boyfriend, even though she was eighteen. Anyway, she construed a fantasy that she and Edward were an item, as they used to say.

"At the end of the summer, Violet discovered Edward was interested in an off-island visitor named Catherine something-or-the-other, I can't remember her last name. Apparently, Edward had taken photos of her in a swimsuit on the staircase to the beach near the cottage. Violet was so furious she tracked them down at the yacht club and threw Catherine's camera in the water. She caused a terrible scene, yelling and screaming about how she was a better match for Edward than Catherine was. When he denied that he'd ever had any feelings for Violet, she tore up the Hathaway family's ration book of gasoline stamps, which they needed to buy fuel for their boat.

"Keep in mind, your great-aunt was ordinarily so shy and reserved that when she was in school, she'd earned the nickname 'Shrinking Violet.' The Hathaways knew how meek she usually was—she'd been their trusted babysitter all summer. They also knew that she didn't have a mother to give her advice about boys and dating. It wasn't right of her to destroy the ration book, but it seemed the Hathaways could've exercised a little mercy and de-escalated her meltdown. Instead, they summoned a couple of nearby Coast Guardsmen, who carted her off to their headquarters.

"After she agreed to reimburse Catherine for her camera and Violet's father gave the Hathaways his ration of gas, the authorities dropped the matter. But Hope Haven was a tiny community and several of Violet's peers had witnessed her outburst. The gossip about what she did spread like wildfire. The kids even came up with a new nickname for her—'Violent Violet.' She was either so ashamed of making a public spectacle of herself or so brokenhearted about being jilted by Edward that she sequestered herself away in the cottage for weeks on end.

"Meanwhile, her brother, Frank, had to endure cruel remarks and exaggerated rumors about her behavior. Since no one saw Violet for a while, his classmates made up wild stories. They claimed that after she'd gone crazy at the yacht club, she'd been confined in an asylum.

"But it was what people said about Violet tearing up the ration book that infuriated her brother the most. You see, the islanders prided themselves on doing everything they could to contribute to the war effort. In fact, your grandpa Frank was a volunteer blackout warden. He'd ride his bicycle from one end of Highland Hills to the other in the dark, checking to make sure the residents were complying with the blackout requirements. There was such a strong sense of community spirit, that many people thought it was unpatriotic for Violet to destroy her neighbor's ration book, no matter why she did it. Your grandpa Frank's peers made terrible slurs against her—against the entire family—and he got into daily fistfights defending their reputation.

"On top of dealing with taunts and black eyes, he had to cope with his father's declining health and his sister's emotional breakdown. Every evening he could hear her crying in her bedroom. At first, he felt sorry for her, but when it kept up night after night, week after week, he began to lose tolerance.

"You have to understand, he was only fifteen or sixteen and he'd never dated anyone, either. So he became angry at Violet for carrying on like that over a man he considered a chicken, as well as for disgracing their family name. He was also angry at the Hathaways for treating his sister so harshly and angry at the islanders for mocking his family. Who knows, maybe he was even angry because his father was going blind. And because he was powerless to change their family's situation.

"In any case, he dropped out of school, left Hope Haven and caught a train to the Midwest, where he got a job working in the stockyards. He missed his family, but he didn't miss Dune Island—it held too many upsetting memories for him. The only time he returned was to attend his father's funeral, about four years later.

"By then, Edward had also died—in a skiing accident, I believe. Violet apparently had never gotten over being rejected by him and scorned by her peers. It wasn't as if she never spoke to anyone on the island again, but she'd become very reclusive. She worked at home, taking in sewing projects to earn a living, and she only left the property when it was absolutely necessary.

"Over the years, your grandpa Frank and Violet drifted further apart, but there wasn't any animosity between them. It was as if she accepted that he didn't want to come back to the cottage and he accepted why she didn't want to leave it. They sent birthday cards to each other every year and my mother always mailed Violet a Christmas newsletter. So, she heard updates about our family, including about the four of you, but she never replied with news of her own.

"After many years, my mother eventually grew tired of trying to keep in touch with her—I think she felt rebuffed—so she stopped reaching out. I'd never met Violet and I didn't want to force a connection since she clearly wasn't interested, so I never wrote to her, either. Everything I've learned about the last part of Violet's life is from what her attorney recently told me after her death.

"He said she was still living on her own in the cottage until about ten years ago. Then she fell and broke her hip and had to move to an off-island care facility. During that time, she rented her Dune Island home to temporary tenants. Three years ago, she had a stroke, and after that, she never regained her ability to speak. Last month, on February twenty-third, Violet died. She was ninety-nine years old."

Sherry paused to take a long swallow of water. For a moment, no one dared to say anything for fear of being scolded for interrupting. Paige had heard bits and pieces about her great-aunt and grandfather's difficult years as teenagers many times before now, but until today she'd never heard the entire account all at once. She found her ancestors' history to be deeply upsetting and it was also sad to imagine Violet spending her final years alone in a nursing home, even if she hadn't wanted any family members to visit her. But she could tell from the way Christopher's eyes had glazed over and her brother was fidgeting that they weren't moved by the story. They probably wished Dustin had never asked to hear more about their great-aunt.

Finally, Sherry set down her glass and said, "So, now that you know who Violet was, I'll let Paige share her news."

It seemed almost irreverent to jump right into talking about the inheritance, but Paige knew she wouldn't be able to hold the guys' attention much longer and she cut to the chase. "Violet's attorney recently contacted me and it turns out I've inherited her estate. Over the years, the cottage has become run-down, but the property is on the waterfront, so it's probably worth a mint—"

The words were barely out of her mouth before Dustin cut in. "You? Why you? You didn't know her any better than the rest of us did."

"She wanted to leave the house to a female family member," Paige started to explain.

Again, she was interrupted by an outcry of protest from Dustin, and Tara whined, "But *I'm* a female family member and I'm older than you are. Why didn't she leave the property to *me?*"

"Because you're married and I'm not," Paige said.

"Exactly!" exclaimed Tara. "I've got three children. My family needs a summer cottage more than you do. Glenn and I could rent it out and use the money to—"

Paige shut her down. "Listen, could everyone please stop getting bent out of shape and let me finish explaining the terms of Violet's trust? I think you'll all be very pleased."

"Doubtful," muttered Dustin.

But he was the first to cheer after Paige told them about her plans to sell the estate and split the proceeds equally among them. Even before she had the chance to ask for help, he volunteered to accompany her to Dune Island to assess what improvements needed to be made before putting the cottage on the market. Rick, Christopher, and Tara all agreed to come and give her a hand at some point during her stay, too.

Their excitement bolstered Paige's confidence that selling the estate was the right decision, and it made her feel more enthusiastic about the trip to Hope Haven. *It won't be the same as going to a resort on Lake Tahoe*, she thought after the call ended. *But maybe with everyone helping, in between making repairs and cleaning the cottage we'll have enough time to enjoy a little R&R together as a family...*

TWO

Paige stood at the bow of the ferry's car deck, craning her neck and squinting. She was trying to catch a glimpse of Dune Island in the distance, but the dense fog prevented her from seeing more than thirty yards ahead.

Seems fitting, she thought wryly, because so far her excursion wasn't exactly going according to plan.

Back in March, when she'd first told her brother and cousins about the inheritance, they'd seemed sincere about helping her make Violet's estate more appealing to prospective buyers. But once summer rolled around, they supposedly all had compelling reasons why they couldn't spend any amount of time, not even a long weekend, at the cottage. So now, three months after their initial offers to pitch in, Paige was making the trip by herself.

I hope the weather isn't usually this damp because I haven't brought enough warm clothes, she thought, pushing her bangs to one side. The moisture in the air had collected on the ends of her wispy brown hair, making it limper than usual. She really should've gotten it cut before she'd left home. It was going to hang in her eyes for the next two to three weeks, unless she visited a salon on the island—and going to a new stylist was always a hit-or-miss experience.

I'd better just clip it back, she decided, even though the idea of a makeover was appealing. Not only did she need a haircut, but as her cousin Tara had so helpfully pointed out recently, Paige could probably stand to lose a few pounds. There were shadows beneath her eyes, too.

Almost thirty-eight years old, she didn't have any hangups about her weight or complexion, the way she did when her cousin criticized her as a teenager. But as a nurse, Paige recognized she could benefit physically from changing her eating habits and getting more exercise and sleep.

I guess I haven't done myself any favors with all that stress-eating in the breakroom. Or by binge-watching TV at night to unwind, she admitted to herself, just as her phone buzzed. Unsurprisingly, it was Tara.

"Do I hear the ocean? You were supposed to call me as soon as you got there. Is the cottage as ramshackle as my mother said it was?" she asked, clearly more interested in hearing about their great-aunt's home than in whether Paige had a smooth thousand-mile road trip from Illinois to Massachusetts.

"That's not the ocean, it's the wind and I haven't arrived at the cottage yet. I'm standing on the ferry deck."

"Working on your tan already?" Tara clucked her tongue. "Too much sun will give you wrinkles, you know."

Too much sun can do a lot worse damage to someone's body than that, Paige thought. "No danger of that happening. I always wear sunscreen. Besides, it's so foggy I can hardly see my hand in front of my face."

"You're lucky it's not raining cats and dogs like it is here. Cami and I scored a last-minute tour of The Landing because there was a cancellation, so it had better stop raining by tomorrow morning."

Tara's twenty-year-old daughter, Cami, had just become

engaged to be married the following June, which is why Tara claimed she couldn't help Paige at the cottage. She was throwing an engagement party for Cami in late August, and she was on a mission to find the perfect lakeside venue for it.

"Hopefully, it'll clear up overnight," said Paige. "But if it doesn't, at least you'll have a realistic idea of what to expect if the weather's crummy on the day of the party."

"Thanks a lot." Tara huffed. She'd always been high-strung, but lately she seemed to take offense at the smallest thing, especially if it was related to the engagement party. And somehow, *every*thing was related to the engagement party. "You shouldn't even mention the possibility of rain on Cami's big day! Don't you know how much money Glenn and I are pouring into this event?"

It was a rhetorical question, since Tara had already told her several times what their budget was for the celebration. Paige could hardly imagine spending that amount on a wedding, much less, on an engagement party and to her, it seemed like a frivolous expenditure. But to be fair, Tara probably couldn't imagine spending the amount of money that Paige had spent getting her nursing degree, either.

"I know—it's a small fortune," she responded. "And it should go without saying that I really hope Cami and Dylan's day is all clear skies and bright sunshine. I only meant that if it rains tomorrow, you can check out what the indoor area and view of the lake will be like in the *unlikely* event of bad weather on the day of the party."

There was a momentary pause before Tara sighed. "Yeah, I guess you're right. See? This is why I wish you weren't out of town during the initial planning stage. You think of practical things I'm too stressed to consider."

Tara wasn't a fan of delegating, so it was futile to suggest she hire an event planner. Knowing that what her cousin really wanted was someone to help her make decisions, Paige gamely offered, "If you text me photos, I'm happy to chime in with my questions and opinions."

"That's not the same. You can't get a true sense of a place unless you're there in person."

Although her cousin's grumbling was getting on her nerves, Paige kept her response light. "I agree but unfortunately, I can't be in two places at once, and this is the only time I could get away since I'd already scheduled time off. Your mom's just a couple miles down the road from you. Now that she's back from visiting her in-laws in Michigan, she'll be thrilled to help you plan the party." Paige couldn't help adding, "If anyone's going to need help during the next few weeks, it's *me*."

Her complaint seemed to sail right over Tara's head. "Yeah, too bad you and Trevor aren't still together. You could've recruited him to help you with the repairs—although he didn't seem like the kind of guy who'd be very handy swinging a hammer, did he?"

Paige had been seeing Trevor, a literature professor at a local college, for almost a year when he'd split up with her in January. The breakup had come as a shock to Paige because other than a few minor quibbles, there hadn't been any hint of conflict between them. His laid-back personality had been the perfect complement to her ambitious nature, and vice versa—everyone had said so, including Paige and Trevor themselves.

They'd seemed so compatible that when he'd announced he had something important to discuss, she'd thought he'd wanted to talk about marriage. Instead, he'd told her that as much as he cared for her, he'd realized he just wasn't ready to be in a serious relationship after all. She'd been stunned, since he'd never expressed dissatisfaction before then.

"I don't get it," she'd exclaimed. "If you were unhappy with the way things were between us, why didn't you talk to me sooner, so we could've worked it out? Why jump to something drastic like breaking up?"

She'd still wanted to discuss whatever changes the two of them might make to improve their relationship. But Trevor had given her a twist on the classic it's-not-you-it's-me excuse, claiming there was nothing either of them needed to do or change, it was just the way they were. Once he'd made up his mind, he wouldn't reconsider. He wouldn't discuss it further, either.

A few weeks later, Paige was floored again when Trevor left Illinois to spend a semester teaching in Ireland. There'd been an unexpected opening in a study abroad program, and he'd jumped at the chance to go. It was almost as if he was running away. Or running scared, according to Paige's best friend Mia.

"Maybe the problem isn't that he doesn't *want* to be in a serious relationship. Maybe it's that he's *scared* of being in one," Mia had surmised. "He's probably never been this close to anyone. Maybe it's freaking him out."

"Freaking him out? He's forty, not fourteen!"

"Exactly. He's forty and he's never been married or in a relationship that's lasted over a year. Sounds like he's got a fear of intimacy."

"Careful there." Paige resented the stereotypes assigned to people over a certain age who'd never been married or made a long-term romantic commitment. "I'm almost forty and I'm still single, but I don't think *I* have a fear of intimacy."

"No, but your boyfriend does, trust me."

"My *ex*-boyfriend," Paige had mumbled sadly.

She'd wept off and on for about a month following Trevor's departure. But eventually she'd come to realize she was more frustrated than brokenhearted about him ditching her out of the blue and for no good reason. By March, she'd accepted the fact —even if she didn't fully understand it—that he simply didn't think they were a good, long-term fit.

But on some level, she must have been harboring unsettled feelings toward him because she felt queasy when Tara mentioned his name just now. Or was that from motion sickness? She wrapped her arm around her waist. She had already promised herself that she wouldn't think about work while she was away, because she wanted this trip to be as relaxing as possible. She made a mental note not to think about Trevor, either.

"Hello? You still there?" Tara asked and Paige realized she'd lost the thread of their conversation.

"Sorry, can you repeat that?"

"I said it just occurred to me that if you were the one who'd gotten engaged instead of Cami, then she would have inherited the cottage. So in a way, it's to your advantage that Trevor broke up with you."

Yeah, lucky me, Paige thought drolly. *Another breakup.*

"How is that to my advantage? If Cami had inherited the cottage, she wouldn't have wanted to relocate to Dune Island to live in it, either. That means *she'd* be the one responsible for fixing it up and putting it on the market. She'd still have to split the profit with the rest of us. So as far as I can see, the only 'advantage' of inheriting the cottage is that I've also inherited all the work of selling it."

"Oh, c'mon. You might have to do a little cleaning or painting here and there, but we all agreed you could hire contractors for the heavy lifting and deduct their fees from the profit of the sale. It's not as if staying at one of the most beautiful vacation spots in the country is a hardship," scoffed Tara. "I'd give anything to spend the next two weeks lolling about on the beach. But as you know, I've got a major party to plan *and* I simultaneously need to start researching Cami's options for the wedding. My head feels like—"

Her sentence was thankfully drowned out when the overhead loudspeaker crackled with static, followed by an announcement instructing drivers to return to their vehicles.

"Listen, it's almost time to disembark. I've got to go," Paige said. "I'll call you later."

"Don't forget to text photos. I want to see if the estate is truly worth what everyone seems to think it is."

"Right. Bye." Turning around, Paige headed down the narrow lane between the parked vehicles. Just as she was removing her key from her pocket, the ferry blasted its whistle. She flinched and dropped the key fob, which skittered across the slippery deck, disappearing beneath the expensive imported convertible parked to her left.

Paige crouched down and tilted her head, but she couldn't see the key. She dropped to her knees and peered beneath the car; the key was out of reach. Groaning with frustration, she lowered herself flat on her stomach on the damp, cold surface and stretched her arm as far as she could. But the key lay just beyond her fingertips.

Now what? She supposed she could ask another driver if they had a long object, like an umbrella, that she could use to sweep the key from beneath the convertible.

"Hey, you there! What do you think you're doing? That's my car!" someone shrieked, clapping her hands as if trying to frighten away a pesky animal.

Paige lifted her head to see a pair of metallic-pink stiletto sandals and ten perfectly pedicured toes pointing in her direction. Clumsily hoisting herself onto all fours, she explained, "I dropped my key and I can't reach it. Do you have an umbrella I could use to push it out?" Paige rolled back onto her heels and looked up to meet the woman's eyes, but she was wearing dark sunglasses.

"No. I don't want you poking around under my car with an umbrella," she objected. "You'll have to wait until the line starts moving and I can pull forward."

"She can't do that, Lexie," said a man's voice. Paige had been so dismayed that she hadn't noticed he'd come up behind the woman and was peering over her shoulder. "If she isn't in her car when the traffic starts disembarking, she'll be fined for holding up the vehicles behind her."

"Sorry, not my problem," said Lexie with a shrug.

The man made an exasperated growling sound. "Arg. *I'll* get it for her."

He pushed past the woman, scowling. He was wearing a white Oxford shirt, a blue silk twill tie, and dark slacks. The couple looked as if they might be coming from—or going to—an important meeting or event.

Feeling guilty, Paige protested, "I don't want you to get your clothes dirty. Like I said, if I had something long to use, I could swipe at it. It doesn't have to be an umbrella—even a rolled-up newspaper would work."

The man ignored her and dropped to the deck with the agility of someone who was accustomed to doing a hundred pushups before breakfast. Tipping his head of thick, close-cropped blondish hair, he peeked beneath the car and swiftly scooped up the key. In one fluid motion, he hopped up and deposited it into Paige's open palm.

"Thank you," she said, rising to her feet, too. They were standing almost face-to-face, and his blue-gray eyes met hers long enough for her to notice the golden fleck in his right iris before he looked away and shifted closer to the convertible.

"No problem," he muttered, but his tightly clenched jaw indicated the opposite. For someone so handsome, he sure had an unattractive attitude.

Paige squeezed past him and Lexie. *If those two are an example of how most summer people on Dune Island behave, it's no wonder Grandpa Frank never wanted to visit his hometown,* she thought as she hurried to her car. *Fortunately for me, I'll only be here for a couple weeks, not an entire lifetime.*

.   .   .

From her online research, Paige had learned that the collective Dune Island community known as Hope Haven was comprised of five individual towns: Port Newcomb. Lucinda's Hamlet. Benjamin's Manor. Rockfield. And Highland Hills—that was where her great-aunt's cottage was located.

She'd also read that Lucinda's Hamlet was called "Lucy's Ham" by the locals. The other four towns were commonly referred to as hamlets or villages, too, which struck her as pretentious. As if they were trying too hard to sound quaint. But after disembarking the ferry and catching her first glimpse of Port Newcomb, Paige decided that "hamlet" was appropriate after all.

Even though it was Hope Haven's biggest and busiest town, Port Newcomb was tiny compared to the cities and suburbs Paige had lived in. Its crescent-shaped Main Street hosted a row of shops, galleries, eateries, and bars on one side. On the other side, the port, yacht club, and jetty were almost completely obscured by fog; only the lighthouse's rotating beam shone through it.

As she pulled onto the primary thoroughfare to cut across the island, Paige glanced at her dashboard. It was almost 5:30. She'd have to hurry to pick up the housekey from the attorney, Steve Reagan, whose office was in Rockfield. Although she'd programmed her phone's GPS navigation to guide her, the narrator's voice kept cutting in and out. Because of the low visibility, Paige almost missed the turn-off for the town center.

Rockfield's Main Street looked like a smaller version of Port Newcomb's, except it didn't run alongside the harbor. In addition to the boutiques, bakeries and restaurants Paige drove by, she passed two inns, a library, and a small Congregational meetinghouse. She parked parallel with the town green and hurried along the brick sidewalk, past the picket fences overflowing with hydrangeas, azaleas, and rhododendrons, to a stately old home that had been converted into the attorney's office.

"First of all, welcome to Hope Haven," Steve said after she'd taken a seat in a plush armchair across from his desk. "But I'm sorry you're here under these circumstances,"

"Thank you," Paige replied, even though it felt odd to receive condolences for the loss of a relative she'd never met.

"We've already discussed the most important matters over the phone and email, but it's always a pleasure to meet a client in person," he remarked conversationally, obviously in no rush to leave the office for the weekend. "Especially a client who also will be a neighbor—my wife, Gretchen, and I live in Highland Hills, too."

"Close to Violet's house?"

"Relatively speaking, yes. I live about eight dunes to the south." He bobbed his head and grinned as if he'd made a joke, but Paige didn't get the punchline.

"Have you lived in Highland Hills all your life?" she asked.

"No. I grew up in Rockfield. Then I went to college and law school in Boston. After I came back, I felt like I needed some, uh, some breathing room from my parents. I got lucky and found a house for sale in Highland Hills."

Smiling at the personal nature of his admission, Paige relaxed again. "How far apart are Rockfield and Highland Hills?"

"Not very—the two towns border each other. But sometimes it's the illusion of distance that matters. Trust me, Highland Hills feels like it's a million miles away from everything and everyone."

He explained that the park service owned most of the territory in Highland Hills, so private residences were few and far in between. While the other four Hope Haven towns were primarily bordered by calmer waters, Highland Hills faced the wide-open Atlantic Ocean. Steve suggested it was this rare combination of extreme solitude plus its extraordinary vantage point that made Violet's property so breathtaking.

I wonder if that's his way of emphasizing the positive instead of focusing on what's wrong with the cottage, Paige mused.

"Your great-aunt was a rarity, you know."

His remark seemed to come out of the blue and Paige's guard went up, remembering how deeply the small-town gossip had affected her grandpa Frank and Violet. "I thought you said you'd never spoken to her."

"I hadn't. By the time I bought my place in Highland Hills, she'd already been admitted to the nursing facility off island. Even if I'd moved sooner, we probably wouldn't have connected. I don't think she was a very social person, especially not after—"

He abruptly stopped talking, but Paige realized that as someone who'd grown up on the island, he'd probably heard gossip about Violet. She completed his sentence for him with a vague reference, saying, "Especially not after her father got sick when she was young."

"After her father got sick, yes." Steve's ears were flaming red. "What I meant about Violet being a rarity is that not many people live year-round in Highland Hills. It's too isolated. As I said, there are some artists' cottages and a few big summer homes, but there are only a handful of residences that are inhabitable in the winter. Your great-aunt's home is weatherized, but just barely. It takes a certain kind of person to live in such a far-flung area during the winter."

"*You* live there during the winter," Paige pointed out.

Steve nodded agreeably—he seemed to do that a lot. "I like to think of myself as a rarity, too," he said, and Paige realized he'd intended his remark about Violet as a compliment, not an insult. "It took my wife a while to get used to the solitude, but now she loves it that our home is surrounded by nothing but heathland and dunes on both sides, and the ocean in the front. Violet's property is the same way."

"But doesn't she have summer neighbors next door?" Paige

hinted, hoping to find out whether the Hathaways would be vacationing while she was there, without directly asking Steve about them.

"Ah, yes, the Hathaway family is up the hill. If they haven't already arrived to open their house for the season, they should be there shortly. The extended family comes and goes throughout the summer. One of their grandchildren is getting married on the island in August, I believe."

"Sounds like you know them pretty well, even though they're not here year-round," remarked Paige.

"It's a small island. During the winter, we locals don't have a lot to do except gossip about each other... and about the summer people." He was undoubtedly poking fun at himself and the full-time residents, but Paige recognized there was a grain of truth to his jest, too. "Besides, everyone knows about the Hathaways. They were born-and-bred Dune Islanders for at least a century before their descendants moved away. Now, even though most of them only visit during the summer, you'll notice several streets, parks, and buildings named after them. They definitely left their mark on Dune Island."

They definitely left their mark on my family's life, too, Paige thought, chewing her bottom lip. Although she'd known the Hathaways were very wealthy, she hadn't realized they'd had such longevity and widespread influence as islanders. *That's probably another reason Grandpa Frank didn't want to come back after what happened between Edward and his sister... He must've felt intimidated.*

Steve wrapped up the subject by saying, "Anyway, I'm sure you'll get a chance to meet them."

"That will be nice," she fibbed.

He leaned forward and showed her a paper map, using a highlighter to trace the best way to get to Violet's cottage. "Once you exit the main route, you'll turn right onto the scenic road. Usually, I'd tell you to follow that until you reach the Hathaways' house, because it's so obvious, you can't miss it. But today the fog's as thick as pea soup—or, as we islanders like to say, as thick as clam chowder."

He caught Paige's eye, and she couldn't be sure if the residents really used that expression or if he was joking. Either way, it made her smile at him.

Steve continued, "So instead of using their house as a landmark, I'd say go about two miles. Eventually, you'll see a low stone wall running just beyond the shoulder of the road—it marks the perimeter of the Hathaways' property. Right after you get to the far corner of the wall, there's a sign for Spindrift Lane. It's a dirt road that blends in with the terrain, so it's easy to miss. Follow it down the hill to Violet's cottage."

"Great," said Paige, as he handed her the map. "This will come in handy if my GPS cuts out."

"It's not a matter of *if*. It's a matter of *when*," insisted Steve. He held up a key ring. "These two bigger keys are for the cottage. This smaller one is for the padlock on the shed. As you know, the property management company moved Violet's belongings off-site to make room for the tenants. Unfortunately, that storage facility was flooded and everything in it was completely ruined. She may have left a few things in the shed, but I'm afraid they're probably not in very good condition after all these years."

"Thank you," she said, accepting the key ring. She was ready to leave but Steve had another question for her.

"I'm curious... Did you happen to inherit your great-aunt's aptitude for sewing?"

"No. Sewing buttons is about the extent of my skill," Paige admitted.

"Ah, that's too bad," Steve replied. "Your great-aunt's talent was in high demand on Dune Island. Even into her late seventies, Violet always had a waiting list of clients who wanted her to make custom-designed garments for them. In fact, she made all the bridesmaid dresses for my second cousin's wedding about twenty-five years ago."

"Really? That's cool." Paige had known that her great-aunt was a seamstress, but no one had ever mentioned how talented she was.

"One final item of business. I received a call from the nursing home this morning. They're sending Violet's personal effects to me here at the office. I don't think they'll be of much value. Probably whatever she'd been wearing when she was admitted to the hospital. They apologized for the delay. In any case, I'll bring them to you as soon as they arrive here."

"You don't have to go through that trouble. If you give me a call, I can pick them up."

"It's no trouble—I drive by Violet's property on the way home every day. Besides, phone service is spotty throughout Dune Island, and it's virtually impossible to get a signal in Highland Hills." He grinned, as if this drawback were a badge of honor.

"So how does anyone in Highland Hills ever get in touch with the outside world?" Paige asked facetiously, feeling a little inconvenienced that she couldn't use her cell phone. "Carrier pigeons?"

"Nope." His grin broadened. "Carrier seagulls."

Paige chuckled. Steve was more affable and laid-back than any attorney she'd ever met. Standing to leave, she said, "Thank you for all your time and help, and for emailing me that list of contractors and real estate agents, too."

"You're welcome. As I mentioned, you won't have any problem finding a buyer. But be forewarned. Once the community learns that Violet has passed on, the local real estate agents will start swarming your cottage like sharks."

"People here don't know that Violet died yet?"

"I doubt it, but if they do, they found out from combing the off-island obituaries, not from me. I don't discuss my clients' business with anyone unless I'm given express permission." As he walked her to the door, he added, "Feel free to stop by if there's anything else you need. Remember, we're neighbors now."

For the next few weeks, anyway, Paige silently corrected him. She'd taken off the full amount of vacation time she'd accrued, in case there was a delay in putting the cottage up for sale. But she hoped to return to Chicago within fourteen days, so she could spend the rest of her leave unpacking the boxes that she still hadn't emptied after moving into her condo last winter. *I've got so many other things I'd rather do that I'm not going to spend a minute longer on Dune Island than I need to,* she thought.

But because it was clear how much the attorney loved his hometown and hoped she would, too, she just smiled and said, "Thanks, Steve. See you soon."

THREE

Of course, Steve was right: Paige lost her GPS connection a mile from the center of town. Using the paper map as a guide, she traveled on the main thoroughfare until the exit for the scenic route, as he'd suggested. The narrow road had so many curves, dips, and inclines, and the fog was so thick that Paige had the sense she might drive off the edge of the earth at any moment.

Luckily, by the time she reached the Hathaways' stone wall, there weren't any vehicles behind her—no oncoming vehicles, either—so she could safely reduce her speed to a crawl. Even then, she almost missed the sign and she had to make a sharp turn onto Spindrift Lane. It was a gently sloping but deeply rutted road, and she bumped along so slowly that it seemed to take forever before she reached the end and Violet's home came into view.

The driveway, a wide, sandy square of flat land, was located to the side of the cottage, which presumably faced the ocean, although in this weather, who could tell? The small, rectangular one-story dwelling had gray, weathered shingles, a crumbling chimney, and white, flaky trim around the windows. The gutter had come detached from one end of the roof and it was dangling precariously above an outdoor wooden shower stall, which surprisingly appeared more robust than the house itself.

Remembering that Steve had mentioned the tenants who'd lived there during the off-season had been utility company employees, Paige consoled herself: *If nothing else, I can count on the electricity working.*

As soon as she stepped out of the car, she could hear the ocean, even though she couldn't see it. She could smell it, too; the scent was even stronger here than it had been on the ferry deck. As someone who'd grown up going to her grandparents' cabin on the lake every summer, Paige was used to a freshwater smell, not a briny one. The salty air wasn't an unpleasant odor, and she had fond associations with it from her travels, but the difference was striking.

To enter the house, Paige first had to pass through a porch, and she noticed that half of its screens were either torn or missing altogether. *That explains why there's so much sand in here*, she thought, glancing at the floor. *It must have blown in after the tenant vacated the cottage last week.*

Before she even opened the interior door and stepped inside the kitchen, she was overwhelmed by the reek of alcohol. While there weren't any bottles or cans visible, the linoleum floor was sticky when she walked across it and she figured the winter tenant must have hosted a party in the cottage recently.

He'd been required to clean the house prior to his departure, but his standard of cleanliness obviously differed from Paige's. There were coffee grounds—she hoped that's what they were—scattered across the counter, the stovetop was noticeably streaked with grease, and something orange was crusted in a dripping pattern down the front of the fridge. Most of the cupboard doors were left ajar and there was only a single chair at the square table.

Paige tentatively passed through the kitchen and peeked

into the living room. It was barely large enough to contain a dark-green-and-brown plaid couch, a coffee table, and a rocking chair. The walls were paneled with dark knotty pine and the brick fireplace was a drab shade of maroon. Although a large picture window faced the ocean, either it was too streaked, or the weather was too foggy to counterbalance the room's general gloominess.

Starting down the hall, Paige noticed the knob to the front door was rimmed with black duct tape, as if to hold it in place. She shook her head and crept toward the bedrooms. Two of them were furnished with full-sized beds, and a pair of bunk beds was stacked in the third. Lopsided and stained, the mattresses made Paige's skin crawl just to look at them.

She turned to go back to the kitchen, but she forced herself to peek inside the bathroom first. The sink, toilet, and tub were so grimy they made the kitchen look as sterile as an operating room in comparison.

On the plus side, at least this is a nice deep clawfoot tub, she thought. *I'll have to give it a good scrubbing before I use it, though. Looks like I'll need to buy a shower curtain, too. But where am I supposed to hang it? There's no rod...*

That's when Paige realized the bath didn't have a shower nozzle—it was only a tub. *The summer tenants must have showered outdoors, but what did the winter tenants do, shower at a gym or something?*

No matter how amazing the view might have been and regardless of what a terrific rate the renters supposedly had gotten on Violet's cottage, Paige thought they'd all been ripped off. She recognized that the property management company had replaced Violet's original furniture with the bare essentials, but she'd seen more comfortable cots and chairs in the ERs she'd worked in.

Even before she'd left Illinois for Dune Island, the idea of sleeping in a bed that countless other tenants had been using for umpteen years had struck her as unhygienic. So she'd brought an inflatable mattress to use while she was here. However, now that Paige saw how dirty the floor was, she felt hesitant to lay the mattress on it. *I suppose I could place it on top of the bed,* she thought.

But she was hungry and after a second long day of traveling, she really wanted to take a nice, long hot shower. By the time she drove to town, purchased groceries and cleaning supplies —*and* found someplace where she could get a signal long enough to call Tara like she'd promised she would—she was going to be too drained to disinfect the bathroom and set up her inflatable bed.

There was another alternative: she didn't have to stay here tonight. *This is the only vacation I'll get this year, so I deserve to treat myself to a night at one of those grand old inns I saw in Rockfield,* she decided. *I might even order room service...*

On the way back to Rockfield, Paige made a wrong turn and somehow wound up in Lucinda's Hamlet. Frustrated and tired, all she cared about was finding lodging before dark. Rather than backtracking, she followed the taillights of the car in front of her through the fog. When she spotted a neon sign that read BOARDWALK MOTEL, she abruptly pulled into the parking lot.

The clerk mentioned she was lucky there was a vacancy because tourist season didn't officially begin until the next weekend. Paige didn't *feel* especially lucky when she saw the condition of her accommodations, which were only marginally more contemporary than those at Violet's place. But the room was spotless and the cell signal was strong, so after a long, luxurious shower, Paige lounged on the bed, devouring the leftover cheese and grapes she'd found in her cooler.

She tapped Tara's name in her phone's contact list, but it

was Tara's mother who answered the call. "Hi, Aunt Sherry. I'm surprised to hear your voice. Is everything okay?"

"Not really. I dropped by with supper because Tara's got one of her headaches again. She's lying down, which is why I answered her phone. I think the stress of planning Cami's party is getting to her."

"Oh, I'm sorry to hear that."

"Don't worry, it's not your fault, dear. She understands why you can't be here to help," Sherry assured her, even though Paige had been empathizing about her cousin's headache, not apologizing for her own absence.

"I'm sure it's a big relief to have *you* back in town to help her again. Hopefully Cami will become involved with the decision-making process, too." She refrained from adding, *It is her party, after all.* Even though she thought that Tara took on too many of her children's responsibilities, Paige recognized it really wasn't any of her business to comment on it.

Instead, she inquired about her aunt's trip to visit her in-laws. After Sherry described her sister-in-law's retirement community by the lake and reported how many fish their husbands had caught, she said, "Enough about me. I want to hear about *your* trip. Did you make it to the island in time to meet with the estate lawyer today?"

"Yes, but just barely. The attorney, Steve, was very helpful and friendly—he told me something interesting about Violet. He said she was kind of famous on Dune Island for her sewing. She had a waiting list of people who wanted her to make clothes for them."

Paige had expected her aunt to be impressed or at least surprised, but Sherry simply said, "Fame is relative, especially in a small community." Then she asked, "Is Violet's cottage really as tiny as my father claimed it was?"

"Yes, it's very small. Very dirty and dilapidated, too," she answered. "The last tenant left it in a mess. And the property management company has done a lousy job of maintaining the exterior."

"That's a shame." Sherry made a *tsk*-ing sound. "My father used to say that the cottage's one redeeming quality was that Violet had always kept it as neat as a pin. She should have sold it after she broke her hip, instead of hiring a management company to maintain it for her. Then she would've been able to afford a better nursing facility and the cottage wouldn't have gone to ruin. But I suspect she was afraid that if she put the estate on the market, the Hathaways would have wanted to buy it."

"Why would the Hathaways want to buy her property if they already owned so much land in the same location?"

"Because hers has direct beach access, and theirs doesn't. But Violet was a stubborn woman and right up until the end she refused to sell it. She really cut off her nose to spite her face." Sherry clucked her tongue in disapproval. "Can you imagine harboring a lifelong grudge just because the boy next door rejected her when they were teenagers?"

"Well, I suppose I wouldn't want to sell my property to one of my exes or to his family, either," Paige replied, chuckling.

"No, no. I doubt you'd ever be that bitter. You're far too emotionally healthy," Sherry contradicted with a seriousness that surprised her niece. "You may have inherited big brown eyes and straight brown hair from your grandpa Frank's side of the family, but you certainly haven't inherited Violet's temperament."

The harder her aunt tried to reassure Paige that she wasn't like Violet, the more it sounded as if she was trying to convince herself. Paige recognized that she intended to be complimentary, but Sherry's remarks made her bristle.

Oblivious, she continued to offer proof of her niece's stability. "No matter how many men have broken up with you, I've never once seen you display the kind of behavior Violet demonstrated. Oh, sure, you might have a few choice words to say about them. Or you might be teary-eyed and go heavy on the comfort food for a while, but after a month or two, you always bounce back."

Deeply offended but too tired to think of a diplomatic reply, Paige yawned exaggeratedly. "Oh, excuse me! All of a sudden, I can hardly keep my eyes open. I'd better go now. Please let Tara know I called, and I hope her headache goes away soon. Also, could you tell her I haven't taken photos yet, because of the fog? And if she doesn't hear from me for a while, it's because I can't call from the cottage. There's virtually no signal."

"Okay, dear, I'll do that," said Sherry. "Nice chatting with you."

But their conversation left a bad taste in Paige's mouth that persisted long after she'd brushed her teeth and changed into her nightgown.

Aunt Sherry glossed right over what I told her about Violet's reputation as a seamstress, she ruminated. It reminded her of how her family often seemed dismissive of Paige's work as a nurse—unless they needed a medical opinion or referral, or wanted her help caring for them when they were sick. *Being married and having children might not be the* only *thing that matters to them... but it's definitely the thing that matters the most*, she silently grumbled.

Paige's grandmother and aunt Sherry had both married the first men they'd ever dated. Tara's husband had proposed to her in college, and now, Cami was following in her mother's footsteps by getting engaged a few months before her twenty-first birthday. Since they'd all gotten married so young, Paige didn't expect them to fully understand what it was like to be single in their late thirties, or to go through multiple breakups.

But their insensitive comments—like those her aunt had made just now—were maddening to Paige. They'd kept her awake and brooding many times in the past. Luckily, tonight she was too exhausted from her journey to dwell on them, and she fell asleep almost as soon as her head hit the pillow.

FOUR

Tara called Paige at 7:15 a.m., which was surprising, since it was only 6:15 a.m. in Illinois. While she was glad to hear that her cousin's headache had lifted, Paige would have preferred to sleep in, especially since she didn't have much to say to her beyond the message she'd asked Sherry to relay the previous evening.

Tara, however, jabbered on at length about how excited she was about touring The Landing with Cami now that the weather had cleared. Still drowsy, Paige half-listened, murmuring in agreement when she sensed it was appropriate.

After fifteen minutes of blathering away, Tara announced, "Oh, here's my sleepyhead daughter now." Then she promptly ended the call, as she often did when the opportunity to speak to someone else presented itself.

Paige couldn't fall back asleep, so she packed up her things and checked out of the motel. Although the fog had lifted, the air was still nippy, and the sky was the same drab whitish-gray color of the seagulls drifting by. Paige zipped her hoodie and briskly strode across the street to the boardwalk.

The bay appeared tarnished and listless, barely rippling as

it lapped the shore. Except for an elderly couple walking a dog and a man swiping a metal detector from side to side above the sand, the beach was deserted.

I'll bet this place really comes alive during tourist season, thought Paige as she passed numerous arcades, souvenir shops, and an assortment of diners and food stands. *Not my cup of tea, but families with children probably love coming here.*

After ducking into a coffeehouse and then making a quick stop to purchase groceries and cleaning supplies, she drove back toward Violet's cottage. Because she took the main thoroughfare instead of roaming through the neighborhoods, Paige saw little more than trees on either side of the single-lane road. It wasn't until she exited onto the scenic route and crested a high hill that she caught her first glimpse of the wide-open Atlantic.

Unlike the bay, the pewter-hued ocean on this side of the island was rollicking with whitecaps and its sheer vastness took Paige's breath away. She lifted her foot from the gas pedal, coasting slowly past the tall dunes comprised of sun-bleached sand, bright green beach grass, and fuchsia-pink rosa rugosa.

As she wound her way up and down the hills, she'd occasionally spy a house or cottage. Regardless of their design or size, or whether they were tucked behind a slope or perched atop a cliff, the weathered, shingle-clad homes all melded with the natural landscape. So when Paige rounded a bend and saw the Hathaways' sweeping, verdant lawn and monumental residence looming in the distance, her first thought was, *What showoffs!*

Drawing nearer, she tried not to stare at the white, imposing Georgian-style home. It was comprised of a three-story main house, flanked by two slightly smaller wings. Paige counted six chimneys—four on the center building and one apiece on the adjacent sections—and each rooftop also hosted a widow's walk with a glass-enclosed cupola. There was a detached garage or guest house situated to the right of the mansion, and both were bordered with impeccably pruned shrubbery. The lawn was so meticulously maintained that Paige marveled, *I doubt there's a single bent blade of grass on their entire acreage.*

Immediately after reaching the far corner of the low stone wall, she turned left onto the dirt road leading down the hill to Violet's cottage. Spindrift Lane ran parallel with the Hathaways' backyard—or was it considered the front yard because it faced the ocean?—and Paige couldn't help rubbernecking at her neighbor's balconies, patios, and solarium.

A symmetrical maze of stone walkways and steps wove through the terraced backyard toward an elaborately landscaped garden. In its center was a raised gazebo that seemed almost as large as Violet's cottage. Beyond the gazebo and garden, the expansive, pristine lawn sloped gradually toward the back section of the old stone wall.

Good thing there's a distinct dividing line or I might not be able to figure out where their property ends and Violet's begins, Paige thought sarcastically as she surveyed the disarray of beach grass, wildflowers, and ground cover sprouting from her greataunt's land.

Now that the fog had lifted, she was relieved to see the cottage wasn't as close to the edge of the cliff as she'd thought it was. The land extended another fifty or sixty yards in front of Violet's home, so there wasn't any imminent danger from erosion. Her parcel of land also included the heathland to the left, which stretched the length of the Hathaways' back wall.

A third of the way across the heathland stood a single, stupendous tree. It wasn't bearing leaves, and its bare branches and twigs created an intricate lacey pattern against the sky. Paige couldn't identify what kind it was, but she guessed it must have been over one hundred feet tall.

Halfway between the tree and the driveway a shabby little shed seemed to teeter on the brink of collapse. To the far right, Violet's cottage didn't appear much sturdier. Yet there was something about the raw and rugged appearance of her great-aunt's property that Paige found more appealing than the Hathaways' palatial estate.

It's too perfect, almost like a stage, she thought as she parked her car. *And for all its grandeur, like Aunt Sherry said, their property doesn't have direct beach access—but Violet's does.*

Paige surveyed the rim of the cliff until her eye homed in on the staircase to the far left. In one of their email exchanges, Steve had said the dunes that sandwiched Violet's and the Hathaways' land were owned by the park service. However, since there was no way for the public to descend to the beach below, it was often deserted, which he'd confided made it his favorite place to walk during the summer months when most of the other beaches were swarming with vacationers.

Maybe it'll warm up and if I make enough progress in the cottage, I'll go exploring later, Paige decided.

Entering the kitchen, she was again overpowered by the smell of stale alcohol. She opened the windows and brought the only chair out to the porch. Paige sat for half an hour, finishing her coffee while she watched a curtain of dark clouds slowly lift from the horizon and listened to the ocean thrashing against the shore.

If the view is this captivating now, I can only imagine what it looks like when the sun is shining. No wonder the property's so valuable, she admitted to herself, reluctantly rising to go inside.

According to Steve, zoning regulations prohibited anyone from increasing the size of Violet's cottage. However, the new owners would be allowed to redesign the interior, so Paige figured there was no sense in spending money and effort on renovations they might redo anyway. But she still had a lot of work to do if she was going to make the cottage presentable for a showing.

She started by scrubbing the kitchen floor on her hands and knees, working her way backward from the door, which she left open, toward the living room. She was just about finished when she glanced up to see a very large tan-and-brown animal sniffing its way across the damp linoleum, its long ears dragging across the floor as it approached.

Paige was so stunned that she momentarily froze. The slack-faced, dark-muzzled dog—a bloodhound, she guessed—sniffed both of her shoulders and then nuzzled against her, knocking her sideways.

"Blossom," a man called as Paige struggled to regain her balance. "Come here, boy. Come!"

Paige hardly had time to absorb the dog's humorous misnomer before the man appeared at the threshold of the kitchen door. He was wearing a wetsuit up to his waist, exposing his tanned, muscular arms and sculpted upper torso. Paige noticed his golden chest was beaded with moisture.

And everyone always says that men like him don't just show up on your doorstep, she thought before she realized she was gawking. She quickly looked away.

"Blossom, come!" the man repeated, but the animal ignored him and planted itself on its hindquarters in front of Paige, thumping its tail on the floor and gazing expectantly at her.

Amused, Paige stood up and simultaneously reached forward to scratch the dog's neck. She told the man, "I don't think Blossom's ready to leave yet. You can come in."

"You sure? I'm wet. I don't want to drip on your nice, clean floor."

Her attention still focused on petting the dog, Paige shrugged. "A little more water won't do any harm."

The man came forward. "I really am sorry we messed up your floor," he apologized.

For the first time they looked directly at each other, and Paige did a doubletake when she recognized that he was the guy from the ferry. What were the odds? *I guess that explains why*

he had no problem dropping down and leaping up from the deck
—he's a surfer, she realized.

Even though the man and his traveling companion, Lexie, hadn't been very gracious yesterday, Blossom's friendliness more than compensated for it this morning. "It's all right. The floor was so dirty I was going to have to give it a second scrubbing anyway."

The man nodded, but he was giving her a quizzical look, which Paige took to mean he couldn't remember how he knew her. "Are you...?"

"I'm the woman on the ferry whose keys you retrieved from beneath your car yesterday. My name's Paige."

"Oh, yeah. Right, right," he stammered. "I'm Seth and this beast here is named Blossom."

"Blossom has already introduced himself—he's very friendly," Paige said, smiling at the dog's droopy face as she continued to stroke his head.

"Yeah, sometimes he's *overly* friendly. Sorry he barged in on you like that, but there's no screen on the bottom half of the porch door and he got used to coming right in. The guy who lived here, Owen, used to give him a treat on Saturdays."

Seth was so apologetic, and he seemed so much more congenial than he'd been the day before that Paige couldn't resist needling him. "Your dog knows what day of the week it is?"

"Sort of. Saturday's my surfing day so that's the day he comes with me to the beach. And beach day is treat day—but he's never charged up here without me. He knows he's supposed to wait until I'm done before he climbs back up the stairs." Seth leaned forward and lowered his voice. "But please don't let the property management people know we were on the staircase. They don't want non-tenants using it—probably because we haven't signed a liability waiver."

He chuckled, and Paige interpreted his remark to mean Violet's staircase was as decrepit as her cottage. It was probably a fair assessment but coming from someone who traveled in a luxury convertible, it struck her as a little stuck-up.

"They don't want pets inside the house, either," Seth continued. "Not that it would make much of a difference—as you've noticed, Owen was a total slob. You've really got your work cut out for you today. It's no wonder Delene isn't coming back."

"Who's Delene?"

"The housekeeper who cleaned the cottage in between summer tenants." He tilted his head. "Aren't you replacing her?"

Paige recognized why that would be a logical assumption and she answered, "Sort of, but I'm not the housekeeper. I'm the house *owner*."

Seth took a step back in apparent disbelief. "You *bought* this house?"

She could only speculate why he was so incredulous. Didn't he think anyone would want the cottage? Or was it that he didn't think she could afford the land?

"No. I *inherited* this house from my great-aunt," she clarified.

"Oh-hhh," he said knowingly, drawing out the word. "Violet Atkins was your great-aunt?"

"Yes. Did you know her?"

"Not personally, no. But my great-grandparents did. My grandparents did, too." He motioned toward the back window. "They own the house up the hill."

Paige's stomach dropped to her knees. "You're a *Hathaway*?"

"My last name's Hathaway, yeah." He rubbed his chin, appearing as astounded as Paige was. "You said you inherited the house. Does that mean your great-aunt...?"

Now that she knew Seth was a member of the Hathaway family, Paige felt even more uncomfortable discussing her great-aunt with him. "Yes. She died last spring," she said curtly.

"I'm sorry to hear that." He sounded genuinely empathetic, but Paige remained guarded.

"Thank you." She picked up her scrub brush to indicate she wanted to get back to work, but Seth kept chatting.

"I didn't realize Violet had any relatives. Who are alive, I mean," he bumbled. "So does this mean you're moving in for the summer?"

"For part of it, yes." Paige deliberately kept her answer vague. She'd only just met Seth, and after hearing Sherry's stories about the neighbors' attitude toward the Atkins family, she was hesitant to share her plans with him. Paige knew she was probably being overly cautious. Most of the Hathaways who were old enough to remember what happened in the 1940s were gone now, so it wasn't as if they'd treat *her* the same way they'd treated Violet. But she intended to keep her distance from the neighbors anyway. She bent down and dipped her brush into the pail of soapy water and Seth took the hint.

"We should let you get back to work," he said, gently nudging Blossom to rise. "It was nice meeting you."

"You, too." Paige had to force a smile at him, but her voice was genuinely pleasant when she gave the hound's head a final rub. "Sorry I didn't have any treats for you, Blossom."

After they left, Paige got back to scrubbing and she tried to make sense of her second impression of Seth Hathaway.

On one hand, he seemed sincerely contrite about Blossom's trespass and sympathetic about Violet's passing. On the other, Paige was bothered by his remarks about the staircase. Not necessarily because he'd implied it was in shoddy condition; but because before he'd realized she was Violet's great-niece, he'd asked her not to tell the property management staff he'd been using it. Did he feel entitled to break the rules simply because he was a Hathaway?

He doesn't seem *like he's that arrogant,* Paige thought. *Although the woman he was with on the ferry, Lexie, sure was haughty, and it's usually true that birds of a feather flock together...*

She'd noticed Seth hadn't been wearing a wedding band and she wondered if Lexie was his girlfriend. *Maybe he's the one that Steve mentioned is getting married on the island this August?*

Not that it mattered to her what the Hathaways did—although, she didn't want them using Violet's staircase if it wasn't safe. And as lovable as Blossom was, Paige hoped he wouldn't visit her at the cottage in the future, because if he did, it meant Seth would be close behind.

One of the first repairs on my list is re-screening the porch, she resolved. *That should keep the two of them from coming in unexpectedly again.*

While cleaning the cottage, Paige noticed what may or may not have been mouse droppings. She wasn't afraid of mice, but as a nurse, she was keenly aware of their potential to carry germs. So that evening she didn't feel comfortable laying her inflatable mattress on the floor. Instead, she set it on top of the bed in the tiny room facing the ocean.

Usually, sleeping on the inflatable mattress made Paige uncomfortably warm and she could only doze in fits and spurts because the fabric squeaked and woke her up whenever she rolled over. But tonight, even though she'd turned up the thermostat and pulled on a hoodie over her pajamas, Paige still felt chilled. She curled into a ball, pulled the summer quilt over her head and, despite the continuous thudding of waves against the shore, she quickly sank into a deep slumber.

When she woke, Paige surprisingly felt so well-rested that it seemed as if she'd been hibernating for three months instead of dozing for eight hours. She sat up and pushed the flimsy, faded curtain away from the window at the foot of the bed. Once again, the sky was a white wall, and condensation had collected on the pane, but at least it didn't appear to be raining. She dared to hope, *Maybe today we'll have warmer weather.*

But when she hopped down from the high stack of mattresses and her feet hit the hardwood floor, she yelped aloud, "Brr! That's *freezing.*"

She danced from foot to foot as she rummaged through her suitcase for a pair of socks—she still hadn't unpacked because she wanted to wipe out the dresser drawers first. Once she'd put on her clothes, Paige touched the radiator: it felt as cold as the floor. The previous evening, she'd set the thermostat at seventy degrees, so she figured something either must be wrong with it, or with the furnace. *I'll ask the inspector to check it out when he comes to evaluate the cottage on Tuesday.*

At the moment, Paige was just grateful that the water heater appeared to be a separately functioning unit from the furnace. *I suppose after I disinfect the tub, I could take a bath to get warm. Or I could use the outdoor shower, although I sure wouldn't want that gutter to come loose and knock me over the head while I was in there,* she thought as she padded into the kitchen to make breakfast.

Even after drinking two cups of coffee and eating a bowl of steaming hot oatmeal, she couldn't bring herself to go outside. Since there was no shortage of tasks to accomplish inside the cottage, she got right to work and by noon, she was so warm she was sweating. She kept telling herself she'd take a lunch break in ten minutes, but one project inevitably led to another, and the next thing she knew, it was nearly time to make supper.

She pulled a pot from the cupboard and peeked beneath the lid. "Ug," she groaned when she saw how dirty the inside was. The rest of the pots and pans she found were even more disgusting, so she set them all on the countertop.

She was about to fill the sink to wash them, when a woman's voice sang out, "Hellooo? Anyone home?"

Paige hurried across the kitchen threshold into the porch and nearly collided with Seth's traveling companion, Lexie, who was holding a bottle of wine in one hand and a cardboard bakery box in the other. She was wearing a black cutout halter-neck minidress and strappy beaded sandals, as if it were eighty degrees and bright sunshine outside instead of fifty-eight and drizzling.

"Hello." Paige adjusted the white-and-purple bandana she'd tied around her head to keep her hair out of her eyes.

"Hi, there. I hope I'm not intruding. Seth told me we have a new neighbor, so I wanted to meet you. I'm Lexie."

"We already met on the ferry the other day," said Paige, unwilling to allow Lexie to pretend she didn't remember her. "I'm Paige Taylor—as I'm sure Seth has told you."

"Yeah, he did. What a strange coincidence that the same woman we helped on the ferry ended up being Violet's great-niece and summering on Spindrift Lane, isn't it?" Lexie marveled.

"Mmm." *It's even stranger you seem to be forgetting that you weren't willing to help me at all. Seth was the one who rescued my keys from beneath the car*, thought Paige.

Lexie seemed to read her mind. "By the way, I was having an unusually awful afternoon on Friday. We'd missed an earlier ferry from Hyannis, which meant I was running late for an important meeting here on the island."

Lexie's explanation of her circumstances was hardly the same as an apology for her rudeness, but Paige decided to let it slide. "How frustrating."

"Yes, it was, especially since the meeting was with my wedding photographer." She smiled brightly and added, "I'm getting married in August."

I guess that means I was right about Seth. Paige felt a

strange spasm in her stomach as she offered her congratulations.

"Thanks. I'm on pins and needles." Lexie suddenly thrust the bottle and box at her. "I almost forgot. These are for you. A little housewarming present."

"Thank you—oops." Paige hadn't expected the box to be so heavy and she nearly dropped it. She quipped, "This must be a pound cake."

"No. It's half a dozen mini fruit tarts from Sebastian's. You know, the bakery off Main in Benjamin's Manor? He's doing my wedding cake and it's so pricey that I swear he's using the money to put his daughter through college." Lexie laughed. "The expense is worth it to me, but I think he feels guilty because whenever I meet with him, he insists on giving me a box or two of samples."

"Oh. That's nice of him," Paige said. And she supposed it was nice that Lexie was passing them on to her, even if she'd told her they were freebies. Paige didn't particularly want to extend her neighbor's visit, but it seemed rude not to offer her one of the treats. "Would you like to have one now?"

"I'd *love* to. But I can't. I'm counting every calorie from now until August eighteen. But you go ahead and help yourself. I'm happy to watch and enjoy the taste vicariously."

Paige had no intention of eating alone in front of her. "I think I'll wait until after I've had my supper. It'll be a reward for finishing all the chores on my list today," she said, hoping Lexie would take the hint about how busy she was.

"If you're going to wait that long, you'd better put the tarts in the fridge to keep them fresh. I'll give you a hand." Lexie took a step forward to enter the house which was the exact opposite direction Paige wanted her to move.

"No, thanks. I can manage. The kitchen is in shambles, and I wouldn't want you to trip on anything." Paige stood firm, blocking her way.

"Okay. I'll wait here." She took a seat on the only chair on the porch.

Paige dashed into the kitchen and set the wine on top of the fridge so she could open the door to slide the box onto a shelf. When she returned to the porch, Lexie was standing again, staring at the ocean.

"What an amazing view. Obviously, it's incredible from up the hill, too, but we can't hear the surf roaring quite as distinctly as you can down here. Which is probably a good thing because we wouldn't want the ocean drowning out our vows." She sighed, wistfully twirling a strand of hair as she turned toward Paige. "The ceremony is going to take place in the garden. We're holding the reception on the grounds, too."

"That sounds like it will be lovely." Paige took a deep breath, preparing to directly tell Lexie she needed to get back to work, but she waited a beat too long and her neighbor rambled on.

"When I was a little girl, I used to pretend I was a bride getting married in the gazebo, so it's like a dream come true."

Even though Paige really didn't have the time to listen to Lexie's trip down memory lane, her interest was piqued. "You used to play at the Hathaways' house when you were a little girl? Does that mean Seth was your childhood sweetheart?"

"Seth? No way! He's my *cousin*." Lexie wrinkled her nose at Paige's error. "My fiancé's name is Grant Farnsworth. He was supposed to join me here in Highland Hills this weekend, but at the last minute, he couldn't make it. Seth agreed to hop on a passenger-only ferry and meet us in Hyannis instead, so we could discuss the landscaping and gardens—he's been preparing them for our wedding. That's why we were traveling back here together."

Paige's eyes went wide. "Seth's a gardener?"

"A landscaper, yes. He owns a local landscaping business."

"He lives here year-round?"

"Not here-here, on Spindrift Lane. But here on the island,

yes. He lives in Rockfield." Lexie must have caught the note of curiosity in Paige's voice, because she added, "And he's *very* single, so if you're asking because you're interested—"

Paige cut her off. "No, I'm not. Not at all."

"Because you're already seeing someone?" Lexie pressed.

Paige was so flustered she blurted out, "No, because I don't have any intention of getting involved with someone from—" She almost slipped and said "your family," but she caught herself and changed it to, "Dune Island."

"I get it. When you reach a certain age, you figure, 'Why waste time on a summer fling,' right?" Lexie asked. "Two years ago, I told myself that if I didn't start getting serious about who I dated, I'd still be single when I was thirty!"

Lexie reminded Paige more of Tara by the minute. "What a horrible prospect," she mumbled. Her sarcasm went right over Lexie's head.

"Isn't it, though? I mean, don't get me wrong. I'm not sorry I'm getting married later in life. Grant was worth the wait. No, my one and only regret is that... well, to be honest, it's that the big beech tree died before our wedding." Lexie shifted and gestured toward the large tree a third of the way across Violet's property. "It used to be so lush and healthy, but now it looks kind of like a woman with a big mass of tangled hair, or something." Her gaze noticeably flickered to Paige's bandana.

"I think it looks more like hundreds of lightning bolts," Paige remarked with a shrug.

"That's even worse." Lexie's voice had a distinct whine to it and Paige couldn't understand why she was so distraught about the tree. Then she exclaimed, "I don't want to subject my wedding guests to an ominous image like that."

Resisting the urge to laugh at Lexie's melodramatic comment, Paige tried to make a helpful suggestion. "Could you angle the chairs so the guests are facing in that direction?" She pointed to the opposite side of the yard.

"No. It's a late afternoon ceremony. If they're facing that way, they'll be squinting into the sun, which also means the lighting will be terrible for my photos." Lexie nervously twisted her engagement ring around her finger. Why hadn't Paige noticed it before now? It was practically blinding. "So, you can see my dilemma, can't you?"

Paige was confounded. "You're not suggesting I cut the tree down, are you?"

"Oh, no, I'd never suggest you do that!" objected Lexie. "Cutting down and hauling away a tree that size is a significant expense. It wouldn't be fair to ask you to pay for removing a dead, unsightly tree just because it affects the aesthetics of *my* dream wedding. All I'm asking is for you to give *us* permission to remove it. We'd cover the costs in full."

Paige rattled her head. "I don't know. I'd really have to give it more consideration before I could let you do something like that."

"Really, there's no need to give it a second thought—it's a drop in the bucket compared to the cost of the rest of my wedding," boasted Lexie, with a dismissive wave of her hand.

Clearly, she thought Paige was hesitant because of the expense, but what Paige had meant was that she couldn't agree to let Lexie or anyone else make a major alteration to the property without giving it serious consideration first. For all she knew, the tree might not truly be dead—maybe it was only temporarily diseased—and its presence on the heathland might make the estate *more* appealing to prospective buyers.

She repeated, "As I said, I'll need to think it over."

"Okay, but the sooner we schedule it, the better. The trucks, excavator, and woodchipper will probably make deep grooves in the ground, so we'll need to give the land some time to recover. Obviously, we'll pay to replant whatever gets damaged, too. If there's anything else you want removed or spruced up around here while we're at it, we can do that for you, as well. For example, the shed looks like it might collapse at any second. If you're not using it, we could haul it away, no problem."

On the surface, Lexie's offer might have sounded generous, but underneath it was a bit offensive and Paige replied sharply. "I've only been here a couple days, and I haven't even had time to walk around the property or take a good look at the beech tree yet. I can appreciate that you're on a tight schedule because of your wedding, but for the third time, I need to think it over."

"Sure, sure, I understand." Lexie nodded agreeably. "You absolutely should go out on the heathland and take a good look, first. Personally, I don't know much about trees, so I kept hoping it might be in a dormancy phase or something, but Seth said no, it had died a couple years ago. If it would be helpful, he could come explain to you how he confirmed that it's dead?"

She just doesn't give up. Paige gritted her teeth, imitating a smile. "Thanks, but I'll let him know if I have any questions after I've examined the tree for myself."

"Perfect!" enthused Lexie. "Alrighty, I'm going to skedaddle now so you can finish your chores and then dig into those fruit tarts."

"Good idea, thanks," was the most gracious response Paige could muster. But as she watched Lexie prance away in her high heels, she thought, *Not only do I need to get the porch door re-screened, but I've got to install a hook and eye latch on it, too.*

In the kitchen, she furiously began washing the pots and pans, sloshing sudsy water over the side of the sink and down the front of her shirt.

What a condescending phony, she fumed to herself. *The wine and re-gifted fruit tarts weren't a housewarming gift—they were a* bribe. *A way of trying to sweeten me up after she'd behaved so rudely on the ferry. Does she honestly think I can't see through her act? Or that I'd be so grateful that she's willing to pay to "spruce up" other parts of Violet's property that I'd jump at the offer? I happen to* like *the way things look on the heath-*

land, including the beech tree—and maybe a potential buyer will like it, too. If Lexie doesn't appreciate the view, then she shouldn't have planned to hold the ceremony in the gazebo.

It occurred to Paige that if her great-aunt hadn't died, Lexie wouldn't even have the option of asking to remove the tree. Because for the last three years of her life, Violet was unable to communicate, and the property management company didn't have the legal authority to make decisions of that magnitude on her behalf.

So until Lexie found out Violet died and I was here, she only had two options. Her guests could either face the sun or they could face the tree. Unless... unless the Hathaways planned to find a way to chop it down without permission. They wouldn't have tried to do that, would they? Paige wondered, remembering what Seth had said about not telling the property management people he was using the staircase to the beach. She didn't like to assume the worst about anyone, but Lexie's manipulative behavior, coupled with Sherry's stories about the Hathaways, made Paige feel suspicious.

I suppose it doesn't matter what they may have been planning *to do,* she finally concluded as she stooped down to put away the last clean, dry pan. *All that matters now is that it's my decision, not Lexie's, whether the tree is removed.*

Paige shut the cabinet door with an authoritative click and then she straightened up so fast she felt dizzy. She grabbed the handle of the fridge to steady herself, causing the bottle she'd set atop of it to teeter and crash to the floor. It sprayed wine and glass everywhere.

Utterly exasperated, she didn't have the patience or energy to mop the floor and deodorize the kitchen all over again. Paige swept the shards into the puddle of wine and threw a rag over the entire mess. Then she opened the fridge, removed the box of fruit tarts and selected two—one to eat for supper, and the other for dessert.

FIVE

Monday dawned brighter yet even chillier than Sunday. As Paige was getting dressed, it occurred to her the temperature outside might be higher than inside the cottage. She made coffee, poured it into her thermal mug and zipped up her hoodie.

Almost as soon as she exited the porch and came around to the ocean side of the cottage, she was warmed by the bright, eastern sunshine. She scanned the area, looking for the best way to reach the staircase landing, where she could sit while she drank her coffee. There were only two trodden paths through the thick ground cover. One led to the beech tree in the side yard. The other meandered across the heathland toward the ocean, looped around a trio of fat junipers, and then ribboned along the edge of the cliff. Paige took that one.

To her surprise, when she reached the other side of the juniper trees, she found three wooden chairs matching those in Violet's kitchen. *Owen must have left these out here,* she thought, rolling her eyes. *Good thing they're so sturdy.*

Other than being a little damp, they were none the worse

for wear. Paige wiped one off with her sleeve and plunked herself down on it. Immediately, she understood why this spot was so appealing to the former tenant. Not only did the bushy juniper trees create a cozy buffer of privacy behind her, but the vantage point was spectacular.

To the left and right, bright white, yellow, and pink wild-flowers accentuated the heathland's brown-green palette, where wrens, warblers, chickadees, and sparrows flitted among the grass and shrubs. In front of her, the sun-dazzled ocean danced with diamonds of light, and overhead the sky was a ceaseless, unblemished blue.

Soaking it all in, Paige tried to remember the last time that she'd deliberately sat still like this, doing nothing. Usually, she tapped her snooze alarm so many times that when she finally rose from bed, the rest of her day was *go, go, go,* until she fell asleep again. But this morning, she lazed near the cliff, allowing her thoughts to drift for more than an hour.

Maybe when I get back home, I can make a practice of starting my day with at least five minutes of quiet contemplation, she thought when she finally stood up again.

Remembering she hadn't taken any photos of the scenery to send to Tara yet, she clicked half a dozen shots. Then she picked up a chair and carried it to the cottage, leaving the other two where they were. *I suppose I could buy a lawn chair, but why bother? I'm only going to be here for a couple weeks at most and those kitchen chairs are practically indestructible. They'll be fine out here.*

A few minutes later, she was on her way to the center of Highland Hills, where there were twice as many art galleries as there were shops or restaurants. About a block before she reached the library, Paige's phone started pinging rapid-fire on the passenger seat beside her. *Must be the backlog of messages from Tara coming through,* she thought.

Sure enough, after pulling over to park, Paige saw she had received dozens of new texts, which included photos of The Landing, from her cousin. The messages were so long that it took Paige fifteen minutes to read through them and look at all the pictures—only to discover in the final message that Tara and Cami had rejected the venue.

Regardless, when Tara answered Paige's call, she rehashed her previous comments, detailing the minutiae of The Landing's shortcomings, including the inferior quality of the table-cloths and what she considered to be unsightly fern panels in the lobby.

"You sound like Lexie grumbling about the tree," Paige muttered, not realizing she'd spoken aloud.

"Lexie? Who's Lexie?"

"She's one of the Hathaways next door. She's getting married in their backyard in August, but the gazebo overlooks an enormous beech tree on Violet's property. She thinks it's unsightly and that it'll ruin the guests' view, as well as her photos. She's offered to pay to have it removed, but I'm not sure that's a good idea." Paige was getting a little tired of talking about other people's weddings and she tried to change the subject. "Did you get the photos I sent of Violet's property yet?"

Tara wasn't distracted. "They just came through. I'll look at them in a sec. Tell me more about Lexie's wedding. The Hathaways could probably afford to hold it at any venue they chose. Their grounds must be really beautiful if they're hosting it in their backyard. Describe it to me."

Paige could hear envy—and a note of admiration—in her cousin's voice. Aware that Tara had a love-hate fascination with people who were wealthier than she was, Paige tried to keep her description generic. "It's a big yard, obviously, and it has a perfectly manicured lawn. There's a fountain in the front and like I said, they've got a large gazebo in the back. The grounds sort of look like a state park or public gardens or something. But in my opinion, the one thing that makes their property so special is its water view."

"That doesn't really tell me anything," Tara griped. "Did you take photos?"

"No way! It's their home, not a tourist attraction." The Hathaways probably had security cameras everywhere and the possibility of being caught on film while snapping photos of their mansion made Paige cringe. "But I've taken lots of photos of Violet's cottage. If you look at them, you'll see that her view is incredible. And unlike the Hathaways' property, hers has direct access to the beach. I haven't made my way over to the staircase to take photos of it yet, but I did snap a few distant shots of the ocean."

Tara was quiet, obviously scrolling through the photos. "Eww, is that the cottage?" she jeered. "I can't believe that's where you've been staying. You're such a germaphobe. How do you sleep at night?"

"I cleaned it out, first," Paige said. "I've been working really hard on it—that's why I sent you before and after photos, so you could see the difference."

"Some of these are *after* photos?"

Paige ignored her criticism. "Did you see the ones of the heathland yet?"

"I'm looking at them now—ug! Is that the beech tree? No wonder Lexie doesn't want it in the background of her photos. It's going to stick out like a sore thumb. The rest of Violet's property looks grubby, too. Isn't there any lawn or is it all just sand and weeds?"

"Those aren't weeds. They're wildflowers and ground cover."

"Whatever. The yard still looks neglected. I feel sorry for the other homeowners in the neighborhood who've had to put up with it all these years."

Growing aggravated at Tara's negativity, Paige crossly informed her, "There isn't any *neighborhood* on Spindrift Lane. There are only two houses—the cottage and the mansion. Besides, most homeowners in Highland Hills live on dunes just like Violet's. If anything sticks out like a sore thumb it's the Hathaways' lush, rolling lawn. I can't even imagine what a drain it puts on their resources to maintain it."

Her cousin snorted. "I doubt they're worried about paying their water bill."

"I didn't mean money—I meant *natural* resources," snapped Paige. Her cousin didn't seem to get it: not everything was about superficial appearances. "The dunes have very fragile ecosystems."

"Okay, okay, I get it, their lawn is bad for the environment," Tara retorted. "But I still think Violet's yard looks unkempt and that tree is hideous. And you're really going to have to work wonders on the cottage before any potential buyers come to see it."

Paige figured that conceding was easier than arguing. "You're right. I've got an awful lot to do to make it presentable, so I'd better get to it. I'll talk to you tomorrow or the next day."

"Wait. You can't go already," Tara protested. "You haven't heard about the other venues I'm checking out for Cami's party, now that we've eliminated The Landing as our top choice."

"You can tell me about them while I drive." But after about a mile, they lost their connection, and for the first time, Paige considered Dune Island's inferior cell phone service to be a benefit, instead of an inconvenience.

Paige sat on the porch, eating her lunch, which consisted of an avocado and tomato crostini, as well as a bowl of peach and apple slices. Her gaze wandered over the random sandy patches and varied greenery in the side yard, past the dense thickets of fuchsia-petaled, yellow-centered wild roses near the edge of the cliff, to the uproarious royal-blue waves in the distance. Yes, the seascape was unruly, but that was what was so wonderful about it.

She was astounded that her cousin didn't seem to recognize the inherent beauty of the heathland. *It seems so obvious to me, but maybe it's not as obvious in a photo. Like Tara herself said the other day—you can't get a true sense of a place unless you experience it in person,* she thought. *Kind of like how you can't get a true sense of another person's life unless you walk a mile in their shoes...*

As she slowly twisted her neck from right to left, taking in the panoramic view, Paige wondered how many times her great-aunt or grandfather had sat out here eating sandwiches when they were young.

Although she'd never met her great-aunt, and her grandfather had died when Paige was a little girl, there was something about staying where they once lived, and looking at what they once saw, that made her want to know more about them, beyond the stories she'd already heard from her aunt and grandmother.

I wish Violet had left behind an early family photo album. Then I could see what she and Grandpa Frank looked like when they were children, she thought. *But all of Violet's things have been cleared out of the cottage and I can't even get a sense of her decorating style. It's almost as if she were invisible.*

Paige suddenly recalled Steve mentioning that Violet might have stored a few belongings in the shed. She took the key he'd given her from her purse and followed the narrow, sandy path through the side yard. Located halfway between the driveway and the beech tree, the shed was angled so that its door faced the Hathaways' property.

I hope Lexie doesn't see me and come down to ask if I've made any decisions yet, she thought. *Maybe when I'm done poking around in the shed, I'll go take a closer look at the tree.*

As she lifted the key to unlock the rusty padlock, Paige discovered it was already hanging open, so she removed it from the latch and set it aside. The door wouldn't budge at first but after several failed attempts, she gave it a swift, hard tug and it came right off its hinges, nearly causing her to fall over backward. A large bag full of bottles, plastic containers and flattened cardboard boxes tumbled toward her and split open at her feet.

This is really the last straw, she thought when she saw the shed was crammed with more bags of recyclables, from floor to ceiling. Paige was both disappointed that the little building didn't contain any of Violet's possessions, and peeved that the former tenant hadn't taken what appeared to be half a year's worth of his refuse to the recycling center.

Aunt Sherry said Violet always kept the cottage very neat, she recalled. *She would've been appalled to see the condition of her home and shed. It seems so disrespectful that Owen didn't take better care of her property.*

Paige trekked back to the cottage to get fresh bags, but she only had one to spare. She stuffed it as full as she could without ripping it, and there were still glass bottles leftover. Tossing them into a heap beside the shed, she figured she'd pick them up after she bought more plastic sacks. Meanwhile, she shoved the full bag on top of the others inside the shed and leaned the door against the frame.

I'll deal with this when I have time to make multiple trips to the recycling center, she thought, and the scope of her annoyance grew to include her brother and cousins. *It really would've been nice if even one of them were here to help me.*

She returned to the cottage, intending to wash her hands and then to go back outside to examine the beech tree like she'd promised Lexie she would. But suddenly, Paige felt too drained to make the effort for her neighbor. And the idea of a mid-afternoon nap was so decadently tempting—especially if she didn't even set an alarm—that she couldn't resist.

· · ·

It was almost 5:00 p.m. when she woke, and Paige felt refreshed and motivated. She sauntered out onto the side heathland again, stopping to pick a fluffy lavender wildflower and tuck it behind her ear. Passing the shed, she continued until she came to the beech tree.

She scanned the circular area of infertile ground beneath it for fallen nut husks, but she didn't find one. Peering up, Paige searched the innumerable branches for even a single leaf-bearing twig—again, she couldn't see any sign of life. *It looks dead to me, but I'm no expert*, she thought, reaching out to touch it.

Its thin, blue-gray bark had faint, horizontal striations and resembled an elephant's hide. Irregularly shaped, the tree's trunk was probably three feet wide and as she slowly circled it, Paige had to duck to avoid knocking her head against the lower limbs, while also taking care not to trip on the thick, exposed roots sticking out like toes near the base.

When she'd come around to the oceanside of the trunk again, Paige leaned against it. She imagined that when the tree was thriving, its immense canopy had created a shady oasis. But as she leaned against its trunk, she was grateful its bare, massive limbs provided little protection from the elements. She felt warmer now than she'd felt since she'd arrived at the cottage, and she closed her eyes, basking in the glow of the sunshine.

Once again, her thoughts wandered to Violet and Frank. *When they were children, Violet was probably too afraid to climb this tree, but I bet Grandpa Frank did. I wonder how close he got to the top branch...*

Her musings were interrupted by a male voice calling, "Hi, Paige."

She opened her eyes expecting to find that Steve had arrived to deliver Violet's personal effects, but it was Seth.

"Hello," Paige called back, watching him approach. Wearing khaki crew shorts, a green, short-sleeved polo shirt, and boots, he looked every bit as attractive in his work uniform as he did in slacks, a tie, and a button-down dress shirt. But what was he doing here again?

He seemed to answer her unspoken question. "Lexie mentioned she talked to you about removing the beech tree. Even though I'm a landscaper, not an arborist, she said you wanted me to stop by and explain how I know for certain that the tree is dead."

"No, I didn't." Paige rolled her eyes at Lexie's statement, not caring if Seth noticed. "Asking you to talk to me was *her* agenda, not mine."

"Arg. I should have known." He shook his head, wearing the same disgruntled expression he'd worn on the ferry. Was it possible on that afternoon he'd been irritated at Lexie—not annoyed that he'd had to fetch Paige's key? "Sorry for disrupting your solitude."

He pivoted to leave but Paige stopped him. "Wait. As long as you've come all the way down here, I'd like to hear how you know the tree's definitely dead and not just diseased or dormant."

"It was easy—an arborist told me." He grinned, but his answer gave her pause.

"Why was an arborist evaluating this tree?" she asked, suspicious that Lexie might be involved. "Did he—or she—have permission to be on my great-aunt's property?"

The grin faded from Seth's face. He held up his hands and took a step backward. "Hang on a sec. Alex—that's the arborist —technically didn't evaluate anything on your aunt's property. We're friends and when we hang out, we occasionally talk about the plants and trees in Hope Haven. This one's a distinct land-mark for anyone who drives along the main road, which is what

Alex was doing a couple years ago when he noticed it didn't look healthy."

Seth ran his hand over the trunk, almost as if stroking a pet. "He thought it had the symptoms of a fungal disease that had already killed several other beech trees in Hope Haven. I remember him saying he hoped this one didn't die because it's one of his favorite trees on the island—mine, too. Like I said, it's got sort of an iconic presence. But the following spring, Alex said he could tell that it was dead from a mile away. And as far as I know, a mile away is as close as he ever got to looking at it."

Touched by Seth's appreciation of the tree's beauty and chagrined that she'd sounded so wary, Paige apologized. "I'm sorry. I shouldn't have made an assumption about the arborist—about your friend Alex, I mean."

Seth blew the air from his cheeks in a hard puff. "It's okay. I can understand why you might be worried about trespassers, especially after I admitted that Blossom and I have been using your great-aunt's staircase without permission." He met her eyes. "Just to be clear, I only used it when I went surfing with Owen this past spring, but I should've stopped that practice when he moved out. I guess I justified it to myself because the only reason the property management people don't want non-tenants on the staircase is they don't want to be held liable if there's an accident. But I knew the chances of my falling are slim-to-none and the chances of me suing if I did fall are absolutely zilch."

He sounded so remorseful that Paige intuitively trusted he meant what he said. "Thank you for explaining. If you really think the stairs are safe enough to use—"

Seth cut in to assure her, "They're perfectly safe, they're just really steep."

"Then feel free to keep using them at your own risk. I trust you not to sue me." She hesitated before deadpanning, "The question is, can I trust *Blossom*?"

Seth threw back his head and laughed. "Listen, I know first-hand how, ah, how aggressive my cousin can be when she wants something. Personally, if I were getting married, I wouldn't be thinking about whatever's going on in the background. All I'd be thinking about would be the woman standing in front of me."

His romantic sentiment was so open and unexpected that Paige inhaled sharply. Luckily, Seth didn't seem to notice and he went right on talking.

"But Lexie... well, she has different priorities than I do. A different focus." Seth's remark reminded Paige of how she felt about Tara and herself. "Obviously, this is your property and your tree, so the decision's up to you, not Lexie. But if you're open to hearing it, I'd like to suggest you consider something..." He paused, an eyebrow raised, seeking her permission.

"What's that?"

"You might want to talk to an arborist, either Alex or someone else, and get their professional opinion about how much longer they think this tree will remain standing. Because if it tips over in the wind or a rainstorm, it might land on your shed and crush everything in it."

Paige had to laugh. "That shed is filled to the ceiling with recyclables. If those got crushed, it would make it a lot easier for me to haul them to the recycling center."

"Yeah, but it wouldn't be easy to haul away the dead tree—and it would cost thousands of dollars. My point is, if a professional arborist tells you it's probably going to fall soon anyway, then why not let Lexie pay to have the tree removed now?"

"Hmm, I hadn't considered that." *But a potential buyer might, which could decrease our asking price for the property...*

"If you decide you'd like to talk to Alex, I can give you his contact info. He's in high demand during summer, but I'm sure he'd stop by and give you his opinion on how much longer this old beauty will remain upright."

As Seth gave the tree another pat, Paige noticed the white

insignia on his shirt directly above his heart: it depicted a dog with long ears. Was that supposed to be Blossom? When she realized that once again, she was staring at his chest, she shifted her focus to the limb just behind Seth's shoulder. Something caught her attention and she pointed. "Hey, what are those markings?"

He turned to look. "Where?"

Paige stepped closer. The lines were faint and shallow, and it almost seemed as if they were merely an abnormality of the natural striations in the bark. But as Paige traced them with her fingers, she recognized they were in the shape of a heart, which encircled a word. Or part of a word.

"It's an L and a T, I think." There was a third letter, too, but she couldn't quite make out what it was.

"No, that's not an L—it's an E. There are two more lines, here and here. And this lowercase T is actually a plus symbol. I think it says E + V." As if there were any question about whose initials they were, he added, "Edward plus Violet. My great-uncle and your great-aunt."

Feeling a bit uncomfortable discussing the subject with a Hathaway family member, Paige continued to study the bark so she wouldn't have to look directly at him. "So I guess you've heard stories about... about what happened when they were teenagers?"

"Yeah. I mean, it's not something my family talks about very often. But I know that Violet was in love with Edward, even though he only liked her as a friend. When she found out he was interested in someone else, she apparently, uh, she... she created a scene."

It was obvious that Seth was measuring his words so he wouldn't offend Paige, which made her feel both grateful and embarrassed. She was trying to think of a way to end the awkward conversation when she was struck with a realization. "That's what I've always thought happened, too. But I guess this carving sort of turns that narrative upside down, doesn't it?"

"How so?"

"It proves that Edward must have had romantic feelings about Violet at some point after all."

"Not necessarily. How tall was Violet?"

"She was average height, I think."

Paige's guess was based on a conversation she'd overheard when she was a young girl. Her grandmother was telling Sherry that Paige's mother had looked a lot like Violet, and that Paige resembled that side of the family, too. She'd called them "Plain Janes," and said the only feature that stood out about them was their bee-stung lips. The phrase had confused Paige for the longest time, as she'd never been stung by a bee. But she hadn't wanted to ask her grandmother what she'd meant because then it would've been obvious she'd been eavesdropping. "Why are you asking me about Violet's height?"

"Because unless she was unusually petite, *she* could've been the one to carve these initials, not Edward," he suggested. "Just because she was a female doesn't mean she didn't know how to use a pocketknife."

"And just because she was a female doesn't mean she was delusional about a man's feelings toward her," Paige shot back.

"I'm not implying she was *delusional* about Edward. I'm just saying, that if all those stories about what happened between them years ago are true, it's possible she misinterpreted his friendship for something else. I made that same mistake more than once when I was young—especially about summer people."

His admission was disarming, and Paige backed down. "I guess it's possible that Violet could have been the one to do this," she conceded, tracing a finger over the heart shape a second time. "I used to doodle my initials and the initials of boys I liked in my school notebooks all the time."

"Either way, it's cool that it's still legible all these years later, considering the extreme weather we get out here on the dunes," remarked Seth. "This tree has been through a *lot*, so when I say I think you should consider having it removed, I'm not making that suggestion lightly."

"I know you're not," acknowledged Paige. "But I'm curious about something. Lexie knew a long time ago the tree would interfere with her wedding photos and the guests' view. So what's her plan if I say I want to leave the tree standing where it is?"

"That's been a source of debate during many of our meetings. But I've got a couple backup plans, so we'll work something out." Seth rubbed his left temple in a slow circle with his palm. Clearly it was a stressful subject and Paige sympathized, but she couldn't let her emotions influence this decision.

"Good. Because like I said, I still have to decide whether I even want to consult an arborist," she reiterated.

"Sure. Take your time." Seth glanced at his watch. "I'd better get home and feed Blossom."

Paige smiled. "I like his name, by the way. Great use of irony."

"Irony? You mean because it's a pretty name for a homely dog?"

"Those are your words, not mine," she said, quickly backpedalling. "But why did you decide to call him that?"

"I didn't—my ten-year-old niece did."

Paige thought it was sweet that Seth allowed his niece to name his dog. "It suits him."

Seth grinned. "I'll let her know you think so, although she'll be embarrassed by it now that she's twenty-one." He said goodbye and started down the path with a wave.

Paige lingered at the tree, studying the initials. She wasn't entirely convinced that Seth was right, that her great-aunt had authored the engraving. Even though what he'd suggested was consistent with what Paige's family had always told her about Violet and Edward, she had an inkling there was more to the young couple's relationship than what other people knew.

If you could talk, I bet you'd tell all kinds of stories about what happened out here on the heathland, she silently addressed the beech tree, before heading back to her great-aunt's cottage.

SIX

Even the tip of Paige's nose was cold. She pulled the summer quilt up to her ears, dreading getting out of bed. *I really need to shower this morning so I can wash my hair,* she told herself. *The inspector's coming today, and I don't want him to be biased toward the cottage just because I look so disheveled.*

Yet it took another half hour of snuggling beneath the covers before she could bear to step onto the cold hardwood floor. She hadn't packed any slippers, but she immediately donned her flip flops. Then she grabbed her bathrobe from the hook and her toiletry bag and towel from the bathroom. Darting outside before she lost her nerve, Paige glanced up the hill toward the Hathaways' mansion.

They can't see me from here, can they? Not that it mattered that much; the showering area was enclosed by a wooden stall. Still, she didn't relish the idea of them looking down from their ivory tower and catching a glimpse of her dashing from the cottage to the shower in her pajamas.

But as soon as the spray of steamy water doused her head and shoulders, the concern dissipated. All she could think about was that she'd never take a hot shower for granted again. *Even with the gutter hanging loose overhead, this shower is the cottage's second-best feature, right after the porch*, she thought.

When she was done, she slowly made her way back inside, stopping twice to listen to birdsong she'd never heard in Illinois, before shuffling into the kitchen for coffee and breakfast.

She was savoring it on the porch when the inspector arrived, an hour early. For the past few days, Paige had spent much more time alone than she usually did, so she was very glad to see him. Hoping he'd chat for a while before he began inspecting the cottage, she offered him a cup of coffee, but he turned it down.

"Thanks, but I've got a full schedule today. I'd better get started ASAP."

"Right. Well, I should mention that the furnace doesn't seem to be working, although I'm sure you would have caught that," Paige said. "Is there anything else I can point out or do to help you?"

"I've got it covered, but you're welcome to accompany me and ask questions." He shifted his weight from foot to foot. "I'll start with the exterior, to give you time to, uh, get ready for the day. I arrived kind of early, so I probably threw you off-schedule."

Only then did it occur to Paige that she was still wearing her bathrobe and she had a towel wrapped around her head. "I appreciate that," she said sheepishly. "I'll be out in a few minutes."

As soon as the flimsy porch door banged shut behind the inspector, Paige flew into the bedroom to change out of her bathrobe, fretting, *If I'm not careful about how I present myself, I'm going to get a reputation for being as socially awkward as Violet was!*

. . .

Paige wasn't surprised by any of the major renovations, repairs, and purchases the inspector recommended making before putting the cottage on the market. They included updating the septic system, as well as installing a new roof and windows, and a furnace.

"I'll provide a complete written evaluation, of course," he said. "But those are the biggies. There are cosmetic changes that should be made, too, obviously. If you're handy, you can do them yourself. If you're not, I'd suggest lining up the first contractor who has an opening in their schedule. This is a very hectic time for carpenters, so you'll be lucky to find someone who can squeeze you in before October."

Paige took his advice to heart. Immediately after he left, she drove into town to call the contractors from the list Steve had given her. She left messages for three carpenters before she reached one, Nick Armstrong, who answered his phone. He said a couple of his crew members would be available on Thursday morning, although only for a day.

"Full disclosure," he warned. "I'll be sending my son Aidan and a trainee. They're young, but they do quality work. It's guaranteed, so if you're not pleased with the results, let me know."

"Sounds good," said Paige, who figured she couldn't lose. Two young carpenters-in-training would be a lot more adroit than she was. Nick said they'd stop by early the following morning to discuss the projects and take measurements, so they'd be able to purchase the supplies they'd need before Thursday.

After picking up groceries at a tiny market, Paige returned to the cottage to enumerate the minor repairs. Re-screening the porch topped her list. She'd swept it at least twice daily, but it seemed every time she turned around, more sand drifted in. *Why go to the beach when the beach will come to you?* she silently quipped.

She added fixing the cabinet doors in the kitchen to the list, as well as filling in gaps in the baseboards, to help keep mice out of the cottage. Also, although she realized that installing new gutters would be part of the roofing process, she intended to ask Aidan and the trainee to either temporarily secure the gutter hanging over the shower, or to remove it altogether.

I wonder if the stairs leading to the beach are truly as safe as Seth said they are. I should look to see if any of the boards need replacing. Since she was going to check them out, she figured she might as well take a walk while she was at it.

Although the descent to the beach was extremely precipitous, the wooden staircase was sturdier than Paige had expected it to be, and it included a handrail on each side. She only noticed three slightly loose steps and one small gap in the railing, which she figured Aidan could easily fix.

I better remember to save some of my energy for climbing back up when I return, she thought as she hopped off the final step and started down the beach.

She had only trudged a few paces in the soft sand before realizing she could move a lot faster if she removed her socks and shoes and walked on the firmer terrain down by the water. As chilly as the damp sand was between her toes, once she picked up speed, she hardly noticed it. Besides, she was completely enraptured by the ocean's salty, breeze-blown aroma, its profoundly blue color, and the boisterous commotion of waves racing each other to shore.

Paige was so invigorated by her surroundings that she must have walked for forty-five minutes before deciding to turn around. Yet when she reached the cliffs near Violet's cottage, she jogged up the steps. *Why is it that I never feel this energetic after being on my feet for an hour at the hospital?* she thought wistfully.

Just after cresting the staircase, she noticed a car descending the hill and turning into her driveway. It was Steve, the attorney; Paige had been so captivated by the beach that she'd forgotten all about him bringing Violet's personal effects to her.

"Hi, Steve," she called heartily and hurried toward him, her pants still rolled up to her knees, and her ankles and toes encrusted with wet sand.

"Hi, Paige. I see you've been beachcombing. Find any treasures?"

"It's nothing *but* treasure down there," she gushed, making a sweeping gesture with her arms. "The beach and the waves and the sandbars and shore birds... It's all so glorious."

"I'm really happy you like it." Steve grinned as if she'd just complimented him personally. "How about the cottage, have you settled in okay?"

"Yes. I mean, there's still a lot of work to be done, but it's clean and comfy enough for my brief stay," she answered, emphasizing the word *brief*. "You're welcome to come inside. I was about to make a cup of tea and I have some delicious fruit tarts from Sebastian's."

"Sebastian's? That's hard to resist, but my wife wants to take a walk with me during my lunch hour, so I've got to hustle home. I'm just dropping by, as promised, with your great-aunt's personal possessions the nursing home sent me." He reached into his car and produced a parcel about the size of a shoe box.

For some reason, she'd expected the container of her great-aunt's belongings to be bigger. Not because Paige was hoping she'd inherit anything else from Violet, but that it seemed kind of pitiful that her personal effects had been reduced to a small, solitary package. "Thank you."

"Sure thing. And if you need anything else, just holler—literally. Voices travel very well out here," he said, with his usual corny humor. "Also, if you really do end up deciding to sell the cottage, be sure to let me know, so I can hammer out the legalities."

Again, Paige tried to dispel his persistent notion there was a possibility she wouldn't put Violet's place on the market. "I haven't gotten in touch with a real estate agent yet, but as I've said, there's no *if* about it. I'm definitely selling."

"You say that now but wait until the weather warms up enough to go swimming." He bobbed his head up and down knowingly. "Trust me. You'll never want to come out of the water, much less leave Dune Island."

Smiling, Paige gave up trying to argue with him. She wished him a pleasant walk, said goodbye, and ambled to the porch, where she stomped the sand from her feet before entering the cottage. Paige still wanted tea, but a fruit tart no longer appealed to her. Exercising in the fresh air made her want to make healthier food choices, so she chopped vegetables for a salad and then carried it to the porch.

Deliberately nibbling the locally grown produce, she reflected on what a relief it was to have a break from the frantic pace of her life and job in Chicago. *If I were on my lunch break right now, I'd be so tense that I'd devour this so fast I'd hardly taste it.*

Then she remembered she'd made a resolution not to think about work while she was on Dune Island. So she slowly finished her meal and then she went into the kitchen to open the parcel that Steve had delivered. Even though she was disappointed by its size, Paige hoped its contents would provide additional insight into Violet's life.

Folded neatly inside the package was a plain, gray wool cardigan sweater, with darker gray buttons up the front. It seemed clean and barely worn. *Did Violet knit this or buy it?* The question had barely formed in Paige's mind when she noticed the manufacturer's size label.

For someone who worked as a seamstress, she sure had drab taste in clothing, Paige thought, shaking out the sweater and holding it up in front of her. She noticed a small manila envelope had dropped to the floor. Paige picked it up and carefully blew off the grains of sand.

Sliding her finger beneath the sealed flap, she opened it. The first item Paige pulled out felt like a driver's license, but it turned out to be her great-aunt's health insurance card. Paige reached in again, her fingers skimming the seam along the bottom. She fished out a long, tarnished chain, which was looped through two equally tarnished pendants. One was a small delicate cross. The other was larger, heavier, and heart shaped.

"Oh, it has a hinge—I think it's a locket," she mumbled. Using her thumbnail, she pried it open, expecting to find a photo. Although the locket contained two tiny frames on both sides, there was nothing in them except dark smudges.

She clicked the two sides of the silver heart together again and dangled the necklace in front of her face. Paige recalled Sherry mentioning something about Violet being religious and praying a lot. So she wasn't surprised to learn that her great-aunt had worn a symbol of her faith around her neck. But a locket was usually a gift from a sweetheart.

Paige peeked inside the envelope a third time and then turned it upside-down and tapped on it to make sure she hadn't missed anything. It was empty and Paige suddenly felt a bit hollow, too. It struck her as sad that her great-aunt's sweater and jewelry had come back to the cottage, but Violet herself hadn't returned.

With a sigh, Paige slid the necklace and locket back into the small manila envelope before tucking the envelope into a dresser drawer for safekeeping. As she was hanging Violet's sweater in the closet, Paige got the idea that polishing her jewelry might be a small way to honor her great-aunt's past.

I've got a conference call with the guys and Tara to discuss what the inspector said, and I have to go into town this evening anyway. If I leave early, I can stop at that jewelry shop I saw in

Rockfield, and purchase a special polishing cloth, she thought, feeling cheerful again. *Meanwhile, I've got plenty of other things around here to clean and polish...*

Paige arrived at the jeweler's right at closing time, but the woman minding the store kindly advised her about which cloths to purchase and how to use them.

"If you have any problems or concerns, you can always bring in the necklace and I'll demonstrate the proper technique," she offered.

Paige thanked her, but in the back of her mind, she had a trifling worry: if the jeweler saw the locket, she might inquire where Paige got it. And Paige didn't want her to discover the locket had belonged to Violet and make an unkind remark about her meltdown about Edward.

I'm being foolish. That was eighty years ago. No one remembers what happened any more, she told herself. So far—with the exception of Lexie—the islanders had been as helpful and warm as the people in the Midwest, who were known for their friendliness. Yet because she'd heard so many stories about how Dune Island gossip had ruined her grandfather and great-aunt's lives, Paige couldn't quite shake her apprehensive feelings.

She still had an hour before her call and her appetite was raging, so she ducked into a casual Main Street restaurant for dinner. She was seated by the window, where she watched passersby as she savored broiled cod with lemon aioli. The fish was mild and flaky, unlike any she'd had from the lake back home, and after so many days by herself in the cottage she was pleased to be among people again, even if she was dining alone.

When she logged onto her video call, none of the guys were online yet. But Tara was waiting impatiently. "I've been dying to tell you that we've decided to book Lakeside Palace for Cami's engagement party," she announced.

It seemed odd that her cousin tended to omit Dylan's name whenever she talked about the engagement party, but Paige didn't draw attention to it. "Wow. Lakeside Palace. That's quite an upgrade from The Landing."

"Exactly," Tara replied smugly. "Cami's my only daughter and hopefully this will be her only engagement party, so we can't celebrate it at a two-bit venue like The Landing."

As Tara continued to extol the superior qualities of Lakeside Palace, Rick and Christopher joined the call. Paige's brother, Dustin, however, was fifteen minutes late. He had little tolerance for Tara's blathering and despite his own tardiness, he boldly interrupted her to say he wanted to get the meeting started because he was going walleye fishing that evening. In turn, the three guys broke into a side conversation about the pros and cons of using minnow-tipped jigs as lures.

Paige chuckled to herself, remembering a remark her grandmother had made about Grandpa Frank: "You can take the man out of Dune Island but you can't take Dune Island out of the man." By that she'd meant that Grandpa Frank wasn't content unless he was near a large body of water—preferably fishing in it. The same could be said for Dustin, Rick, and Christopher, but Tara had even less interest in hearing them talk about the sport than they had in listening to her talk about Lakeside Palace.

Visibly irritated, she butted in, "Hey, Dustin, since you're in such a hurry to go fishing, we should stay on topic. We're supposed to be talking about what the inspector told Paige she needs to replace or repair before she puts the cottage on the market."

Before Dustin had a chance to make a flippant comeback, Paige spoke up. "There's good news and there's bad news," she announced. "The good news is that, thanks to some recent updating, the foundation and wiring are in great shape. The bad news is that the roof and windows need to be replaced and the septic system should be updated. Also, the cottage needs a new furnace."

Rick gave a low whistle. "That *is* bad news. A furnace alone can run upward of eight to ten grand."

"Yeah. That's what the inspector said, too. He couldn't give exact figures on how much a new roof, new windows, and a septic system update would be—I'd have to get bids on those—but he did provide estimates for what labor and supplies generally cost on the island."

After Paige shared the figures with the group her brother yawped, "Are you kidding me? We can't afford that. Let's sell the cottage as is."

"Not so fast," Paige protested. "Whatever happened to the idea of pooling our resources for the repairs, like we discussed?"

"I've been thinking about that and it doesn't really make good financial sense. Anyone who can afford to purchase the property can afford to overhaul the cottage, too—it'll be chump change to them," answered Dustin. "It's not the same situation as when the repairs need to be made so the buyer can secure financing from their bank."

"He's right," agreed Christopher. "I mean, an aging roof is definitely a red flag for most buyers, especially on a house they'd use as their primary residence. But judging from the pictures you've sent, I think the location is going to be what sells Violet's estate. Something as minor as a busted furnace or drafty windows won't be a dealbreaker for someone purchasing a summer cottage, especially not when it's situated on prime oceanfront acreage."

"I'm not sure I agree with you on that," countered Rick. "But I'm cash-poor at the moment and honestly, I'd prefer not to tap into my assets to help fund any major repairs."

"But... but I thought everyone was on board with making repairs before we put the cottage on the market," Paige said.

"Why did I bother to come all the way here if we're just going to sell the house as is?"

"We were on board with *assessing* whether to make the repairs," Rick clarified. "That's why we chipped in to hire an inspector before we listed the property. And it's why you went out there—to gather the information we needed in person, and to be sure everything was on the up and up. Now that we know we probably won't get a good return on what we'd invest making repairs, you can work with a local real estate agent to get the ball rolling on selling the place. So it's not as if it's a wasted trip."

"Hold on. You three guys might not feel like it's worth it to make the repairs, but I happen to think that having a new roof and energy efficient windows could increase the potential buyer pool, which in turn, could increase the asking price," argued Paige.

"Yeah, but it could take weeks or even months just to get bids for those projects and who knows how long it would take for a contractor to actually put us on their schedule?" asked Dustin. "Listen, as far as I'm concerned, the sale of Violet's property represents found money. A *lot* of found money. If we sold it tomorrow for half of what it's worth, we'd still be a lot wealthier than we are today. So why turn this into a long, drawn-out process?"

Before Paige could point out the flaws in his financial reasoning, Tara piped up, "I couldn't agree with you more, Dustin."

"Thank you," he replied, with a self-satisfied flourish of his hand.

Paige suspected the unprecedented agreement between her cousin and brother had something to do with the fact that Dustin was planning to buy a boat and Tara was planning a wedding. And the sooner the estate sold, the sooner they'd know just how big of a boat or how lavish a wedding they could afford.

However, she also recognized that their motives for rushing the sales process were irrelevant. All that really mattered was that without their financial help, Paige couldn't afford to replace the roof, install new windows, or purchase a new furnace for the cottage.

"If everyone is absolutely certain we should sell the house as is, then I guess I've got no other option," she admitted. "But what about cosmetic repairs? I've already scheduled someone to come on Thursday to re-screen the porch and to work on a few other minor projects."

"That's fine. We don't want the place looking like a complete rat trap for showings." Although Dustin's word choice may have been accurate, it struck Paige as insulting. "How much do you think you'll need for a budget?"

Paige suggested a figure and everyone agreed to split the expenses. The guys told Paige to use the funds at her discretion, and Tara did, too, but she had one stipulation. "Don't use any of the money to remove the beech tree. Since the Hathaways are the ones who want it taken down and they're willing to pay for it, you should let them. I'll be paying plenty for my own daughter's wedding preparations—there's no way I'm going to contribute a single red cent to Lexie's."

After explaining to the men what Tara had meant, Paige assured everyone, "Trust me, I have no intention to pay to chop down the beech tree. I'm not even sure I'll have it removed."

"Great. Keep us posted, Sis. Talk to you all at the same time next week unless something comes up sooner," said Dustin. "Bye."

Christopher and Rick said goodbye and their faces disappeared from the screen in a blink, too. Only Tara remained. "Good, now that they're gone, we can talk about the Palace without being interrupted."

But at that moment, Paige couldn't bring herself to even feign interest in Cami and Dylan's engagement party. It wasn't that she didn't care about the event; it was just that she was maxed out on the subject at the moment.

"Sorry, but we'll have to chat tomorrow. I forgot to pick up a few things earlier today, so I want to get to the market before it closes. I also need to stop for gas. Then I'm headed straight back to the cottage to collapse into bed. I'm exhausted."

"Really? You don't look any more tired than usual."

"Thanks, but I am," she replied, intending to be firm, not sardonic. "Have a good night. Bye."

As Paige approached Spindrift Lane, she noticed there were only two vehicles in the Hathaways' circular driveway and the interior of the mansion appeared almost entirely dark. For some reason, she had imagined the Hathaways would host parties every night of the week, but so far, she hadn't heard any noise coming from their estate.

When she got out of the car in her own parking area, she paused and peered across the heathland. The beech tree's multitude of dark limbs and twigs against the white, windblown clouds reminded her of thousands of exquisite neurons, and the association with her profession made her smile.

I really do love being a nurse. If only work wasn't so stressful, Paige thought. *But how is that going to happen when our floor is so mismanaged and there's such high staff turnover?*

Shaking thoughts about the hospital from her mind, she went inside. After changing into her pajamas and layering them with a sweatshirt, Paige realized that although her body was bone-tired, her mind wasn't sleepy yet. So she wrapped her quilt around her and brought the polish cloths and Violet's jewelry into the living room, where the lighting was the brightest.

She gently freed both pendants from the chain. Since the cross was smaller and more delicate than the heart, she polished it first, carefully massaging it with the white cloth, as the jeweler had instructed.

It was so fragile that she was worried she might bend it between her fingertips, so she worked slowly. After several minutes, she discovered that the metal wasn't silver, but gold. Once she'd completely removed the outer layer of dirt, she switched to using the gray cloth, and although the cross was flat and unembellished, by the time she finished it was gleaming.

Then she started on the chain, which she quickly learned was also gold. Paige used the white cloth to painstakingly caress it between her thumb and fingers. Centimeter by centimeter, she slowly worked her way toward the clasp, until the entire strand was gleaming. She set it aside and picked up the heart pendant.

Until she began polishing it, Paige had thought the markings in the center of the heart were scratches. But as she wiped away the grime, she realized the fine lines were deliberately etched into the pendant. They looked like... a floral pattern? She squinted at the graceful hairline sketch.

"They're violets!" She gushed aloud, "That's so sweet."

Paige studied the engraving a long time, wondering if Violet's parents had given their daughter this piece of jewelry in honor of her name. It seemed like an extravagant purchase, considering that they'd been a poor family.

Maybe it was a gift from a grandparent, or a friend? Or maybe she bought it for herself as an adult? Paige wondered. *Could a man have given it to her?*

Because the jewelry was so tarnished and fragile, she had assumed it was very old. But maybe it was something Violet had acquired more recently, such as from a fellow patient at the nursing facility, before she'd had the stroke... Paige noticed that the locket was silver, not gold like the chain and cross. Was that significant? She opened the heart and continued polishing.

The tiny interior frames created raised edges, so cleaning the inside took longer than it had taken to remove the grime from the flat external surfaces. As she massaged the left half of the heart, once again she noticed what appeared to be scratches. Paige was hesitant to apply more pressure, for fear of damaging the metal. She wiped the cloth over it in a few more slow, gentle circles and then lifted her thumb to see if the scratches were still there.

Those aren't scratches—they're curlicues. I think it's another etching, she realized.

The tendrils and whorls were so faint and shallow that even when she held the pendant an inch below the lightbulb, she couldn't make out what the image depicted. So she snapped a photo of it with her phone and then magnified the view. She realized she'd been wrong: the lines weren't an etching—they were *words.*

In tiny, elaborate cursive, the inscription read:

Violet, my love
My favourite flower—

Paige was astounded. *So the locket* was *a gift from an admirer... but who?*

She enlarged the image on her phone even more, and then she compared it with the left half of the pendant in her palm. Now that she knew what the inscription said, it was easier to decipher it with her naked eye. Was there an engraving beneath the smudge on the other half of the heart, too? Or had the giver left that side blank so Violet could insert a photo of him there?

Paige shook the hair from her eyes, picked up the polishing cloth, and began wiping the pendant again. Every ten seconds she deliberately forced herself to pause to peek at it. The last thing she wanted to do was rub too hard and erase the engraving.

The cursive she uncovered on the right side of the pendant was less faded than the cursive on the left, but she still couldn't quite make it out. Again she snapped a photo with her phone and enlarged it on the screen. The inscription said:

> Hold me in your heart
> always and forever

Squeezed into the very bottom of the heart was a signature:

> –ED–

"*He* gave this to her?" Paige marveled, astonished. "Edward Hathaway gave Violet a locket inscribed with a poem?"

Maybe not a poem, exactly, but a little verse. A love note, of sorts. An expression of his feelings, and a request for her devotion.

Paige reread the inscription in its entirety:

> Violet, my love
> My favourite flower—
> Hold me in your heart
> always and forever.
> –ED–

She read it two more times—once from her phone and once directly from the locket—to make sure her eyes weren't playing tricks on her. Paige set it down, admittedly feeling very clever. Hadn't she told Seth that the initials on the tree indicated that Edward had cared for Violet after all? Now Paige knew that she'd been right.

But her smugness quickly turned to confusion. *Why did*

Violet allow everyone to believe that her feelings for Edward had never been reciprocated? she ruminated. *Why didn't she just show them the locket and prove that he'd been as serious about her as she was about him?*

She could only imagine that young Violet must have been so dejected because Edward had jilted her for another girl that it was irrelevant whether anyone else knew the truth. Or maybe after her initial outburst, she'd been so ashamed of her destructive behavior that she'd decided not to stand up for herself again.

But why had Edward denied ever having feelings for Violet? Was it because he didn't want the other girl to know, especially if he'd been two-timing her?

It was more likely that he was worried his parents would have disapproved of his relationship with Violet, Paige speculated. *Judging from what Aunt Sherry told me, they probably would have forbidden him to date someone they'd considered to be a poor, unrefined islander.*

Whatever his reason was for lying, she concluded that Edward was a spineless creep. Paige understood why his behavior would have devastated an inexperienced, vulnerable young woman like Violet. After all, what had happened between Paige and Trevor wasn't entirely different from what happened between Violet and Edward. Essentially, Paige and her great-aunt had both been cast aside by men they'd thought loved them more than they did.

But like Aunt Sherry implied the other day, the difference in our response is that no matter how ticked off I felt, I know I'll move on. Even if Violet eventually forgave Edward, she clearly never allowed herself to love or be loved by another man after him.

Maybe Violet had decided it was easier to shut out the world than to risk being hurt again, but Paige still couldn't fathom a lifetime of seclusion. She also found it difficult to comprehend why her great-aunt had kept the locket from him all these years—she'd even worn it to the nursing home in her nineties. It made it seem as if she'd never gotten over Edward, even though he'd denied and betrayed her—and even though Violet was no longer a naïve teenager. Paige thought it was very strange that she hadn't developed a more mature perspective as she aged.

Then again, Edward had died very young, which might have complicated Violet's feelings about him. Maybe she'd saved the piece of jewelry as a tribute to their youth, instead of as a symbol of her abiding affection for him?

It could be that I'm assigning too much emotional signifi-cance to why *she kept the locket,* Paige reasoned as she collected the pieces of jewelry and returned them to the small envelope. *Other than this gold chain and cross, the pendant was apparently her only piece of jewelry. Maybe she simply wore them as a set because it made her feel dressed-up while she was in the nursing home.*

Although disturbing, her great-aunt's reason for continuing to cherish the locket didn't matter to Paige half as much as the fact that Edward had given Violet inscribed jewelry in the first place.

For all these years, everyone—including me—believed an incorrect version of what happened in the past. She yawned and stood up to go to bed. *Tomorrow, I'm going to tell Aunt Sherry and Tara that we were wrong. And the next time I see Seth, I'm going to tell him, too.*

SEVEN

Even though she was as cold as ever, on Wednesday Paige hopped right out of bed because she needed to get dressed, brush her hair, and have breakfast before the guys arrived to discuss the repairs. As soon as they left, she intended to head into town to call Sherry—and Tara, too, since they were probably both at Tara's house.

The young carpenters were scheduled to· arrive between 7:00 and 7:30 before heading to another job. By 8:00, they still hadn't shown up and Paige was growing impatient. She decided that if they weren't there by 9:00, she was going to go into town without speaking directly to them; she'd leave a note on the porch listing the repairs.

However, at 8:55, their truck rumbled down the driveway. Aidan appeared to be in his early twenties, but the other kid, Micah, didn't look old enough to shave yet.

"Sorry we're running late, but there was a detour," Aidan explained. "It caused a major traffic jam."

Paige raised an eyebrow. "I didn't realize there were enough vehicles in Highland Hills to qualify for a traffic jam."

"There usually aren't, but tourist season opens this

weekend and a lot of people have started arriving early to beat the rush. This morning a jogger found a UXO on the beach in Port Newcomb, so the police had to reroute all the ferry traffic through Highland Hills, and since there's only one main road along the coastline, it was slow going."

"What's a UXO?" asked Paige.

"It stands for unexploded ordnance. It's the second one that's been discovered this week, which is weird. It's been, like, five years since the last one was found."

"It's the *second* one this week?" exclaimed Paige. "I didn't realize a small community like this would have such a problem with terrorism."

Micah slapped his knee and cracked up, until Aidan elbowed him in the ribs. He explained, "The unexploded ordnances aren't from terrorists. They're left over from World War Two. The military used Hope Haven for training and the tiny, uninhabited islands in the surrounding waters for target practice. Every once in a while, a storm or erosion will uncover a UXO in the sand."

"Really? That sounds dangerous."

"It can be—some of the warheads are live. But most of them are dummies and fortunately, no one has ever been hurt. There are signs posted at the beaches closest to where target practice took place. So people are aware of what they should do if they find a big chunk of metal while they're, you know, clamming or making a sandcastle or something."

"What *should* they do if that happens?"

"Run!" joked Micah, cracking up again.

Aidan shot him an annoyed look before answering Paige's question. "They should call 9-1-1. Then the police will notify a bomb squad—and possibly the Navy—who will come out to collect the UXO so they can detonate it."

"Wow. I knew there was some military presence here during the war because my grandfather used to assist with the blackout drills," said Paige. "But I had no idea they used the area for target practice."

"Yeah. There's an exhibit at the museum in Port Newcomb if you want to learn more about Dune Island's history during the war," Aidan told her. "Personally, I think it's kinda fascinating when people find UXOs, but the vacationers usually aren't happy about the beach closures. My clients don't appreciate it when I show up late, either..."

Paige took the hint and quickly began discussing the lists of projects she hoped they could accomplish the following day. Aidan assured her they'd do their best, and the estimate he gave her for the cost of supplies and labor was well within her budget.

Since they'd advised her against going out on the main road for a couple more hours, Paige postponed her phone call to Sherry, happily opting for a walk on the beach instead. Today she headed in the opposite direction, and once again, she felt energized by the ocean's dynamic presence. As she briskly strode just beyond the spray of waves shattering onto shore, she noticed that the cliffs to her left were diminishing in height. Every now and then she spotted a house or cottage enveloped within the lower dunes, but she didn't pass any people on the beach.

Eventually, she arrived at an inlet, which was probably 200 yards wide. Realizing there was no way around the swift, incoming current, she had to turn back even though she felt as if she could have kept walking for hours.

Time never flies like this when I'm on the elliptical at the gym, she thought. Not that Paige was at the gym very often; usually after being on her feet for eight hours at work, she felt as if she could barely drag herself to the train station for her commute home. *Maybe I should start going for walks on the lakefront trails a couple times a week.*

Even as the idea occurred to her, Paige knew it was unlikely she'd follow through with it. Getting to the trail before or after work would add another hour to her commute, and she really needed to spend that time unpacking the rest of her boxes and getting more settled into her condo. Maybe if she personalized the décor, it would feel more like her own home instead of just the place where she slept in between hospital shifts.

Paige smiled as she imagined painting her living room walls a brilliant, ocean blue, and installing carpeting the same shade of neon green as the beach grass. She wouldn't do it, of course; in her experience, colors that were striking in the natural world were seldom as aesthetically appealing indoors. But maybe as a compromise she could buy some throw rugs that were the color of sand?

An especially large wave bounded onto shore and as Paige scampered to higher ground, she noticed the receding water had worn branch-like patterns in the slope of wet sand. Instantly, her mind went to the beech tree. Should she consult an arborist or not? And if they suggested removing the tree, would that end up being a big hassle for her as she prepared to sell the cottage?

She was so lost in thought that she almost didn't notice a woman setting up an easel near the dunes.

"Good morning," the artist called. Dressed in a flannel shirt and jeans, the blonde woman appeared to be around the same age as Paige was.

"Hello. That's a terrific easel. Is it an antique?"

"Yes, it is. Good eye. Are you an artist, too—or an antique dealer?"

"Neither. I'm a nurse. But I dated an artist once, and he had an antique easel, too."

"What a coincidence—I'm an artist and my husband, Lucas, is an ER pediatrician." The woman tipped her head, a hopeful expression on her face. "Is there any chance you've moved to the island to work at Hope Haven Hospital or another medical facility?"

"No. I'm just here to... to clean up my family's cottage," Paige faltered. Even though she planned to contact a real estate agent after Aidan and Micah completed the minor repairs, until then she didn't want the word to get out that she was selling Violet's estate. "Besides, I already have a job working at a hospital—in the in-patient department."

"Oh, that's too bad. I mean, it's good for you, obviously. It's just that the island is always in need of essential employees, like teachers and utility workers—and especially medical professionals. So I thought maybe you were a traveling nurse."

"No, but I used to be," said Paige. "It's surprising that there's a staffing shortage here. Most of the nurses I know would love to work in a beautiful location like this."

"Yes, the scenery here is unbeatable... but the salaries aren't. Which is doubly unfortunate since the cost of living is so high and it's virtually impossible to find affordable housing."

"Yes, I've noticed that everything here is almost as expensive as where I live in Chicago."

"You're from Chicago, too? Another coincidence—I grew up near Chicago. I'm Emily, by the way."

They chatted about their hometowns a little and then Paige said, "Dune Island is a huge change from the city. Highland Hills is so quiet that I can go an entire day without talking to anyone other than myself."

Emily giggled. "That's what I like about it—I'm a total introvert. My husband's the opposite, so he gets his social interaction at the hospital during the day, while I enjoy the solitude of the beach." She glanced at the water. "In a way, though, I've found that the ocean has a presence of its own. Not exactly like a person, but it keeps me company."

"Then you come here often to paint?"

"Not as often as I'd like. But this morning after I dropped Lucas off at work, I was rerouted because of the UXO—did you hear about that?" She paused and Paige nodded. "I had my easel and supplies in the car, so I pulled over at the nearest public beach, about a mile from here. I wanted to paint the waves breaking on these sandbars, so I figured it was worth the hike. But now the tide's probably going to chase me away before I even finish setting up."

"I'd better let you get to it, then." As she turned to leave, Paige had an idea. "If you need to finish your painting, you're welcome to park in my driveway and use my staircase. It's steep, but it's a lot closer to these sandbars than the public beach is."

"You live close by?"

"Yes. On Spindrift Lane." When Emily showed no sign of recognition, Paige added, "It's the tiny cottage down the hill from the Hathaways' house."

Again, Emily looked blank. "Sorry, I should pay more attention to street signs and residents' last names, but around here we identify ourselves by landmarks and first names. As in, 'I'm Emily from four dunes northeast of the inlet.'"

Paige chuckled. "Yeah, I've noticed that, but I'm still not in the habit of counting dunes. I'd say my family's cottage is about a third of a mile that way... There's a big beech tree in the yard, so you can't miss it."

Emily grabbed Paige's sleeve. "That's *your* beech tree? I *love* her!" she exclaimed, as if she'd just discovered they had a favorite relative or a beloved schoolteacher in common. She released Paige's sweatshirt. "Sorry, it's just that the tree is so majestic."

"I think so, too." Paige was tickled that the beech tree had made a more memorable impression on Emily than the Hathaways' mansion had. "Unfortunately, as you've probably noticed, it appears to be dead, so I may have to have it cut down."

"Aww, I'm very sorry to hear that." Emily wrinkled her forehead. "I can understand why it might be a safety hazard. And it would be a mess to clean up if it fell unexpectedly. But the tree's presence will be missed."

"Thank you," replied Paige with a sad smile.

Yet oddly enough, Emily's appreciation for the old beech tree made it easier rather than more difficult for Paige to decide she was ready to consult an arborist. Granted, Seth had essentially expressed the same regard for the tree's beauty and resilience that Emily had expressed. And he'd also stated concern about the tree falling.

But that was different, coming from him. Even though he'd mentioned that having the tree removed might be financially beneficial to Paige, she couldn't lose sight of the fact that Seth was working for Lexie. So he had a vested interest in getting rid of the tree, too. And after what she'd discovered about Edward giving Violet a locket, Paige felt a little wary about letting down her guard since the Hathaways were involved.

Instead of talking to Alex, I think I'll consult a completely impartial arborist, she decided.

However, when she went into town later that afternoon, Paige quickly learned it was as difficult to reach an arborist directly as it had been to connect with a carpenter. She tried four tree service companies before someone answered their phone.

After listening to Paige's request for an arborist to evaluate the beech tree, the staff member said, "We're booked solid through August. Our first opening is September fourteen—but that's only if we don't get hit by a hurricane before then. If we do, we'll push our scheduled projects out so our crew can help with emergency tree and limb removals. In that case, you might be waiting until October."

"Oh. Well, then, I hate to ask this, but... do you know of any arborists who might be able to help me out, instead?"

The woman snorted. "Nope. It's the same situation across the island. That's what happens when all you summer people wait until the last minute to schedule your seasonal yard cleanup."

I'm not a summer person and I don't need my yard cleaned, Paige silently argued, but she thanked the woman for her time. After disconnecting, she decided she'd ask Seth to put her in touch with his friend Alex after all.

Then she called her aunt Sherry, who mentioned she was at Tara's house, helping her select a design for the engagement party invitations. Apparently, Cami—who was characteristically absent—had told her mother that she'd prefer to send evites. Tara had balked at that suggestion, so Cami had compromised, agreeing to use printed cards if her mother chose the design and hand-addressed them by herself. Or, more accurately, without Cami's help; Sherry undoubtedly would assist Tara, instead.

"I'll put you on speaker phone, so we can both hear your opinion at the same time," Sherry offered. "Tara, text her photos of these two and she can tell us which style she prefers. The bold and modern or the floral and romantic."

"Or we could also opt for a photo of Cami and Dylan," Tara reminded her mother. "Or one of their hands, with Cami's engagement ring showing."

The three of them spent a full hour discussing the pros and cons of the various designs, typography, overlays, and stationery. Yet somehow, by the time Paige said she needed to return to the cottage, they'd increased their options two-fold instead of narrowing them down.

"Before I go, I wanted to tell you something interesting I discovered," she began. "Yesterday the estate attorney stopped by with Violet's personal effects that the nursing home had sent him, including a piece of jewelry. I was—"

Tara cut her off, pummeling Paige with questions. "The inheritance included jewelry? What kind of jewelry? And why didn't you mention it when we were on our conference call last night?"

"Because we had limited time to talk and our priority was discussing the inspection," Paige calmly reminded her. "Besides, I didn't think the guys would be interested in hearing about a necklace and a pendant—"

Once again, Tara didn't let her cousin finish. "She left a necklace *and* a pendant? Take a photo and text it to me."

"I'll have to send photos later—I didn't bring the jewelry with me." Paige had photos of the interior of the pendant, of course, but she didn't want to spoil her announcement by texting the inscription to them. She wanted to recite the verse aloud to her aunt and cousin.

"Then describe the jewelry," insisted Tara. "And not in the useless way you described the Hathaways' grounds, either."

"Yes, I want to know what they look like, too," Sherry chimed in. "An antique necklace or a pendant might be just what we need. This morning Tara and I were discussing how it's not too early for Cami to begin collecting what she'll need for 'something old, something new, something borrowed, and something blue' for her wedding."

"The jewelry would definitely fit into the 'something old' category," said Paige. "It's very fragile, though, especially the necklace and cross. I think they're gold or gold plated."

"Ah, that would've been the necklace she inherited from her mother, who died when your Grandpa Frank and Violet were just children," Sherry told her. "I remember my father telling me Violet treasured it so much she never took it off. She was afraid she'd lose it, though, so she always wore it tucked inside the collar of her blouse."

"Since it came from Grandpa Frank's mother, I really want you to have it, Aunt Sherry," Paige insisted. Even though she figured Tara would reject it once she saw the necklace wasn't a priceless heirloom, she added, "That way, you can offer to let Cami use it as something old, or something borrowed."

"That would be nice. Thank you," her aunt replied graciously.

"Didn't you say there was a pendant, too?" pressed Tara.

"Yes. It's a heart-shaped locket. I think it's sterling silver, and it's probably only worth two hundred dollars, at most. But it has an inscription. It says, 'Violet, my love, my favorite flower—hold me in your heart always and forever.'" Paige paused for dramatic effect before adding, "It's signed *Ed.*"

"Edward Hathaway wrote that to Violet?" Sherry sounded more amused than amazed. "Humph, how about that? I guess he liked her more than he wanted to admit."

That's an understatement. For some reason, her aunt's blasé reply made Paige feel more impassioned about the subject. "Yes, he did. Can you imagine how hurtful and maddening it must have been for Violet when he denied ever having a relationship with her? Especially because everyone on the island, including their families and peers, believed *him* instead of her. They all thought Violet was just a pathetic, deluded teenager for imagining someone like Edward could be interested in someone like her. And that impacted her whole life! I mean, decades later, even *we* believed that she was misguided about his feelings for her."

"Hey, that's not *my* fault," Sherry replied in surprise. "I was only repeating the stories I heard from my father. How would he have known any differently? Apparently, Violet never told him or anyone else about the locket."

"I didn't mean to sound like I was blaming you or Grandpa Frank, Aunt Sherry," Paige apologized. "I know that neither of you would deliberately mislead anyone with your stories about Violet. But now that we know more about her life, doesn't it cast her—and Edward Hathaway—in an entirely new light?"

"I think you're overestimating the importance of that

inscription, Paige. Whether Edward Hathaway liked Violet or not doesn't change the fact she had some major... *issues*." Sherry seemed to be trying—but failing—to choose her words carefully. "Most people don't go into seclusion for their entire lives just because a teenage romance went wrong. They get over it. They move on. The very fact that Violet kept the necklace from Edward all these years—especially since he denied ever liking her—shows just how odd she was."

"The operative word here is *was*," Tara crassly interjected. "Violet's gone now, so I don't see any point in analyzing her character or dwelling on something that may or may not have occurred between her and Edward Hathaway eighty years ago. What happened in the past doesn't affect the present."

"I'm not *dwelling* on it, but I think it bears mentioning that we were all wrong about her," insisted Paige. "Yes, her reclusive behavior was... idiosyncratic, but she *wasn't* confused about Edward. He liked her romantically. He wouldn't have given her an engraved locket otherwise. That's all I'm saying."

"Yes, that's a good point," admitted Sherry, but Paige had the feeling her aunt was placating her. Or maybe it was that Sherry still felt a little insulted that Paige had pointed out the error in their family's beliefs about Violet?

Tara expertly redirected the conversation to her favorite topic. "You know, those lines Edward wrote about holding him 'in her heart always and forever' actually have a nice ring to them. Maybe we can include something like that on Cami's invitations? If we choose the overlay with a heart design on it, that might work, right?"

Paige politely endured another fifteen minutes of being an audience to Tara's indecision before she said she had to get back to the cottage to start washing the windows.

"I'll text you both a photo of Violet's jewelry soon," she promised, even though she doubted that either of them was very interested in seeing it.

. . .

For the rest of the afternoon and into the evening, Paige grappled with feelings of disappointment about her conversation with Sherry and Tara.

What did I expect? she asked herself. *I knew before I called them that they're too involved with party planning to really pay attention to anything else.*

But their self-absorption wasn't the only thing making her feel so prickly. Paige was also annoyed because she'd come to recognize that her great-aunt deserved a lot more empathy and respect than anyone—especially her own family—had given her.

And I suppose that has included me, too, she thought regretfully.

EIGHT

After Aidan and Micah arrived on Thursday morning, Paige carried her second cup of coffee across the heathland, intending to drink it on the other side of the junipers, where she wouldn't hear their hammering. But when she rounded the fat, bushy trees, she was surprised to find an elderly man occupying one of the wooden chairs. He was wearing a long-sleeved button-down shirt, dark trousers and a matching vest, as well as a newsboy cap, and Paige noticed he was resting one hand on the cane propped beside him.

"Beautiful morning, isn't it?" he asked cheerfully.

"It's gorgeous," she agreed.

"My name is Joseph Hathaway." He half-rose from the chair, extending his hand. "You must be Violet Atkins' great-niece?"

Someone at the mansion has been talking about me, she thought warily as they shook hands. *Was it Seth or Lexie?*

"Yes, I'm Paige Taylor."

"Ah, yes, that's right. Paige. Lexie told me your name but I'm afraid it slipped my mind. I'm very sorry to hear about your great-aunt's passing."

"Thank you."

"I hope you don't mind if I sit here a while. I ambled down from the hill and I need to catch my breath before I climb back up it again."

"Please sit as long as you like. Should I bring you a glass of water? Or is there something else I can get for you?" Concerned about his well-being, she hesitated before suggesting, "I'm a nurse, so if you're feeling winded, I could take your pulse, or..."

"Thank you, but that's not necessary. I'm not having a medical emergency. I'm just old and someone moved the beach farther away since the last time I was here," he complained, causing Paige to giggle and relax.

Settling into the chair beside him, she asked, "When *was* the last time you visited Dune Island?"

"About eighty years ago."

"Eighty years?" Paige repeated, with admiration in her voice. *How wonderful that he's returned after so much time. He's got to be almost ninety—no wonder he feels a little winded from walking all the way down the hill. It must have been very important to him to see the ocean up close again.*

"Yes, it was the summer of 1943."

She winced inwardly. *Does that mean he was here in August, when Violet made a spectacle of herself?* She didn't particularly want to discuss her great-aunt's life with another Hathaway family member. But at the same time, she was curious about whether Joseph might remember anything about Violet or her grandpa Frank.

"The summer of 1943?" she repeated as nonchalantly as she could.

"Yes. I'd been sent to Dune Island for several weeks because my mother was ill with rheumatic fever. My aunt and uncle agreed I could stay with them and their family. But I was a very active child and they were so consumed with their social calendar that they ended up hiring your great-aunt Violet to watch me."

"*You* were the boy she babysat that summer," Paige exclaimed.

"Yes, I was indeed. I take it she's already told you about our time together?" Joseph looked so pleased that Paige regretted having to tell him she'd never met or spoken to Violet.

"She didn't really keep in touch with our family. My grandpa Frank—her brother—moved away from Dune Island when he was a teenager. He died when I was three, so he never directly told me about their life here, either." She added, "But I've heard the stories he passed down, including that Violet was a babysitter for one of the Hathaway boys."

"She was more than a babysitter to me—she was like a second mother. I absolutely adored her," he raved. "She was a very gentle, quiet person, but she never tried to make *me* be that way. I wasn't much of a swimmer, and neither was she, but we'd spend entire days walking the beach. I'd run up ahead, racing the waves and throwing stones into the water, and she'd saunter along behind me, combing the sand for treasures. When we got hungry, we'd stop and eat jelly sandwiches. She made the jelly from beach plum she'd picked right here on the heathland..."

Joseph's voice trailed off and Paige could tell from the way he was gazing at the water that he was reimagining those afternoons. It was fascinating to hear about Violet from someone who had known her—from someone who had *adored* her—and Paige felt a pang of regret that she'd never met her great-aunt years ago.

"Do you remember anything else about that summer?" she asked.

Joseph nodded, his green eyes sparkling like the ocean in front of them. "I remember that Violet didn't have two spare pennies to rub together, but she sewed an army of soldiers from scraps of fabric as a surprise for my birthday. She used itty bitty clam shells that she'd collected for their faces." He chuckled, "After she gave me my gift, a portion of our time on the beach was always devoted to constructing military forts in the sand. And my toy soldiers would try in vain to defend them from the incoming tide."

Paige threw back her head and laughed. "I can just picture it," she said, marveling at his sense of recall.

"I also remember the time I found half of a dried-out horse-shoe crab shell down by the inlet. It was just the front part—its legs and tail were no longer attached. I thought it looked like a soldier's helmet, so I kept it." He gestured toward the water with his cane. "During the war, the Coast Guard and Navy patrolled the beach and woods around the clock, did you know that?"

"Not that, specifically, but I'm aware that the military had a strong presence here in the early forties."

"Well, I admired the servicemen almost as much as I adored Violet. She had a high regard for members of the US military, too. So after we washed the shell and bleached it in the sun, she made a chin strap to keep it from slipping off my head. I tell you, I wore that helmet proudly. Of course, I could only wear it when I was with Violet because..." He shook his head as if he'd said too much, which made Paige even more curious.

"Because why?" she asked.

"Let's just say that my aunt and uncle considered *proper attire* to be more important than a young, homesick boy's imagination." Joseph heaved a sigh and Paige's eyes smarted from his poignant recollection.

They were both quiet a moment before he asked, "I trust you know that an earlier generation of the Hathaway family showed very little regard for your great-aunt when a... a *misunderstanding* arose between them and her?"

Paige could tell by the delicate way Joseph was phrasing the question that what he was really asking was if she'd heard about

Violet's outburst in Port Newcomb. She swallowed before admitting, "That's what I've been told, yes."

He frowned and shook his head. "What a shame that whole situation was. Violet deserved my aunt and uncle's appreciation, not their scorn. At the very least, they could have exhibited more grace—"

He was interrupted mid-sentence by someone calling in the distance. "Uncle Joseph! Uncle Joseph!"

"Uh-oh. I'd better let them know I'm here."

As he used his cane for leverage to rise from the chair, Paige leaped to her feet and stepped to the side of the juniper trees. Waving her hand at a woman standing beside a black convertible in Violet's driveway, she called, "He's over here—we're coming!"

She and Joseph made their way along the path, as the woman hurried toward them. When they met halfway, the woman scolded, "We were so concerned about you. Why didn't you tell us where you were going?"

"I'm sorry I worried anyone. I wasn't aware I needed to sign out before leaving the premises for an hour," he apologized drily.

Joseph introduced Paige to the woman, his great-niece Tabitha, and the three of them continued toward the driveway. Just before getting into the car, he said, "It was delightful chatting with you, Paige."

"I enjoyed it, too. I'm leaving the chairs out by the junipers, so please feel free to stop by any time."

She couldn't believe she'd been so fortunate to encounter someone who had known her great-aunt and she cherished hearing his stories about their time together. Other than Steve mentioning what a talented seamstress Violet had been, Joseph was the only person Paige had heard speak highly of her great-aunt. And as the car sped up the hill, she thought, *I hope that's not the last time I get to see him.*

. . .

Paige was amazed by how much better she felt about the cottage after Aidan and Micah re-screened the porch and made a few small repairs. *This is the kind of TLC Violet's home needed*, she thought. She was so encouraged by the changes that she decided she'd paint the wooden kitchen cupboards. Maybe she'd paint the paneled walls in the other rooms, too.

The new owners will probably renovate the interior anyway. But meanwhile, if it's freshly painted in bright colors, it will help prospective buyers to see its potential to become a "cute and cozy" cottage, she thought. Besides, Paige found painting to be a relaxing, mindless activity, especially when she wasn't under a tight deadline to complete it.

Before heading to the hardware store, she snapped a photo of Violet's jewelry to text to Sherry and Tara while she was in town. Then she carefully put the gold necklace and cross into the manilla envelope again. But she held the locket to the light, admiring the tiny flower etching before opening it to examine the elegant engraving.

I should wear this so the next time I see Seth, I can show him proof that he was wrong about his great-uncle, she thought as she snapped the two halves together. Paige had only brought one necklace to Dune Island, and its chain was silver and durable. So she exchanged her birthstone pendant for Violet's heart-shaped one, and clasped the chain around her neck.

As she drove, she reflected on the memories Joseph had shared with her. Once again, Paige felt a bit ashamed that she'd accepted some of the stories she'd heard about her great-aunt at face value. She considered what else she'd always believed about her that might not have been true.

Maybe Edward's denial of her initially triggered her retreat from society, but there must have been other circumstances that contributed to her seclusion, too, she thought. *Like her father's declining health.*

Paige knew firsthand the emotional toll that caregiving could take on a person. Not only because she was a nurse, but also because she'd cared for her grandmother during the final year of her life. She considered it a great privilege, but it was also emotionally and physically draining.

Violet didn't have any other family members to help her, since Grandpa Frank left the island when he was sixteen, she thought.

Sherry had always implied that Violet and Frank were both content with their estrangement, but now Paige wondered whether Violet might not have become so withdrawn if she'd had her brother's support caring for their father.

She couldn't imagine what it must have been like for her grandfather and great-aunt not to be close to each other. Paige's mother had died when she and Dustin were young. A few years later, their father married a woman who wasn't necessarily strict with them; it was more like she was utterly indifferent.

Dad was on the road all the time for work, so he didn't realize how lonely it was for us at home. I don't know what Dustin and I would have done if we hadn't been able to spend so much time at Grandma's or Aunt Sherry's houses, playing with our cousins, Paige reminisced.

It wasn't just that her extended family supported her when they were kids, either. When she was twenty and commuting to college, her father died and her stepmother more or less kicked Paige out of the house. If Tara and Glenn hadn't allowed her to live with them, she wouldn't have been able to finish earning her nursing degree.

Another time, when she was living in Michigan and her apartment was on the verge of flooding, Dustin and her cousins, Rick and Christopher, drove for six hours and moved out all of her stuff in the middle of the night so it wouldn't get ruined.

So, she appreciated how fortunate she was to have the family she had—but she was still irritated at Sherry and Tara. *It'll pass, but on second thought, I think I'm going to postpone texting photos of the necklace or calling them for another day or two. And when I do talk to them again, I'm not going to mention Joseph's anecdotes about Violet,* she decided. *His memories are very special and he shared them with me, not with them. Besides, they wouldn't appreciate them anyway, which would just annoy me all over again...*

On Friday evening, Paige sat on the porch where the paint smell wasn't as strong as it was inside the kitchen. *The cottage is really shaping up,* she thought with a self-congratulatory sense of satisfaction. *I could see myself vacationing in a place like this now.*

She was even getting used to the sparseness of the furnishings. The simplicity of the interior décor seemed to complement the serenity of the natural surroundings. *Maybe when I get back to Chicago, I'll downsize my belongings. I've managed just fine for six months without unpacking those boxes in my living room, so I must not need any of the stuff inside them...*

As she was musing, she heard a noise coming from the Hathaways' backyard. She twisted around to look, but she didn't see anyone.

I really need to talk to Seth about contacting Alex, she thought. *I should go up to the house to ask if he happens to be there.*

But Paige felt too intimidated to drop by the Hathaways' house unexpectedly. Besides, she reasoned that Seth had better things to do on a Friday evening than prepare the grounds for his cousin's wedding, which was still six weeks away.

Lexie said Seth was "very single," so he's probably not on a date, but maybe he's hanging out with Alex or some other friends.

Paige wondered about what the nightlife was like among the locals on the island. Steve had seemed to indicate everyone in Hope Haven knew each other, just like they did when Violet and Frank were growing up there.

I wonder if Steve and his wife ever socialize with Emily and her husband, she reflected. Then she wondered whether the islanders mingled with the summer people, and if they had some off-the-beaten-path bar or restaurant or beach where they all got together. *Does Seth ever hang out with them, too?*

Paige found it curious he wasn't involved with anyone. *He's successful, good-looking, and on the surface he has a nice enough personality,* she thought. *Maybe there just aren't very many single women on the island? Or maybe he doesn't want to see anyone right now? If that's the case, then good for him for knowing his own mind instead of getting involved with someone and then telling her a year later that he doesn't want to be in a serious relationship after all, the way Trevor did to me.*

Now that he'd popped into her mind again, she felt the old familiar flicker of resentment in her gut. It may not have burned as intensely as it once had, but it was still smoldering. She absent-mindedly lifted the pendant from where it hung against her chest and caressed its violet etching with her thumb, ruefully thinking, *Maybe I don't bounce back as quickly as Aunt Sherry thinks I do, after all.*

In the middle of the night, Paige was woken from a deep sleep by a thunderous boom. It was so powerful the entire cottage vibrated from the sound. A moment later, a torrent riveted the roof and windows, driven by a rushing wind.

Even though she'd grown up in the Midwest, where tornado alarms were a routine part of her summer experience, Paige was uneasy. All she could think about was whether the roof would be torn off the cottage or the beech tree would get struck by lightning.

By the time the deluge eased into a steady rain, she realized something that else she'd always believed about her great-aunt had been inaccurate. *Violet might have seemed timid by outward appearances*, she thought. *But she was braver than most people to live in such a flimsy little abode her entire life...*

Paige had learned to leave a pair of socks on the end of her bed so she could put them on before touching her feet to the floor when she got out of bed. But the air was so damp on Saturday morning that she knew she'd need to wear more than just her customary hoodie to keep her torso warm.

Shivering, she pulled on her jeans and then searched her closet for a long-sleeved top she could layer over her T-shirt. She needed something that was casual enough that she wouldn't care if it became stained while she continued her household projects. Her eyes immediately settled on Violet's gray wool sweater.

Why not? It looks cozy. The yarn felt a bit scratchy against her wrists, but the tight-knit sweater was toastier than her sweatshirt and it fit her perfectly.

It's better than driving around in my car with the heater on, she told her reflection in the mirror as she brushed her teeth. Her self-talk was interrupted by a muffled thump coming from the direction of the porch. *That's weird. I must not have pulled the kitchen door all the way shut—or else the wind blew it open.*

She stuck her head out into the hall, listening. Were those footsteps she heard crossing the kitchen floor? *Click, clickety, click-click,* they went, like high heels. Was it a woman? Lexie? Feeling both annoyed and nervous in equal measure that someone had entered the cottage uninvited, she summoned her sternest voice as she started down the hall.

"I don't know what you're doing in here without my permission, but you need to—*oh, Blossom!*" she abruptly cooed when she recognized the large dog. The animal was so excited he thwacked his tail against the white fridge, spattering it with mud. Paige knelt in front of him, scratching his neck until he settled down.

"It's so good to see you, boy. You must have known I bought you organic doggy treats, didn't you? But if your owner's still on the beach, how did you get in? Did the wind blow *both* doors open?"

By way of answering, Blossom stuck his nose in the air, sniffing, and a big string of slobber dripped from his upper lip. Paige pulled a treat from the bag—as well as a rag from the cabinet. After he'd eaten the snack and she'd wiped his muzzle, she scratched his neck again, delighting in the way his dark-rimmed eyes and sagging jowls made him appear comically woeful.

"You're lucky my cousin Tara can't see you. She'd criticize your skin care regimen, like she does mine." She exaggeratedly imitated her cousin. "You've got unsightly dark circles and your pouchy skin makes you look ten years older than you really are. Have you considered getting an eye lift?"

"Uh, hello?" Seth called from outside the porch. "Paige?"

Mortified that he may have overheard her, she cleared her throat and answered in a regular voice, "We're in the kitchen. Come on in."

"I can't," he called back. "The screen door's locked."

"How can that be?" As Paige stepped onto the porch, she immediately spotted the answer, but Seth explained anyway.

"Blossom must have charged right through the bottom half of your screen door." Instead of a wetsuit, this Saturday he was wearing a navy-blue jacket and jeans. With his damp hair flattened against his forehead and his nostrils pink from the cold, he looked as forlorn as one of her pedi patients suffering from the flu. "I'm sorry. I'll repair it right away."

"Not *right* away—you'd better wait till it stops raining, first," Paige said good-naturedly as she crossed the porch to unhook the latch. Because the old dog obviously hadn't been hurt, the entire incident struck her as funny. "I'm glad Blossom dropped by because there's something I've wanted to talk to you about. I'll make coffee. We can sit in the living room."

But Seth insisted he didn't want to get her kitchen floor dirty a second time—not that it mattered, as Blossom had already beat him to it—so Paige brought the coffee and another chair out to the porch, along with a towel so he could dry himself off.

"That was quite a storm last night, wasn't it?" she asked when they were both seated, with Blossom stretched out on his side in between them.

"Yeah. It kicked up some epic waves." He used his chin to gesture toward the frothy, roiling ocean in the foreground.

"Is that why you're not surfing?" she asked. "Are the waves too big?"

"No such thing. Those waves are *ideal*. I might not see surf like this again until late August, when the tropical storms and hurricanes start rolling past." He frowned and took a long pull from his mug. "But I can't get out there this morning. Lexie and Grant are in town and I've got a breakfast meeting with them."

"Oh. Then I don't want to keep you—" Paige started to say but Seth interrupted.

"You're not keeping me. They can wait." From the sound of his voice, it was clear he wasn't pleased about something. After another swallow of coffee, he leaned back in his chair and explained, "Lexie and Grant weren't awake when I arrived, so I took a jaunt down to the beach alone to see what I was missing. Nobody likes the smell of a wet dog, so I put Blossom in the garage—he's not allowed inside the main house unless I'm with him. Anyway, someone must've opened the garage door because when I got back, Blossom was gone. Since I hadn't crossed paths with him at the beach, I figured there was only one other place he'd go. Lucky you."

"Like I said, I'm glad he came by. I hope you don't mind that I gave him a treat?"

"It's fine with me, but now you're never going to get rid of him. He'll be back every Saturday morning."

"In that case, maybe you shouldn't re-screen the bottom half of the door after all," teased Paige. "I wouldn't want him getting hurt."

Seth assured her it wouldn't be an issue, promising her for a second Saturday in a row that he wouldn't allow Blossom to enter the cottage without her explicit permission.

"He's always welcome to visit," said Paige. "So are you—and Joseph is, too."

He cocked his head. "Joseph visited your cottage?"

"No, I met him out on the heathland by the junipers. He was sitting in one of the chairs that Owen left out there. We had a very nice chat."

"I didn't realize he'd come down here. I'm sorry you've been inundated by the Hathaway family. Is that what you wanted to talk to me about? 'Cause I can remind everyone that this is private property."

"No, no, like I said, I enjoyed meeting Joseph. What I wanted to tell you is that I've decided I'd like Alex to give me his professional opinion about the beech tree. I'd appreciate it if you could put me in touch with him."

"Sure. He owes me a favor, so how about if I make the arrangements? Does it matter when he drops by?"

"No, anytime that's good for him is good for me."

"Great. Thanks for being willing to seek his advice."

"You're welcome." Paige suddenly felt ambivalent about discussing the necklace with Seth, but she forged on. "I also wanted to mention that I've discovered something else that makes me think your great-uncle and my great-aunt were in a romantic relationship after all."

"Another engraving?"

"Kind of. My great-aunt's estate attorney brought me this pendant the other day. It was among Violet's personal effects at the nursing home. There's an inscription inside."

Paige unclasped the chain from her neck and carefully pried it open before handing it to Seth. She'd expected to feel smug when she proved him wrong about Edward, but now she proceeded carefully. After hearing Sherry's reaction, Paige was more sensitive about how difficult it might be for Seth to realize he'd been wrong about his family's history, too.

He squinted at it for a moment but then he slowly shook his head and gave it back to her. "Sorry, it's too small. I can't read it."

Paige recited the verse from memory. She ended by pointing to the signature squeezed into the bottom of the heart and saying, "The signature says *Ed*."

"Really?" He scratched the side of his head. "That's kind of hard to believe."

"Why?" Paige challenged him. "Is it so unthinkable that Edward might have been infatuated with Violet just because she was poor and he was wealthy?"

Staring into his coffee mug, Seth slowly nodded. "Yeah, actually, it is."

Paige hadn't expected him to admit it outright, and she was too dumbfounded to reply.

"I mean, it's not unthinkable to *me*," he clarified. "But I know what some of my family members are like, especially the older generation. They have very deeply ingrained attitudes about socioeconomic status. The Hathaway mindset was that it was acceptable to employ members of the working class, but not to socialize with them."

"That's offensive," Paige muttered.

"No kidding. Fortunately, my parents' generation, including Lexie's parents, didn't perpetuate that kind of discrimination. But I thought my grandparents were going to disown me when they found out I'd dropped out of law school to take up land-scaping." Seth chuckled, but his eyes were downcast.

Resisting the urge to reach out and give him a comforting pat on the shoulder, Paige murmured, "That must have been hurtful."

"Yeah, but it didn't stop me from following my heart. And apparently it didn't stop Edward from following his, either. Which is really surprising, considering that it wasn't just my relatives who were against the idea. Your fam—"

He abruptly stopped speaking but he'd said enough that Paige got the gist. "My family what? They were against the idea, too?" When he didn't answer, she urged him, "Please don't hold back. I'd really like to know what you've heard about my family."

"Even if it's not very flattering?"

Paige didn't know if anything could be less flattering than what had already been said about them, especially about Violet. "Yes."

Seth pressed his lips together and shook his head, but then he began, "Well, according to the stories my family used to tell, Violet's younger brother, Frank—"

Paige cut in to clarify, "He was my grandfather."

"Right, well, supposedly he was one of the people who repeated gossip about Edward. They said he was a draft dodger, which was completely unfounded. My great-uncle couldn't serve in the military because he had a heart arrythmia—that's why he died so young."

"I was always told he died in a skiing accident."

"No. He was skiing when he passed away, but he died from his heart condition, not from an accident." Seth continued, "Anyway, because he didn't serve in the military, some people on the island also spread rumors that he was a Nazi sympathizer, or a German spy."

"What a horrible accusation! Are you sure my grandfather Frank was one of the people who said that about him?"

"I don't know if he repeated that rumor, or if he just believed it. The reason I'm mentioning it is because supposedly, Frank and his father were very protective of Violet. They didn't want her getting involved with the 'wrong' kind of guy—including someone who wasn't what they considered patriotic."

Seth's story wasn't quite the same as the account Paige had grown up hearing, but there was a note of familiarity to it that made her uneasy. All these years, her family had believed that their neighbors had a derisive attitude toward the Atkins family. Was it possible that the Atkins family had been equally disparaging of the Hathaways? Paige wasn't sure whose rendition of the past to believe, but she continued to listen to Seth without interrupting.

"Your grandfather Frank was only a teenager at the time, but according to what I've heard, he was a lot stronger than my sickly great-uncle and he wasn't afraid to use his fists. Edward wasn't a draft-dodger, but supposedly in other ways, he was kind of a coward. Or at least, easily intimidated. So I'm really surprised he had the guts to put his feelings for Violet in writing —whether on the tree or in a locket. It seems like he would've been too scared of what Frank might have done to him if he ever saw their initials or read the inscription."

"Maybe that's why Edward denied he'd ever been romantically involved with Violet," Paige speculated, "Maybe he'd felt he'd had to convince everyone that my great-aunt was mistaken about the nature of their relationship, so Frank wouldn't... beat him up or something."

Seth lifted his shoulders and let them drop. "Anything's possible. We weren't there, so I guess we'll never know the full story. To some extent, it doesn't matter any more. Whatever happened back then shouldn't negatively affect the relationship between our families now, should it?"

"No, it shouldn't," said Paige, squirming a little because until now she *had* allowed the past to taint her relationship with the Hathaways in the present.

"Good." He pulled a slightly soggy business card from his back pocket. "When I come back to fix the screen, I'll let you know what Alex says about his schedule. But here's my number, just in case you need it for anything."

Paige's fingertips brushed his as she accepted the card. "S.E. Landscaping?" she read aloud.

"Yeah. It's my first and middle initials. Seth Edward—I was named after my great-uncle."

Knowing that Seth was Edward's namesake made Paige feel even guiltier that she'd been so biased. To her, Edward was the man who'd broken Violet's heart, but to the Hathaways, he was a beloved family member, who had died too young. "I'm surprised you don't use your last name, since I've heard how highly regarded the Hathaways are in Hope Haven. It seems like it would be good for business."

"Yeah, probably. But I want my work to be valued for its own merit, not because I'm related to the people who own the mansion in Highland Hills," Seth explained. The more Paige learned about him, the more she liked him. He stood up and handed her his coffee cup. "Speaking of the mansion, I'd better get up there for our breakfast meeting. C'mon, Blossom. Time to go."

The dog jumped to his feet and exited the same way he'd come in; without hesitation and through the bottom half of the porch door. Paige chuckled, but Seth shook his head. "I can tell I'm going to have to use pet-proof mesh. I probably won't make it to the hardware store today. Is it okay if I re-screen the door on Monday?"

"Sure. No hurry," Paige told him, even though she wouldn't mind seeing him again sooner than that.

It rained for the rest of the day, which gave Paige plenty of opportunity to sit on the porch, staring absently toward the ocean and reflecting on what Seth had told her about Edward and Frank.

Although it was upsetting, she knew she had to acknowledge the possibility that her grandfather had been a bully. *He may have intimidated Edward in a misguided attempt to protect his sister, but it was still inexcusable,* she lamented to herself.

It also saddened Paige to imagine that her grandpa Frank may have been indirectly responsible for her great-aunt's reputation as a mixed-up and emotionally unstable young woman.

Edward still might have broken Violet's heart by going out with another girl. But if Grandpa Frank hadn't been so threatening, then Edward might not have felt he had to lie about liking Violet in the first place. Instead, Edward made it seem as if she'd made up their relationship and then the rumors about her spread like wildfire.

Paige recognized that Edward himself had also been the object of deeply damaging remarks. *I always knew that Grandpa Frank suspected him of being a draft dodger,* she thought. *But I had no idea that he or anyone else gossiped about Edward being a Nazi sympathizer or a spy. That must have been so painful for his family.*

Of course, she had no way of knowing for certain who'd started and perpetuated those rumors or exactly what else had happened in the past. But one thing seemed certain: two young people had been deeply wounded by other people's misconceptions about them.

In an effort to prevent Sherry from getting hurt, too, Paige decided she wasn't going to share what she'd learned with her.

She's already sensitive about the topic and since Grandpa Frank isn't alive to give his version of events, it wouldn't be fair to repeat what Seth told me—even if I believe what he said is true.

On Sunday, Paige drove into town to call Tara. At first, she couldn't understand why the roads were suddenly so crowded, but then she remembered what Aidan had said about this weekend marking the official start to tourist season.

Funny, just a few days ago Paige would have been glad to be in the thick of things again, but this afternoon, the hustle and bustle nearly made her feel claustrophobic. *I guess this is what happens when you become accustomed to having the ocean in your front yard and nothing but sand dunes to your left and right...*

When she called her cousin, Cami picked up instead.

"I grabbed Mom's phone so she wouldn't wake up from her nap," she explained. "She hasn't been feeling good all weekend and she hardly got any sleep last night."

"Oh, no. That's crummy. Is it her summer allergies? You sound a little congested, too."

"No. It's not allergies." When Cami sniffled, Paige realized she sounded nasal because she'd been crying.

"What's wrong, Cam?"

"*Every*thing," the twenty-year-old exclaimed dramatically. "Mom keeps getting headaches and stomach aches and she can't eat or sleep. And it's all because she's stressed about my engagement party. It's like, she can't stop obsessing over every. Single. Detail. It's all she ever talks about. It's all she ever thinks about. Right now, she's probably even *dreaming* about it!"

Paige smothered a giggle with her palm. Cami was dead right about her mother, but Paige didn't want to make it seem as if they were mocking Tara together. "Yes, she's really been putting a lot of time and energy into planning the party," she agreed diplomatically. "But if it's affecting her health, then she probably needs to pull back a little."

"That's exactly what I told her," grumbled Cami. "But she won't listen. She just keeps harping about how there's still so much to do..."

"Maybe if she had more help, she wouldn't feel so stressed?" Paige hinted gently.

"Grandma's already helping her. And you'll be back to help pretty soon, too, won't you?"

Paige ignored her question and made a straightforward suggestion. "I meant maybe if she had *your* help, she wouldn't feel so stressed." She stopped short of adding, *It is* your *party after all.* In some ways, Cami was still so immature that Paige couldn't imagine her living on her own, much less, getting married.

"That doesn't work. We just end up arguing. Like, she's got her heart set on printed invitations, but she couldn't make up her mind about which typography to use. I tried to tell her that I don't care, we should just send digital invites instead. Then we got into a huge argument..."

When Cami burst out sobbing, Paige murmured sympathetically until her niece had gathered her composure again.

"This is so *not* how I want to spend my last summer before my senior year of college. I wanted to spend it waterskiing at the lake with my friends, not fighting with my mother or worrying that she's going to wind up in the hospital. I wish I didn't even have to have a stupid engagement party. That would be a lot better than watching Mom drop dead from a heart attack or something."

Although Tara's anxiety and stress often resulted in unpleasant physical symptoms, she was generally a healthy person, so Paige assured Cami, "I doubt very much your mom will have a heart attack. But I understand why it's worrisome for you to see her so stressed out." She waited until Cami's crying subsided and then she asked softly, "Have you talked to her about how you feel? Have you told her you'd rather not have the party than to see her getting so worked up about planning it?"

"Are you kidding? It would *crush* her if I said I didn't want to have the party. Every time Dad complains about how expensive it's going to be, she tells him, 'Other than announcing when our baby-girl was born, this is the most important announcement we'll make about her life, so we're going to make it in style.'"

"Announcing you've graduated from college will be a pretty big deal, too," Paige said beneath her breath.

"Not as big of a deal as announcing my engagement," replied Cami. She quickly added, "No offense—you know what I mean."

Yeah, unfortunately, I do, thought Paige. "Obviously, your mom's going over-the-top because she loves you, she's happy for you, and she wants to give you the best engagement party she can possibly give you. Maybe if you're open with her about how concerned you are about her health, she'll reconsider hiring an event planner to help her."

"Ha! You know how she feels about that." Cami imitated her mother saying, "Why pay a stranger to mess something up when *I* can do it the right way for free?"

"It's still worth a try," insisted Paige, although she realized her niece was probably right. "But if you decide you definitely don't want the party, it might be better for both of you if you tell her right away, rather than going along with her plans and letting her think you're happy about it." Momentarily distracted by her memories of how Trevor broke up with her, Paige scowled. "Being honest can be difficult, but it's so important in relationships, Cami. In the long run, it will prevent a lot of misunderstanding and hurt."

"M-maybe you're right," she sniveled, just as Paige's phone vibrated on her dashboard.

"Uh-oh. I'm getting a call from the tree service guy. I've got to take it. Let your mom know I hope she feels better and I'll call tomorrow, okay?"

To her surprise, Alex told Paige he'd stopped by the cottage about an hour ago. "Sorry we didn't get a chance to meet, 'cause I would've liked to show you a few things about the tree." He explained in detail the obvious and not so obvious signs that it was dead, not merely diseased or dying. "It's understandable if you're reluctant to have it removed for aesthetic reasons. It still cuts a stunning silhouette on the heathland, especially in the moonlight."

"Yes, it does." Paige was impressed that he'd noticed the same thing she'd admired about it—unlike Lexie and Tara, who felt the tree *should* be taken down for aesthetic reasons.

"Removing it would be a big financial investment, too. Sometimes when a client has the amount of open land that you have, I understand the appeal of letting it fall in its own time, as long as leaving it standing doesn't pose a safety hazard."

"But the beech tree does?"

"Let me put it this way. It already has a slight lean to the south and it's got a lot of rot, which means it's waterlogged. To be honest, I'm surprised it's still standing. If it fell, it would crush the shed and it might nick any vehicles that happen to be near the farthest edge of the parking area, and I'd recommend avoiding that area if it's windy. But it's nowhere near landing on the cottage, so you don't have to worry every time there's a storm."

"That thought did cross my mind on Friday night," Paige admitted, making Alex chuckle.

"Nope, not going to happen."

She tried to make her next question sound hypothetical, since she still didn't want the word to get out that she was putting the estate on the market. "Suppose I decided to sell the cottage at some point in the future... Would leaving the tree where it is diminish the property value?"

"Definitely. Any buyer is going to require you to remove it or to reduce the list price."

She thanked him for his opinion and asked how she could pay his fee, but he told her there was no charge. "Seth helps me out with my clients' landscaping questions all the time, so I'm glad to return the favor. He's a really good guy."

Paige was starting to think that, too. She felt a little foolish that she'd been concerned about consulting Alex just because he was friends with Seth. The arborist had seemed completely impartial and after he disconnected, Paige sat in the car with the engine off for nearly half an hour, contemplating what Alex had told her. Even though it saddened her, for all the reasons they'd discussed, she knew removing the tree would be the wisest course of action.

Additionally, she figured that cutting down the tree would make Lexie happy and it would alleviate Seth's stress, too. She saw her decision as a mending of the rift between the Atkins and Hathaway families.

It'll be like extending an olive branch—or a beech tree branch, she thought, giggling to herself.

Rather than waiting until the following day when Seth came to repair the screen door, she entered his number into her phone. *Even twenty-four hours might make a difference in whether he can schedule a tree service, especially if Alex isn't available and he has to search for someone else to do the project.*

When she told him he could arrange to have the tree cut down, he sounded surprised. "You've decided already? That was fast."

"After talking to Alex, it kind of seems like a no-brainer."

"Well, Lexie will be thrilled and I really appreciate it, too. You have no idea how much easier you've made my life."

"Why? What were you going to do if I said no? Transport the gazebo to another part of the property with a crane?"

"No—with a helicopter." He laughed. "Just kidding. Moving the gazebo actually would have been a lot easier than what Lexie suggested. She wanted me to relocate virtually all the flowers and shrubs in the garden to clear a place for the guests' seating. I would've had to plant several small trees, too. But hey, no pressure, so if you change your mind—"

Paige cut him off. "I'm not changing my mind, so you can put your shovel away."

NINE

Paige smiled when she woke to sunshine on Monday morning. Not only was she happy to see blue skies again, but she was glad that today she'd get to see Seth, too.

Yet a small misgiving tugged at her conscience when she stepped outside to shower and spotted the mighty beech in the distance. She brushed it off by reminding herself of the principle that most choices involve a loss, too.

After her morning walk, Paige headed to town to check her phone for texts from Tara. She hoped by now her cousin was feeling better than Cami had indicated she'd felt yesterday. For a variation in routine, Paige decided that instead of parking behind Highland Hills' library to get a signal for her phone, she'd drive to Port Newcomb.

But just before she reached Main Street, she noticed a sign that said: DUNE ISLAND MUSEUM & HISTORICAL SOCIETY. Recalling Aidan's recommendation, she abruptly made a right-hand turn into the parking lot.

The museum was hosted in a three-quarter Cape-style house that looked like *it* should be in a museum. It had low ceilings and wide-planked floorboards that creaked when Paige walked across them toward the docent's desk to pay the admission fee.

"Sure is a beautiful morning," commented the white-haired woman, whose nametag read *Marge*. "I think you and I might be the only two people on Dune Island who aren't at the beach today."

Paige smiled. "I've already been to the beach. Someone recommended I see the World War Two exhibit, so I figured now would be a good time to pop in—no crowds."

"Ah, you're right about that. The World War Two exhibit is in the back room, there." She pointed to a door on the opposite side of the wall. "Of course, your admission entitles you to explore the entire museum, so feel free to poke around. I'll be upstairs replacing a plaque in the children's section, but if you need anything or have any questions, just give me a shout."

Paige thanked her and then breezed into the room housing the World War Two exhibit. In the center of the floor, a large glass enclosure showcased several wartime artifacts, including military medals, service flags, and hand-held weapons and tools. She was particularly interested in the model planes that were used to teach plane spotters how to identify enemy aircraft, and she was also delighted to see a headpiece once used by a Red Cross nurse.

But most of the display consisted of black-and-white photos hung on the walls. There were pictures of summer homes that had served as military headquarters, clifftop bunkers, and tanks. There was even a photo of a UXO—it looked like a chunk of rusted metal—like the one that had recently been found on the beach.

But what fascinated Paige most was what she read on the informational cards posted beside each photograph. She learned that the US military had used Dune Island's high cliffs for military training in preparation for storming foreign beaches, including Normandy. The troops would stage drills during which they'd practice coming ashore, scaling the cliffs, and "overtaking the enemy." Paige had never known that Dune Island had played such a vital role in the war.

She was also enthralled by the photos of soldiers socializing with the men and women from the island, primarily at USO dances. Knowing that her great-aunt would've been the same age as some of the women, she scanned the images for Violet, even though Paige didn't know exactly what her great-aunt looked like and she probably wouldn't have attended a dance anyway.

"It's sobering to think that many of those young people who went off to war didn't come back, isn't it?" asked Marge. Paige hadn't heard her enter the room.

"Mmm," she murmured with reverential appreciation for those who'd sacrificed their lives serving the country. She studied the photo in front of her a few moments longer. Then she took a sideways step and viewed a photo of seven or eight women seated around a large rectangular table, their chins tucked to their chests as they stitched together various lengths of fabric.

Before Paige had time to read the label affixed on the wall next to the photo, Marge proudly informed her that the photo had been donated from her family's personal collection.

"These girls were volunteers who sewed blankets for the Red Cross to deliver to soldiers and POWs overseas." She pointed a bony finger at the young woman seated at the head of the table and boasted, "This was my mother. If you look at the photo in the newspaper clipping displayed to your right, you'll see her pictured with the mayor. She received a special commendation for sewing the second highest number of blankets on Dune Island."

"She must have been very proud of herself," said Paige. "Is this girl beside her the one who sewed the most blankets?"

"No, that's Ginny Williams. She sold the third highest

number. The only person who could sew faster than my mother was a mousy girl named Violet."

"Violet?" Paige repeated in surprise.

"Yes. Violet Atkins. But apparently she was too timid to be photographed for the newspaper. My mother said it was unusual for Violet to even participate in their sewing circle, because she was such a homebody. My mother, on the other hand, was the life of every dance and party at the USO. She received proposals from six soldiers before accepting my father's. Can you imagine being that popular?"

"No, I can't," Paige said absently. She wasn't sure how to take Marge's remarks about Violet. Although they were probably accurate, they weren't exactly complimentary.

The docent kept gabbing. "Neither can I. I was never what you'd call a *looker*, the way my mother was. Beauty, brains, she had it all. She excelled at everything she did. The only time she ever 'came in second place' was the year Violet Atkins sewed seven more blankets than she did." Marge chuckled and shook her head. "Mother never forgot it. Even though she accomplished so much in her lifetime—homecoming queen, business owner, selectman's wife, mother of five—and Violet Atkins wound up a secluded, kooky old maid, my mother was always envious of her sewing skill. Must have been why she told us all that story."

Paige's cheeks burned at the docent's reference to Violet as a "kooky old maid." She felt conflicted between wanting to defend her and not wanting Marge to find out that Violet was Paige's great-aunt. Saying nothing, Paige moved on to look at a framed photo of something called an LCM, or landing craft mechanized, which was used to transport troops, vehicles, and equipment during amphibious assaults. Rectangular in shape, the boat had a waist-high fence-like enclosure around its large deck. Two men were standing near the bow, watching intently as a ramp was lowered into the shallow water.

"Amazing photo, isn't it?" Marge asked, trailing close behind Paige. "During the war, it was illegal for the media to publish photographs of any military operations or equipment. But in the 1990s, when the local newspaper went out of business, they donated their World War Two archives to us, which was very fortunate."

"Yes, it was," Paige agreed. She pointed to the blondish sailor on the port side of the boat. "Why does his cap say HMS on the brim?"

"It stands for Her Majesty's Service. That sailor is from the Royal Navy. You see, a small number of the British military came to Dune Island to help train US sailors and soldiers for beach landings and assaults, including the invasion of Normandy," explained Marge. "Funny, but no one else has ever mentioned spotting those initials on his cap."

"Hmm," Paige murmured noncommittally and shuffled to examine the next photograph hanging on the wall. She was having a difficult time focusing because the docent was so talkative.

"Dune Island could have benefitted from someone like you living here during the war."

They'd only just met so Paige was surprised and confused by the docent's comment. "Excuse me?"

"I mean because you're very observant. Residents were instructed to be on the lookout for anything out of the ordinary, so they could report it to the authorities. Fishermen even carried special radios with them for just that purpose. You see, Dune Island had its share of German U-boats in the area, so the residents kept their eyes peeled." She lowered her volume and her voice took on a conspiratorial tone. "Little did anyone know, but the real danger wasn't in the water. It was on the land. Supposedly, someone who summered on Dune Island, a young person, was suspected of being a German spy—"

Paige assumed she was referring to the gossip Seth told her

that the islanders had spread about Edward Hathaway, and she interrupted the docent. "Was that ever officially verified? Do you have *proof* that someone in Hope Haven was a spy? Or was it merely a nasty rumor?"

"Well, no, it wasn't officially verified—or if it had been, I assume those details would've been classified top secret by the government. I'm only repeating what my mother told me. I don't think she intended to be *nasty*, though. She never named anyone's name, she just told me about the gossip that circulated the island because I was always fascinated by what it was like to live in Hope Haven during the war..." Marge's voice trailed off and her cheeks were tinged with pink.

Paige felt awful for embarrassing her. "It *is* a fascinating subject and your insider's knowledge really makes that time period come alive," she said sincerely. "It's just that I'm hyper-sensitive about rumors because people have made wrong assumptions about my family in the past. And *I've* made wrong assumptions about other people, too. It's been painful on both sides, so I'm trying to be more careful. As my great-aunt used to say, 'We don't truly know the condition of someone else's heart, so we shouldn't judge.'"

Recovering her composure, Marge nodded. "Your great-aunt sounds like one smart cookie."

Yes, thought Paige. *She was a lot wiser than anyone gave her credit for being.*

After leaving the museum, Paige drove to the library to call her cousin. Because she hadn't gotten around to texting a photo of Violet's jewelry yet, Paige decided to make it a video call so she could show her cousin the locket.

"Tara, hi!" she exuberantly greeted her when she saw Tara's face, which appeared drawn and tense. "How are you feeling today?"

"Stressed, as always. And my head is killing me."

"Again? I'm sorry to hear that. Do you want me to call back another time?"

"No. It won't make any difference—I'm probably going to feel this way for the next fourteen months."

Paige would have been alarmed about her cousin's health if she didn't recognize that Tara's comment was just a figure of speech, a way of complaining about how much work she'd have to do until the wedding next year. But to be on the safe side, she advised, "If your headache lasts more than a few days or if it gets worse, you should speak to your doctor."

"I already did. She told me to cut back on caffeine and drink more water." Tara narrowed her eyes. "What in the world are you wearing?"

Paige held the heart-shaped pendant close to the camera lens so her cousin could get a better look. "It's Violet's locket. See the etching on the front? They're violets, of course."

"No. I meant what are you wearing over your T-shirt? It looks like something that not even a one-hundred-year-old woman would be caught dead in."

"Tara! This sweater was Violet's." Paige was appalled because she had the feeling Tara already knew it belonged to their deceased great-aunt when she made the crack. "It's freezing at the cottage and this keeps me toasty warm."

"You're not *at* the cottage. You're in public."

To be honest, Paige had forgotten she was wearing the sweater when she went into the museum on the spur of the moment. "Don't worry, only one person has seen me in it—the docent at the Dune Island Museum, and she was wearing something sort of similar." Paige quickly redirected the conversation to what she'd really wanted to talk about. "Anyway, here's a funny coincidence... the docent's mother knew Violet. It turns out they were part of a sewing circle that made blankets for the soldiers during World War Two. Apparently, Violet sewed more blankets than anyone else in Hope Haven. Impressive, isn't it?"

Instead of acknowledging Paige's discovery, Tara asked, "Why are you out going to museums and getting all hung up with the past when you're supposed to be getting the cottage ready for showings?"

Stung by her dismissal of Violet's accomplishment and annoyed at her bossiness, Paige snapped, "Excuse me, but the cottage *is* ready for showings."

"So you've contacted a real estate agent?"

"No, not yet. The screen door needs to be repaired again because—"

"I thought you just said—" Tara began to interrupt but Paige interrupted *her.*

"For once, would you please let me finish my sentence?"

Ironically, Tara's phone made a beeping sound and she said, "That's the printer calling about the invitations. Talk to you tomorrow at seven."

"Tomorrow at seven?" asked Paige, but her cousin had already hung up. *Oh, right, we've got a video conference call scheduled. I'm supposed to provide an update on the sales process.* Because she didn't want the guys to give her grief about her lack of progress, too, Paige called several real estate agents. She couldn't reach any of them directly.

Doesn't anyone on this island need business enough to answer their phones? she wondered as she waited for the signal to leave a message at the fourth real estate agent she'd tried. Remembering Steve's warning about how aggressive they could be, Paige only provided her first name and phone number, not her address.

I've already got enough greedy sharks in my family, she thought scathingly. I *don't need more of them circling Violet's estate.*

.   .   .

When she returned to Spindrift Lane, Paige was surprised to see Seth traipsing across her driveway, with the screen door tucked under his arm like a surfboard, and a brown paper bag swinging from his other hand. He flashed a grin, waiting for her to get out of the car.

"Hi, Paige. You weren't here, so I hope it's okay if I removed this door and brought it up the hill for a while to work on it? I made sure your kitchen door was pulled shut, so no chipmunks could get in."

"No problem, but if I had known you were coming, I wouldn't have gone out. I didn't expect you to come until much later in the day."

"I'm on my lunch break." He held up the brown bag. "Lobster rolls. I got two of them, if you want to join me?"

"Sure. I *love* lobster," she said.

When they reached the porch steps, he turned the door he was carrying upright and said with mock gallantry, "Please. Allow me to hold the door for you."

Paige smiled at his silly pun and entered the porch ahead of him. "Do you want to eat out here, where we can enjoy the view, or in the kitchen, where there's a table?"

"It's so sunny. Let's eat on the heathland. Do you have a blanket or something we could spread on the ground?"

He wants to have a picnic, she thought. "I'll go get one."

"Okay. Just let me re-hang the door. It'll only take a couple minutes."

Paige went into her bedroom, aware that the only blanket she had was the summer quilt on her bed. But the prospect of sitting on two stiff wooden chairs in the kitchen or on the porch wasn't nearly as appealing as the prospect of stretching out in the dunes. Paige pulled the quilt from the bed and folded it into a neat square.

Before leaving the room, she checked her reflection in the mirror above the dresser. Once again, she'd forgotten she was wearing Violet's sweater. Tara was right; it might be warm, but it looked awful. She quickly exchanged it for a sweatshirt. *Not a huge improvement, but at least it's from this century*, she told herself as she pulled a brush through her hair.

Seth had already finished re-hanging the door when she stepped onto the porch with a large, frosty bottle of iced tea. He was standing on the outside looking in, his beaming face bordered by the wooden frame. "What do you think?"

"Very nice," she said. *Very nice, indeed.*

As she snuggled beneath her freshly laundered quilt later that night, Paige mentally replayed her lunchtime conversation with Seth. She'd told him about living in Illinois and the various nursing jobs she'd held, and a little about her family. He'd told her about his dad, who was now deceased, teaching him to surf when Seth was a kid, and about what it was like growing up on a small island.

"Like anyplace, it has its pros and cons," he'd said. "Obviously, it's a gorgeous location. But that can be a two-edged sword, because it means in summer, we're flooded with visitors. Which again, is both good and bad. Good for our economy, bad for our traffic."

Paige had chuckled. "I've discovered that. Do you live in a busy part of Rockfield?"

"Nah. I don't even live in a neighborhood. I live in the woods, or for what passes for woods on Dune Island."

He'd pulled out his phone and showed her a photo of Blossom sitting on the front steps of his home. It was a standard gray-shingled Cape-style house with the requisite dark green shutters and door. What had surprised Paige most was that there was no front or side lawn; instead, the yard was blanketed in needles and cones that apparently had fallen from the dozens of scraggly, lichen-encrusted pitch pines surrounding the house.

"I pictured your yard being like a smaller version of the grounds up the hill," she'd blurted out. Almost immediately, she'd realized it might have sounded as if she'd been making a comment about him not being as wealthy as his relatives were. She'd clarified, "I mean, I was expecting a lawn and a garden because you're a landscaper."

"Nah. I don't like to take my work home with me," he'd joked. Then he'd explained in a more serious voice, "I do my best to give my clients what they want, within the budget they can afford. I mean, I always steer them toward eco-friendly and sustainable choices, and I'll make suggestions if they want advice, but it's ultimately up to them, not me. That's why my grandparents' yard looks the way it looks and mine looks like this. They want every inch of their property to be meticulously landscaped, but I prefer a more natural look. It might seem a little messy to some people, but to me, the flaws are part of the natural beauty."

It wasn't so much what he'd said, but how he'd locked eyes with hers when he said it, that made Paige flush with warmth when she thought about it now, as she drifted off to sleep.

TEN

The first thing Paige noticed when she woke on Tuesday was that the tip of her nose wasn't cold. She touched her bare toes to the floor: they weren't cold, either.

If the weather keeps warming up like this, I might be able to take a dip in the ocean before I return to Illinois, she thought. *Maybe I could even go on Saturday, when Seth comes here to surf. It's always safer to have a swimming buddy...*

Paige hurried out to the juniper trees, wondering if there was any chance Joseph might have come to watch the sunrise, too. He wasn't there, but she arrived just in time to catch the sun's golden eye peeking over the horizon. It imbued the sky and water with such resplendent hues of orange and purple that Paige felt as if she herself were glowing. She sat in awe long after the colors faded, slowly inhaling and exhaling to the lazy rhythm of the mild waves advancing and retreating on the shore below.

As she circled back to the porch, Paige thought about how much more relaxed she felt than she did only a week ago. This was mostly because she'd had a break from work. It was also that she was more comfortable in the cottage now that she'd given it a thorough scouring. In general, she was eating and sleeping better, and getting regular exercise, too. There was something about life here that seemed simpler than it was at home. In turn, Paige felt calmer. More content. *If only I can hold on to this feeling when I get back to Chicago*, she thought.

Before continuing her painting projects, Paige went to town to check for messages from the real estate agents. There weren't any, which didn't necessarily upset her, but she wasn't looking forward to her brother's and cousins' complaints about it.

Next, she called Mia. Her best friend had been scheduled to return from a medical mission trip last week, so Paige had been giving her time to debrief, but she figured by now Mia had recovered from jetlag and had readjusted to being back in the US.

"Mia! How was Senegal?" she inquired when her friend answered the phone.

"Awesome. Except for the humidity, which made Chicago's weather seem mild by comparison. And the people's hospitality put our Midwestern friendliness to shame." As Mia described her experience in a remote village clinic, Paige completely forgot all about her minor grievances with her family.

When her friend asked how she was doing, Paige told her about the beautiful scenery, as well as what she'd discovered about her great-aunt's skills as a seamstress, especially during the war. Mia was enthralled and she kept peppering her with questions. It was the kind of response Paige had hoped she'd get from Sherry and Tara, so she was delighted that Mia was so interested. She also told her friend about the initials in the tree and her decision to cut it down, and she recited the verse from the locket.

"None of my boyfriends has ever given me engraved jewelry. I don't recall any of them writing me a love poem, either," Paige mused. "Although one time Trevor did trace our initials in the sand at the lake. I guess I should've taken that as a sign our relationship wouldn't be very enduring, either."

When Mia didn't respond, Paige thought she'd lost the connection. "Mia? Did you hear what I said?"

"Yeah."

Paige could tell she was holding back. "Why are you so quiet? Is something wrong?"

"Nooo, not necessarily *wrong...*"

"C'mon, spill it. What do you know that I don't know?"

"Are you sure you want me to tell you, no matter what it is?"

"I'm positive," declared Paige, even though she wasn't.

"I, um, I bumped into Trevor in the airport the other day. He was with someone."

Paige didn't need to ask. "A woman."

"Yeah."

"Oh." She was quiet, letting this information sink in, unsure how she felt about it and reluctant to ask anything else. Mia waited until Paige eventually prompted, "Was it someone I know?"

"No. It's someone he met in Ireland," said Mia and for a moment, Paige was relieved. It couldn't be too serious if he'd only met her this past semester.

"Oh. Is she a faculty member? Will she be teaching in the exchange program at his college this autumn?"

"No. she's not a faculty member. Trevor said that she was visiting so she could, uh, meet his parents."

"What?" yipped Paige. "*I* never met his parents and I live less than two hours away from them!"

"You'd better brace yourself," warned Mia. "There's more."

She swallowed. "Please tell me she isn't one of his students."

"She isn't one of his students." Mia paused. "She's his fiancée."

"You have *got* to be kidding me," shouted Paige, smacking

her palm against the dashboard. "You've just *got* to be kidding me."

"I'm so sorry. I didn't know if I should tell you, but I felt disingenuous *not* telling you. I postponed calling you for days because I didn't want to upset you."

"I know, I know. It's not your fault. I'm angry at him, not at you. No, I take that back. I'm angry at *myself*. How stupid was I to accept that he meant it when he said he was breaking up because he suddenly realized he wasn't ready to be in a serious relationship?" she ranted. "What he meant was that he realized he wasn't ready to be in a serious relationship with *me!*"

Mia made sympathetic sounds as Paige continued, "It's not as if I still have feelings for him—feelings *about* him, yeah, but not *for* him. It's just that I can't believe he practically got engaged five minutes after telling me he wasn't a long-term-commitment kind of guy. It boggles my mind. I mean, what was it about this new woman that he finds so irresistible that he'd decide, over the span of a few months, that he's ready to commit to spending a lifetime with her? Is it her looks? Her personality? *What* is it?"

"Maybe it's her nationality?" quipped Mia, obviously trying to lighten Paige's mood. When it didn't work, she said, "My point is that it could be anything. As much as I love to try to analyze people, who really knows why Trevor decided why he wants to marry her? If he didn't value all *your* amazing qualities and love *you* for who *you* are, then you wouldn't want to be with him anyway."

"Yeah, I know. You're right. Deep down, that's how I feel about him, too. I'm not sad because I'm not with Trevor any more," she assured her friend. "I'm sad because... because I'm not with *any*one."

"Aww, Paige." Mia released a heavy sigh. "I know you hate it when I say this, but—"

"Don't you dare," interrupted Paige, knowing exactly what

Mia's next words were going to be. She'd expressed the same sentiment a dozen times before and she was always wrong.

"The next guy you get involved with is going to be for keeps, you'll see."

Paige slowed as she turned onto Spindrift Lane, trying not to gape at her neighbor's circular driveway. There must have been eight or ten foreign luxury sports cars parked in front of the mansion. Even though her knowledge and interest in vehicles was negligible, Paige's brother, Dustin, was a self-proclaimed "motorhead." She knew he'd never forgive her if she didn't snap a photo.

As discreetly as she could, she idled the car, raised her phone, zoomed in and clicked half a dozen times. Then she examined the display to be sure the photos weren't blurry and that the cars were distinguishable.

The quality's okay but I should take a video, too, she thought, fiddling with the settings. When she looked up again, she caught a glimpse of someone ambling across the lawn in her direction. Mortified that the person may have caught her filming the Hathaway's property, she panicked, dropped the phone on her lap and stepped on the gas pedal.

Barrelling down the bumpy road, she glanced in the rearview mirror to see whether the person had turned around and gone back to the mansion. All she saw was a cloud of dust and sand.

When she reached her parking area, she dashed inside the cottage. *It's not a crime. I haven't done anything wrong. Besides, maybe the person didn't even notice that I was using my camera,* she told herself as she splashed cold water on her face in the bathroom. Regardless, she felt very unsophisticated and immature, and a moment later when she heard a knock, she momentarily considered not answering the door.

But she dragged herself to the porch. A rush of relief washed over her when she recognized Seth's profile on the other side of the screen. Paige wouldn't feel nearly as embarrassed explaining to him why she'd taken the photos as she'd feel explaining it to Lexie, or to any of the other Hathaway family members.

"Hi, Seth," she said lightly, opening the door so he could come inside. He was holding a small, black leather-bound book. "Are you on your lunch break? I was just about to make a sandwich. It's only tuna, not lobster, but I'm happy to make one for you, too?"

"No, thanks. I've got to get back to work—or get *to* work. My family's having our annual Fourth of July reunion this week, so I spent the morning visiting some of the early arrivals up the hill," he said cordially. If he'd seen Paige photographing the cars, he didn't seem upset about it.

"That's right. Thursday is the Fourth of July, isn't it? I've completely lost all track of time," she admitted. "It's nice that you're celebrating with your extended family."

"Yeah, it's always a fun occasion. We have a cookout and clambake on the back lawn and then we head over to Beach Plum Cove to watch the fireworks. Anyway, we were wondering if you wanted to join us?"

We? Who does he mean by "we"? Paige questioned silently. *Does he mean the collective Hathaway family? If so, then that's a nice, friendly invitation. But if he means him and Lexie, then the invitation is probably only because she's so happy I said they could cut down the tree. On the other hand, if he means him and Blossom, then it's almost as if he's asking me out.*

When she hesitated to reply, Seth added, "It won't be just family there, if that's what you're worried about—a lot of our other summer friends are coming, too."

I suppose that answers my question. I'm in the "summer friend" category, Paige thought, which should have been perfectly acceptable. Yet she felt strangely let down, an emotion she attributed to having just heard that Trevor was getting married.

"Thank you. That's a really nice invitation." She didn't have any specific reason to decline, yet she couldn't quite imagine hanging out with the Hathaway clan and their friends, either. "I'm not sure what my plans are yet. Can I get back to you?"

"Sure. We start serving at five, but it's very informal. People come and go all evening, so feel free to drop in any time. Like I said, we head out to the Cove after dark to watch the fireworks display."

"Thanks, I'll keep that in mind."

Seth turned and pointed to the shed across the driveway. "You know, the other day when I was fixing the screen, I noticed the door has come off your shed. You shouldn't leave it unsecured. I can re-hang it for you."

"I appreciate the offer, but that's not necessary," Paige said. "There's nothing in there worth stealing."

"I meant it should be secure from critters, like raccoons and mice," said Seth, causing Paige to involuntarily shudder.

"You really wouldn't mind doing that?"

"Not at all. I'll take care of it this evening since I'll be at my grandparents' house anyway."

"Oh. I've got to go to town for a family conference call around seven, but I can reschedule it if you need my help."

"That's okay. I can manage on my own. Anyway, I'd better get going, but I thought you might like this." He extended the small, leather-bound book. "It's a field guide to Dune Island's plants and animals."

"This is great!" Paige exclaimed, genuinely pleased. "Hope Haven's natural environment is a lot different from what I'm used to seeing in Illinois. There are so many birds and flowers here I haven't been able to identify."

"Yeah, I sort of guessed that when I noticed you were

wearing a wild chive behind your ear the other day." He winked at her and Paige could feel her cheeks burning.

"Do you mean the pale lavender flower that looks like a miniature pompom?" she asked, and he nodded. "No wonder my hair smelled like onions!'

Seth laughed. "Could've been worse. Could've been poison ivy," he joked, before turning to leave. "See you later."

As she watched him head across the parking area, Paige noticed movement by the shed. A mouse? No, a chipmunk. *I keep forgetting to buy extra plastic bags*, she realized. *I really need to start carting away the recyclables. I hope the Hathaways don't see all those glass bottles by the side of the shed and think I've got a drinking problem.*

Then it occurred to her that the Hathaways already *had* seen the bottles—in which case, they'd seen the broken door propped up against the frame, too. Admittedly, it looked trashy and as Seth had suggested, it left the contents vulnerable to rodents. Had Lexie or someone else sent him to repair it before their annual Fourth of July party? Paige was embarrassed by the possibility, primarily because she was so conscientious about tidiness and sanitation. She didn't need a reminder to clean up her yard and she didn't need anyone else to clean it up for her.

Nah, I'm being too sensitive, she told herself. *If they cared that much about how Violet's property looked, they would've sent Seth to fix the gutter that was dangling from the roof when Owen lived here. They probably can't even see the bottles or tell the door is off its hinges from way up there.*

Even so, Paige resolved to stop at the store before her conversation with Tara and the guys that evening so she wouldn't forget to purchase plastic bags for the cans and bottles, as well as a tarp for the trunk of her car.

. . .

As usual, Tara was the first one to log on to the conference call. Without so much as a hello, she launched into an update about her plans for the engagement party. "Did you look at the links I sent you for the envelopes? You'll be relieved to hear I decided on the green one with the gold-leaf seal. If you can believe it, it took me almost as long to choose the envelope as the actual invitation..."

Paige tried to murmur and nod at the right times during Tara's patter, but she found herself becoming more and more annoyed. She felt like asking her cousin, *Why do you expect me to be fascinated with every last detail of your stationery when you can't listen to me talk for two minutes about something I think is interesting, like Violet receiving a commendation from the mayor?*

By the time the guys had logged onto the call—Dustin was late, as usual—Paige's patience had worn thin. She decided she was going to take control of the conversation from the start.

"Before I update you about the cottage, there are a few pieces of news I want to share with you," she announced. "I've already told Tara what I've recently discovered about Violet, but I think you guys should hear it, too, since it's part of our family's history."

"You're not going to tell them about the locket, are you?" Tara whined. "You yourself said the guys wouldn't be interested in hearing about a piece of jewelry."

"Actually, I was going to tell them about Violet sewing a record-breaking number of blankets for soldiers during the war. But thanks for reminding me about the locket. I almost forgot I hadn't shared that with them, either."

"Arg," moaned Dustin. "I thought you were going to give us an update about what you found out from the real estate agent. Can you start with that and save the chitchat for the end of the call? I'm running on a tight schedule here."

Paige didn't appreciate her brother referring to something

that was meaningful to her as "chitchat" and she suggested, "Then you might want to refrain from interrupting while I share a few things I've learned about Violet. They show that we were wrong about what happened between her and Edward Hathaway when she was young, and it casts her in a different light." As an extra warning, she added, "Until I'm finished saying what I want to say I'm not providing an update about the cottage."

Dustin rolled his eyes, but he didn't say anything else, so Paige dived into sharing what she'd learned. Without divulging the specifics of Joseph's anecdotes, she mentioned how thrilled she'd been to meet him and how highly he had regarded Violet as his babysitter. Paige also revealed what she'd discovered about Edward and Violet, as well as about Grandpa Frank's possible interference in their romance. Neither her brother or her cousins seemed fazed by what she told them. They listened without interrupting, but she got the sense they were indulging her in order to move on as quickly as possible.

Paige wouldn't allow herself to be rushed. "Just a sec. I'll text photos of the inscription on the locket so you can see it for yourselves."

After reading it, Dustin scoffed, "Wow, that's embarrassing."

"What's so embarrassing about it?" asked Paige. "I'm sure Diana would treasure it if you wrote a sweet verse like that for her."

"I didn't mean what he wrote is embarrassing. I mean it's embarrassing that he went to all that trouble to get the locket engraved and a word is misspelled. Favorite doesn't have a U in it."

Paige had noticed the variation in the spelling the first time she'd read it, too, but she'd thought nothing of it. "It just seems old-fashioned to me. Or maybe he was using Oxford English," she informed him. "He went to Harvard, you know. He was probably imitating some of the classical poets he studied."

"My, my, aren't we hoity-toity." Dustin pretended to sip from a cup of tea, causing Rick and Christopher to burst out laughing.

"You guys are acting like seventh-graders," Paige said.

"I tried to warn you," gloated Tara. "So now can we discuss the cottage? Have you consulted with a real estate agent yet?"

"Hold on. I'm not done telling everyone about Violet's contribution to the war effort."

"You already told us. She sewed blankets. Lots of them," retorted Tara. "And that's terrific. But the fact is, we didn't know Violet and she didn't know us. That's the way she wanted it. She isolated herself from her family and from everyone else. She *chose* to be a hermit when she was alive, so I don't see any reason to try to get to know what she was like now that she's dead."

What a convenient excuse to justify being so self-focused and grabby. Paige was getting fed up with Tara having such a cavalier disregard for their great-aunt, and the guys turning everything she shared with them into a joke.

She argued, "We don't necessarily know all the factors that caused Violet to go into seclusion. It could've been that she didn't really *want* to be alone, but she felt like she didn't have a better option. Or she was suffering from chronic depression or she didn't have the social skills to change her situation. Who knows, maybe she was just an extreme introvert who would've preferred to spend lots of time alone no matter what else had happened in her life."

Paige's shoulders were tensing up and she could feel her calmness slipping away but she hardly paused to take a breath before continuing, "Regardless of what you think of her being a so-called hermit, there were parts of her life that were admirable and deserve our respect. I mean, we stand to profit over a million dollars from her property, so it seems only fair that—"

Dustin interrupted his sister. "Over a million dollars? Is that per person or total?"

"I didn't mean it literally. I don't know exactly what the estate is worth because I haven't met with a real estate agent yet. I was tossing out a number to make the point that we're benefitting a *lot* from the fact that Violet didn't sell the estate a long time ago and spend all the money on herself. Or she could have donated her property to the local land trust after she died, for that matter. Instead, she left it to us," Paige reminded them. "So it seems to me the least we owe her is to acknowledge that she wasn't just an emotionally unstable teenager who eventually became a batty recluse. And she wasn't mistaken about Edward Hathaway's feelings for her, either. There was obviously a lot more to the story—and more to her *life*—than that."

"Point taken," replied Dustin, a little too quickly. "But why haven't you met with a real estate agent yet? You really need to step it up. A lot is riding on this. None of us can make financial plans for our families unless we have a ballpark figure of what we'll get for the estate."

"And how soon we'll get it," said Rick.

"Not to mention, how soon you'll be coming back to Illinois," added Tara. "I could really use your help here, especially once the RSVPs start rolling in. What's the holdup, anyway?"

"The holdup is that none of the real estate agents has returned my calls yet." Paige was practically shouting with frustration. Her brother and cousins had completely missed her point about demonstrating appreciation for their inheritance by trying to understand Violet better.

She informed them, "Since all you're interested in is how much money you'll receive and when you'll receive it, I'll wait to schedule our next conference call until I've spoken to a real estate agent. That might happen tomorrow, but with the holiday coming up on Thursday, I probably won't hear from anyone until next week. Honestly, *I'm* in no hurry to find out—and I'm not in a hurry to return home, either. And since *I've* been the one doing all the work of preparing the cottage for sale, then I'm going to talk to a real estate agent when it suits *my* schedule, not yours."

With that, Paige ended the call.

For the next ten minutes, she sat in her car with the engine off, seething. Staying in her great-aunt's cottage, as well as hearing Joseph's memories about her, had given Paige new insights into Violet's character. But she recognized she'd been foolish to hope that her brother and cousins might be intrigued about aspects of their great-aunt's life that they'd never known before now, too.

It's regrettable enough that for years, our family was unaware of what Violet was really like and we were wrong about her relationship with Edward. But it's even worse that they're deliberately choosing to remain ignorant now, she thought. *After all, Violet's not only our benefactor, she's also our relative. Yet they act as if it's a nuisance to listen to me talk about her life.*

By the time she returned to the cottage, Paige's temper had cooled a degree or two but she felt like a long hot shower would help wash the rest of her annoyance out of her system.

Unfortunately, Seth was in the driveway, squatting beside a toolbox.

"Great timing. I just finished," he said, standing up as she got out of the car. "The door closes tightly now, see? It doesn't even squeak."

As he demonstrated his handiwork, Paige managed a weak smile. "Thanks a lot. I appreciate it."

"You're welcome. How'd your conference call go?"

"Fine." Backing toward the cottage, she repeated, "Thanks

again for fixing the door. I think I'm going to take a quick shower before it gets too dark."

"Oh, sure. I'll just grab my things and get out of your way." Seth picked up his toolbox, but he didn't leave. "There was one other thing I wanted to put out there for you to consider."

"What's that?"

"As you can imagine, Lexie was thrilled that you agreed to have the beech tree removed. I've been in touch with a tree service. Nothing's confirmed yet, but it looks like they might be able to schedule the project for next week."

"Really?" Paige had hoped they wouldn't be able to come out to the property until after she'd left Dune Island. She wasn't looking forward to hours upon hours of noisy chainsaws. And even if it was sentimental, she still felt a little guilty that she was allowing such a beautiful old tree to be cut down.

"Yeah, why, is next week a bad time for you?"

"No, it's fine. I'm just surprised because I thought all the tree service companies, including Alex's, wouldn't have any openings until after hurricane season."

"Yeah, I had to call in a few favors. Turns out, one of the companies is housing an additional crew of off-island contractors for the summer. It's not guaranteed they can put me on the schedule, but I think it'll work out." Seth licked his lips. Usually, Paige would have invited him to have a drink on the porch, where they could have continued their conversation. But tonight, she wished he'd quit stalling. "Anyway, I wanted to talk to you about, uh, the possibility of putting up a privacy fence."

Oh no! Someone did *see me videoing the cars this morning.* Paige was so embarrassed she wished she could scurry down a burrow, like a chipmunk. She quickly assured Seth, "There's no need for that. I promise it won't happen again, and I wasn't doing it to be nosy. See, my brother's a car enthusiast, so I try to take photos of cars that I think will impress him. But I haven't sent these yet and I'll delete them right now." She showed him her phone, so he could watch her deleting the photos she'd snapped of the Hathaways' driveway.

Seth's cheeks and forehead blotched with color, almost as if he was as embarrassed for her as she was for herself. "No, no. That's fine. I don't care about the photos. I-I didn't mean we're going to install a privacy fence up the hill. I meant we wanted to know if you'd like a fence installed in the back of the cottage. Just a small one that wouldn't block very much of your view in that direction. Lexie would pay for it, of course."

Paige was flabbergasted. "Why would I want to do that? And why would Lexie want to pay for it?"

"Since, um, since our family will be hosting a lot more social events than usual this summer, we thought you might appreciate a little extra privacy. We don't want you to feel uncomfortable because, you know, you'd potentially have strangers looking at you while you're relaxing on your porch or moving about your property..."

Paige was too emotionally spent to censor her response. "Yeah, right. I doubt very much that Lexie cares about *my* comfort. It's more like she's embarrassed to have *her* guests looking at my great-aunt's shabby little cottage. Be honest with me, Seth. Isn't that why you re-hung the door to the shed just now? Because Lexie didn't like the way it looked so she sent you down here to fix it?"

"No, that's not what happened," Seth insisted, shaking his head. "Like I said, I noticed the door was off yesterday and I was concerned about rodents getting inside, so I fixed it for you. Lexie had nothing to do with that."

He seemed sincere enough about the shed door, but she noticed he didn't deny that Lexie's reasons for installing a privacy fence weren't as altruistic as he'd claimed they were. Either way, it had been a long evening and Paige was too maxed out to discuss it further.

"Yeah, well, please tell your cousin that the answer is a

definitive *no*," she said. "Even if she sends you down here a hundred times with food or wine or gifts or whatever, the answer will still be *no*. I don't want a privacy fence and I don't want charity, either. If you'll excuse me now, I need to take a shower."

Then she turned and retreated into the cottage.

ELEVEN

By six-thirty on Wednesday morning, Paige was outside picking up the loose glass bottles she'd left beside the shed and chucking them into a plastic bag. She figured she might as well get started on the chore, since she'd been up half the night stewing about it. She'd also been stewing about how much gall her brother, cousins, and Lexie had.

And here I thought that Trevor was obnoxious for getting engaged a few months after dumping me, she brooded. *But the five of them are so eager to sell or alter Violet's property for their own purposes that they won't even take two minutes to pay tribute to the fact that she lived here for almost ninety years!*

In general, Paige didn't consider herself to be a pushover. Especially not at work, where she had to be very decisive and set firm boundaries with patients and their families almost every day. However, setting limits with her loved ones was a lot more complicated because her emotions—as well as theirs—were involved. So she tried to compromise as often as she could.

But I can see that when it comes to the estate, from now on I'm going to have to take a stronger stance with my family, she decided. *With my neighbors, too.*

Did that include Seth, or just Lexie? Paige was torn. She wanted to believe that the handsome, good-natured landscaper was as trustworthy and considerate as he seemed to be. Yet she couldn't shake her qualm that he'd been going out of his way to be kind so she'd be more likely to agree to Lexie's requests. Especially because last evening he'd been acting very cagey before he'd asked Paige about the privacy fence. It made her relieved that she hadn't told him about her plans to put the estate on the market.

If the Hathaways found out the property was for sale, they'd purchase it in a heartbeat just so Lexie could raze the cottage to the ground before her wedding, she thought.

Paige realized she was probably exaggerating because she was ticked off, yet the scenario she imagined wasn't completely preposterous. As she pitched a bottle into the sack, she was struck with an idea: she could refuse to set a closing date that was earlier than August 31. That way, even if the Hathaways did buy Violet's estate, they wouldn't be permitted to demolish the cottage until after Lexie's wedding. As an added benefit, Paige's brothers and cousins would have to wait longer to split the inheritance.

That would teach them to be more patient and appreciative, she thought. *It would give them a chance to reflect on all that Violet's done for them, even if it wasn't directly intentional.*

Energized by her revenge fantasy, Paige opened the door to the shed. She sang and stomped her feet to scare away any critters as she began extracting the plastic bags of recyclables. More frequently than not, the bags ripped, spilling their contents on the ground. She'd have to stop to collect the sticky refuse and then re-bag it in a fresh sack.

After lining her trunk with the tarp, she loaded in the heavy pouches and drove to the recycling center across the island in Lucinda's Hamlet. As it turned out, she was required to separate the recyclables, weeding out the redeemable cans and bottles. Since she didn't want to drive all the way back to the cottage with the junk she'd just brought there, she sorted it right there in the sandy parking area.

It was a laborious, dirty task and she didn't look forward to repeating it with the rest of the recyclables in the shed. *This is one of those times when it would've been really nice if Dustin, Tara, Christopher, or Rick were here to help me,* she griped to herself.

When she'd finished, she brought the bag of redeemable cans and bottles to the teenage attendant, who counted as he tossed them into the oversized bins. Then he paid her a nickel apiece.

I should divide this money five ways and send it to Tara and the guys. I'll tell them it's their share of Violet's inheritance, Paige thought facetiously, smiling for the first time that day.

By noon she'd repeated the same process several times, and she was hot, grimy, and hungry. And, although she hated to admit she cared, she didn't want the Hathaways to watch her slinging garbage bags into her trunk. She had deliberately avoided looking at the mansion, but she'd heard laughter coming from up the hill.

One more load and I'm going to quit for the day, she thought, even though she'd barely made a dent in the mountain of debris in the shed.

As she stepped forward to hoist another bag from the top of the stack, she stubbed her toe on something immoveable and hard. Paige pushed several bags out of her way and found what looked like an old end table. Waist-high and made of wood, it contained a single drawer with a metal handle that wouldn't open when she tugged on it. *It must be decorative, not functional,* she thought.

Paige wiped the dust from the table's surface with her work glove, revealing a deep crack running from back to front. It was too straight to be accidental, and she quickly recognized that the piece of furniture wasn't a table—it was a cabinet with a top cover that could be opened by flipping it sideways.

I think I know what's inside, she realized with excitement, feeling the perimeter of the cabinet until she located a metal arm, which she swung outward. Then she cautiously lifted the cover sideways until it rested on the metal support. Peeking inside the open cabinet, she reached in and pulled the dark, heavy apparatus upward on its hinges and secured it against a smaller supportive wooden lip.

There it was: her great-aunt's sewing machine.

As she examined it, a lump unexpectedly rose in Paige's throat. *This was the main tool of Violet's trade,* she realized. *It's what she used to earn a living and it's how she made a name for herself as a professional.*

Right away, she knew she wanted to keep the cabinet and machine, even though she herself had no sewing skills. But it was too heavy for her to carry to the cottage, and she had a niggling concern that it was likely to be stolen if anyone happened to peek inside the shed. So, she re-covered the cabinet with pouches of recyclables, and decided, *I'll pick up a new padlock after I drop off this load and check my voice mail for messages from real estate agents.*

There was so much pre-holiday traffic that Paige didn't return to the cottage until almost 2:30. By then, she felt absolutely famished and she smelled as if she'd fallen into a brewer's vat. She clicked the new padlock into the loop on the door and hurried across the driveway.

I don't care if four generations of the Hathaway family watch me from their widow's walk with binoculars, she thought defiantly. *I need a shower and I'm taking one.*

It was a smart decision. Paige planted herself under the hot jet of water until it went lukewarm and then she stayed a bit longer until it turned icy cold. As she wrapped a towel around her head, she could hear the Hathaways or their guests giggling.

Their laughter was so distinct it almost seemed as if it was coming from the other side of the shower stall, but Paige recalled what Steve had said about how well voices carried over the dunes.

I'll probably be hearing their voices and laughter a lot over the next few days, she thought, remembering that tomorrow was the Fourth of July. She still felt ambivalent about Seth's invitation to join the Hathaway celebration. *I'd really love to see Joseph again. It might be difficult to speak to him in private, but I want to tell him about finding Violet's sewing machine. I bet he'd appreciate its significance more than anyone else I know. I might even show him the locket. Maybe he'll remember something about Violet and Edward that would shed light on their relationship.*

She'd kind of like to see Seth again, too. But considering their last interaction, she wasn't sure he'd give her quite as warm of a reception now. And because Paige had turned down the offer of a privacy fence, Lexie might not exactly roll out the red carpet, either. *I'll wait until later to decide whether to drop by or not*, she thought.

Paige cinched her robe around her waist and slipped her feet into her flip flops to trek back to the porch. Just as soon as the shower stall door banged shut behind her, she noticed a man who appeared to be in his early thirties cutting across her driveway. A young boy trotted beside him and an even younger girl was riding on his shoulders.

"Hi, there," he greeted Paige nonchalantly as her towel started to slide sideways on her head. "You don't mind if we use your staircase to get down to the beach, do you?"

Paige used one hand to push her towel back in place and with the other hand she clasped her robe together beneath her chin. "They're extremely steep," she said. "I really don't think they're suitable for children."

"Don't worry. I carry Princess Kayla everywhere she goes."

At that moment, the little girl reached over and grabbed the towel from Paige's head. She giggled before dropping it onto the sandy driveway. The man began to bend down to retrieve it, obviously forgetting his daughter was on his shoulders—not a reassuring move for someone who'd just claimed he'd keep a close eye on the children.

"*I'll* get it." Paige quickly stooped to pick up the towel. As diplomatically as she could, she repeated, "I'm sorry I have to say no, but two children seems like too much to manage on steps like mine."

"It's okay, I'm used to it. I'll hold Reece's hand."

"I don't need to hold your hand. I'm a big boy." Folding his arms across his chest, the defiant child stuck his fists in his armpits.

"You only need to hold my hand on the stairs, Reece. When we get to the sand at the bottom, you can let go."

The boy bargained, "*Ten* steps from the bottom."

"Five," the father compromised.

"I said *ten*," the boy demanded.

"And *I* said the staircase is very steep, so I can't allow children on it, period," Paige stated in her practiced, no-nonsense nurse's voice.

"But I'm Grant's best man and I helped him arrange for the plane to fly by," the man argued as if Paige should understand the reference. "I promised Princess Kayla and Reece we could watch it from the beach."

Paige didn't know what plane he was referring to and she didn't care, either. "No. This is non-negotiable. Children are not permitted on the stairs. It's unsafe. You're welcome to watch the plane from my driveway, if you'd like."

"There it is," the boy wailed, pointing at the sky. A white biplane was approaching from the south, flying northward. "You said we could watch it from the beach, Dad."

His father quickly changed his tactic. "Watching it from up

here is even better. Look, we're practically close enough to touch it." He teased his daughter, "You'd better duck, Princess Kayla, or it might bump into your head."

The little girl started screaming and pitched her torso backward, trying to get off his shoulders. Because the man was grasping her ankles, she didn't fall, but she was hanging upside down on his back. Paige quickly took hold of her and gently lowered her to a standing position on the ground.

"It's okay, Kayla. I've got you," she comforted the toddler. "Look, the plane is way, way, way up in the sky. And we're way, way, way down here. It could never bump into us."

As Kayla buried her face against Paige's bathrobe, Paige craned her neck to watch the plane pass. It was pulling a long banner that read: ONLY 46 MORE DAYS, LEXIE. I CAN'T WAIT UNTIL YOU'RE MY WIFE!

A burst of applause and cheers erupted from the top of the hill, and the man clapped, too. Out of the corner of his mouth, he told Paige, "There's going to be one flying by every time Lexie visits the island. The final one will pass right after the wedding ceremony."

"That's incredible," she replied, which he clearly took as a compliment because he grinned.

"*Now* can we go down the stairs?" asked Reece and Paige realized the child couldn't have cared less about the plane. He'd probably only wanted to go to the beach so he could run in the sand or splash in the water.

Paige momentarily wavered about her decision. *I suppose I could offer to escort one of the children down the staircase and the father could take the other one, but I'd need to get dressed, first...*

"No, it's time for ice cream now, remember?" Reece's father said, and Reece took off toward the mansion. "Okay, Princess. Your chariot awaits. Up you go." The man lifted Kayla into his arms instead of onto his shoulders and they ambled away without another word.

Wasn't it the poet Robert Frost who said, "Good fences make good neighbors"? Paige asked herself as she went inside the cottage. *Maybe Lexie had the right idea after all.*

Never had Paige wished the cottage had a cell phone connection more than she did for the next hour. She was too tired to drive to the library in holiday traffic, but she was dying to tell Mia about her interaction with Grant's best man, the best man's children, and about the appearance of the biplane pulling a countdown banner. It was so outrageous that Mia would have made a hilariously biting comment about it. The two friends would have laughed until their sides ached, something that Paige felt like she hadn't done in years.

But she also wanted to share the situation with her best friend because she needed advice. *What if Reece nags his dad to take him down to the beach when I'm not here, and his dad agrees even though I've told him it's dangerous?* she fretted. *Or what if the Hathaways' other guests let their kids use the staircase? It's so steep. I don't want the children to fall or trip. It would be awful if someone got hurt—and I wouldn't want to be held legally responsible if they did.*

Paige had trusted Seth when he'd said he'd take responsibility for his own safety. But she couldn't extend the same amount of trust to someone as inattentive as Grant's best man, or to other people she'd never met. Yet she loathed the idea of trudging up the hill to the mansion and asking Lexie or Seth or one of the other Hathaways to spread the word that her staircase was off-limits. Driving through holiday traffic into town to leave a voice mail for Seth was only slightly more appealing.

My only other choice is to block off the stairs, she conceded.

Since her supplies were limited, she used the paint she had

on hand and a square of cardboard she cut from an old box to create a NO TRESPASSING sign. Paige didn't have any rope or string, but she did have duct tape, which she fastened in a big X shape across the entrance to the stairs. She strung an extra piece vertically across the top, from post to post. Then she affixed the sign in the middle and stepped back to examine her handiwork.

It looks tacky, like the kind of thing you'd expect an unfriendly, poor old hermit like Violet to post, she admitted to herself. *But appearances aren't everything. The stairs are too steep for children. So if the sign prevents someone from getting hurt, that's all that matters.*

When Paige tried to go for her morning beach walk on Thursday, the Fourth of July, she realized in her zeal to protect the children from falling down the stairs, she'd also prevented *herself* from gaining access to the beach. She'd thought she'd be able to ease herself over the top strip of duct tape, but she had misjudged how high it was above the first step. Every time she tried to slowly hurdle it, she felt uncertain of her footing and gave up. So she spent most of the morning and part of the afternoon painting the trim in the living room and retouching the kitchen cabinets she'd painted earlier in the week.

By three o'clock, she was too hot and drowsy to continue. After washing and putting away her supplies, she carried the rocking chair from the living room into the back bedroom, which was the coolest place to sit. Propping her feet on the bare mattress, she perused the field guide that Seth had given her. She tried to determine whether the buttery-yellow wildflowers that sprouted so abundantly across the heathland were hoary frostweed or bushy rockrose, but she couldn't quite tell the difference.

I should ask Seth. I'm sure he'll know, Paige thought. An

image of him standing bare-chested and dripping in the middle of her kitchen floor flitted through her mind, and despite the nearly stifling heat, she shivered.

Paige must have drifted off because the next thing she knew, she was woken by someone exclaiming, "So glad to see you!"

She'd been sleeping so soundly that she sat up with a start. Blinking, she tried to figure out whether it was daytime or night. Then she smelled a tantalizing aroma and she remembered: the Hathaways were having a party up the hill, which meant it must be close to 5:00.

Once again, Paige considered accepting Seth's invitation to drop in at their cookout and clambake any time. But she'd been feeling more and more regretful about what she'd said to him during their last conversation. She didn't want the first time they talked again to be in front of a crowd—that might be awkward. Besides, Paige hadn't showered today and her hair was flat on one side and sticking out on the other. She didn't want to meet the rest of the Hathaways looking like a stray cat so she decided to stay home.

Her circumstances reminded her of what Tara had said about Violet choosing to be a hermit. *I guess I'm choosing to be a hermit, too*, she realized. *I wouldn't enjoy isolating myself all the time, but today it beats the alternative.*

TWELVE

Paige woke up with the birds on Friday. She immediately headed out to the chairs on the other side of the juniper trees to eat her breakfast. Despite the early hour, once again she hoped she might meet Joseph there.

On the way, she was able to identify plants such as cypress spurge, broom crowberry, and woolly beach heather, because of what she'd learned from the field guide Seth had given her.

I can tell already it's going to be another scorcher today, she thought, marveling that the temperature had shot from the low sixties into the high eighties seemingly overnight.

Knowing she didn't want to spend another day cooped up inside, Paige decided she'd beat the crowds to one of the bayside beaches in Benjamin's Manor. As she tramped back toward the cottage, her eye was drawn to the beech tree. She'd already taken several photos of it from a distance, but it occurred to her she should get a close-up of Violet and Edward's initials for posterity.

Judging from how late she'd heard voices from up the hill last night, Paige figured most of the Hathaways and their guests would still be sleeping, so they wouldn't see her. She left her breakfast dishes inside the porch, grabbed her cell phone, and crept across the heathland.

After snapping several pictures of the engraving, she gazed upward into the complex network of limbs, branches, and twigs. *I hope it turns out the tree service crew isn't available next week after all. I'd really prefer not to be here when they remove the tree.*

It was a wish she'd made half a dozen times since agreeing to have it cut down. Not only would the process be noisy, but it would be *final*. Paige knew the towering beech tree was already dead, but as long as it was standing, it gave the illusion of growth and strength and permanence. She didn't think she could bear to see it lying on the ground.

Unexpectedly, she was overcome by an impulse to weep, something she hadn't done in ages. Aware that the Hathaways and their guests couldn't see her on this side of the thick trunk, she leaned her arm flat against the tree, pressed her forehead to her wrist and allowed her tears to freely tumble down her cheeks.

It wasn't just that she was crying in mourning of the tree. Paige was also crying because of family conflicts and broken romances—both hers and Violet's. And she wept because deep down, she was dreading leaving this beautiful place and returning to the stress of her job. Mostly, she wept as a tension reliever.

It didn't last long and when she'd finished watering the tree with her tears, Paige turned to face the ocean. Resting her back against the trunk, she closed her eyes, and tilted her face upward, allowing the sun to dry her skin.

There's nothing I can do to mend past relationships, she told herself. *But I can work on improving the relationships I have now.* Which didn't mean she was going to give in to everyone's demands and schedules—but that she wasn't going to postpone a closing date on the cottage just to spite her cousins and brother. And she'd already decided she should cut Seth some slack for suggesting a privacy fence. After all, Lexie was his client, as well as his cousin, so Paige understood why he'd advocate for her preferences.

She also realized she was going to have to accept the fact she couldn't force her brother and cousins to be interested in their great-aunt's life or to hold her in higher esteem. But that didn't mean Paige was going to stop acknowledging and appreciating whatever else she discovered about Violet before leaving Dune Island. *It'll be my small way of honoring her memory*, she decided.

Feeling better about her new perspective, she started to walk back to the cottage. She'd only taken a few steps when she noticed Joseph sitting on the low stone wall that ran across the Hathaways' backyard. *Oh, good! This might be my chance to find out if he knew anything about Edward and Violet's romance.*

He was facing the ocean, but when Paige came closer, she noticed that his eyes were shut. She didn't want to startle him if he was asleep, so she softly cleared her throat.

"Ah, Paige, good morning," he said when he saw her standing in front of him.

"Good morning. Is it okay if I join you?"

"Of course. Have a seat." He patted a flat stone beside him, and Paige sat down. "My legs aren't as ambitious as my mind is today. I intended to walk to the cliffside again, but this is as far as I'm going to get."

"Well, the view is wonderful from here, too—and I'm very glad our paths crossed again."

"So am I. Seth mentioned you might drop by the shindig last evening. I was sorry you weren't there."

"Yes, I was going to come, but I, um, I..." Paige couldn't think of a good excuse that was also truthful.

"No need to explain. You had your reasons." Joseph gave her a knowing wink.

Relieved, she remarked, "The party must have been a huge hit—the food smelled amazing."

"Yes, everyone agreed it was delicious, although to be frank, my sense of taste isn't what it used to be. As a lifelong bachelor, I would have been just as content with a ham and cheese sandwich," he replied, his eyes twinkling. "What I enjoyed most about the gathering was taking a trip down memory lane with some of my relatives I haven't seen in decades. The younger generations must have been bored to tears listening to us yammering about the good ol' days."

"I doubt that very much. The memories you shared with *me* were fascinating," Paige enthused. "You're such a good storyteller that I could picture everything you were describing."

Joseph laughed. "Thank you, that's a very generous thing to say."

"It's also very sincere," she insisted. "I loved hearing about my great-aunt from someone who knew her—especially because you liked her so much. To be honest, most of the stories my family told me about Violet haven't been very flattering and I'm a little ashamed to admit that I accepted their accounts at face value."

"Don't be too hard on yourself, or on your family," he suggested kindly. "At some point, we've all believed rumors or held misconceptions about someone else."

"That's probably true, but I still regret not questioning my family's perspective on Violet more than I did." Paige hesitated a moment before confiding, "I haven't told anyone on the island this yet, but I'm putting her property on the market. It's just not practical for me to keep it for myself."

Joseph nodded thoughtfully, but he remained quiet, allowing Paige time to express her thoughts.

"I know how incredibly fortunate I am to inherit my great-aunt's estate. It's an enormous gift. So I feel like I need to—and I *want* to—honor her memory by understanding more about what she was truly like, instead of just accepting my family's descriptions of her as a pitiful teenager or an eccentric spinster. Listening to your stories and staying in her cottage has already given me a fuller understanding of her character and the kind of life she lived here on Spindrift Lane. But I've discovered a few other things that are puzzling to me." Paige shifted sideways so she could look directly at Joseph. "I'm hoping you might be able to shed some light on her relationship with your cousin, Edward."

He furrowed his brows. "I'll tell you what I remember, although from what I personally observed, they didn't have much of a relationship. They were only casual acquaintances."

"That's what I always believed, too—until I inherited this locket." Paige lifted the heart pendant from her neck to show it to him.

Joseph squinted at it. "That belonged to your great-aunt?"

"Yes, and there's an inscription inside that proves Edward was in love with Violet, just like she claimed he was." Figuring Joseph might not be able to read the verse without glasses, she recited it to him. Paige expected him to look surprised, but instead, he glanced toward the horizon and the tips of his ears went pink, almost as if he were embarrassed.

When he looked her in the eye again, he said, "It's a wonderful sentiment, but I don't believe your great-aunt received that locket from Edward."

Paige was taken aback by Joseph's response, but she gently informed him, "The inscription includes his name. And the initials E and V are carved into the beech tree, too."

His eyes widened in obvious surprise. But he still refuted the possibility that Edward and Violet were a couple. "It must have been a different Edward."

That's as unlikely as it being a different Violet. Paige was perplexed by Joseph's denial of the concrete evidence she'd just shared with him. She knew he was mistaken, but she still wanted to hear why he was so insistent that his cousin and her great-aunt hadn't had a romantic relationship.

"What makes you think your cousin didn't give this locket to Violet? Is it because of something you witnessed between them? Or because of something your cousin told you?"

· "No, I was far too young to be interested in my cousin's love life. Most of what I know about what happened that summer, I figured out by putting two and two together when I became an adult." He looked off into the distance, as if he could see the past playing out across the horizon. Paige waited patiently for the rest of his explanation.

"However, one thing I do remember very clearly was when Catherine Brown—the girl whose camera Violet threw into the harbor—started coming to the house. She was a peroxide blonde with broad, square shoulders and even as a youngster, I knew she was a big phony. She pretended to dote on me in front of my aunt and uncle, but when they weren't around, she called me a little pest and told me to beat it. In retrospect, I realize she was pretending to like Edward, too. She was probably only interested in his parents' money, but he didn't have a clue. I can still remember him whistling as he shined his shoes on the days she came over. He was absolutely wild about her."

"That doesn't mean he wasn't dating Violet on the side. Or he might have been just leading her on," Paige argued, her voice quavering with frustration. She also felt a little stung. Even though Joseph had expressed his high regard for Violet the other day, now he seemed to be indirectly discrediting her, just as so many other people had done. "With all due respect, I don't understand why it's easier for you to believe that some other Edward gave Violet the locket than it is to believe that your cousin lied about having a romantic relationship with her."

As Joseph looked into her eyes, an expression of anguish

darkened his features. Then he heaved a sigh. "You're right, that doesn't make any sense. No wonder you're confused," he admitted. "I'm sorry I haven't been forthcoming with the truth. It's just that I've kept it to myself for eighty years because I felt like it wasn't my place to interfere. But Violet's gone now and as her great-niece who's searching for answers, you deserve to know."

Paige's curiosity was piqued and her heart rate quickened. Did Joseph hold the key to understanding what really happened between Edward and Violet? "I deserve to know what?"

"Your great-aunt's secret." He knitted his brows, hesitating.

Paige sensed he was trying to decide how to share whatever information he'd been guarding, and she was tempted to tell him it was okay to blurt it out, but she held her tongue. As eager as she was to hear it, she recognized that Joseph needed to reveal Violet's secret in his own way and at his own pace.

After a moment of silence, he pointed to the beech tree. "The summer I came to visit, on a humid July evening, right around dusk, I climbed that tree nearly three-quarters of the way to the top," he told her. "When Violet caught me up there, she put her hands on her hips and said, 'Joseph Michael Hathaway, you come down here right this minute.' It was the only time she ever used that tone with me." His shoulders slumped at the memory.

"She yelled at you?"

"No, she didn't yell. She might not have even raised her voice—it may have just seemed that way to me—but she sounded so stern that I knew I was in big trouble."

"Was she worried that you'd fall?" Paige guessed.

"Perhaps, although she knew I was a good climber. I think she was more upset because I'd been pretending to be a spy. I was carrying a little notebook so I could jot down everything she was doing. Can you believe I was spying on the one person who'd been so kind to me?" Joseph covered his face with his hand and shook his head, as if remembering how ashamed he'd felt.

Paige tried to console him. "You were only a young boy. Besides, from what I've heard, during the war the residents were instructed to report suspicious activity. So you were probably influenced by what was happening on the island at the time."

"That's exactly right, I was. And Violet understood that about me. But as she explained, there was a difference between 'being nosy' about neighbors, friends, and family members, and keeping an eye out for enemies who might intend us harm," said Joseph.

"That's a difficult distinction for a child to make."

"Yes, that's why she gave me a rule of thumb to follow. She said if I had a question about whether something I noticed someone doing was wrong, I should ask an adult about it. But if I was watching someone on purpose without them knowing, that was spying. I've never forgotten that lesson she taught me."

"She forgave you, though, didn't she?"

He nodded. "She even repaired my horseshoe-crab helmet. You see, I'd scrambled down from the tree so fast I snagged the chin strap on a branch and it tore in half. But Violet stitched it together in no time flat."

The memory returned a small smile to Joseph's lips, and Paige smiled, too. Every detail he remembered increased her appreciation for what kind of person Violet had been. Or at least, who she'd been before Edward had betrayed her, and she'd retreated from society.

Joseph continued, "For my part, I promised I'd never spy on her again. And even though she didn't ask me not to tell anyone else, I've never told another soul what I saw Violet doing that evening."

Her breath bated, Paige waited for what he'd say next.

"She was kissing her boyfriend beneath the beech tree," he confided in a low voice. "And it wasn't Edward Hathaway."

Paige's eyebrows shot up. "Then who was it?"

"I have no idea. He was a tall, lanky fellow, but he wasn't Edward." Joseph elaborated, "I was quite high up in the tree and the young man had already left by the time Violet spotted me and ordered me to come down. So I only saw the top of his head, but I recall his hair was curly and dark. Edward's was stick-straight, like mine used to be." He lifted his cap and ran a hand over his bald skull.

"Are you *sure* it wasn't him? You said it was evening, so it must have been getting dark." Paige felt guilty second-guessing Joseph's memory, but she had to point out, "You couldn't have gotten a very good look at him."

"I didn't need a good look. I slept in the same room as Edward because I was too afraid to sleep alone in that huge house. If it were my cousin beneath the tree, I could have recognized him blindfolded."

"Did either Violet or her boyfriend say anything?" asked Paige, hoping their conversation might provide more information.

"If they did, they kept their voices low. As I said, they were... otherwise engaged." It was clear that even now he was being protective of his former babysitter's privacy.

As much as Paige wanted to believe that her great-aunt's heart hadn't been broken by the wealthy boy next door, there were still parts of Joseph's story that didn't make sense. "If Violet wasn't infatuated with Edward Hathaway and vice versa, then why did she get so angry that he was interested in Catherine?" she asked. "There were plenty of bystanders at the yacht club who witnessed her meltdown. They heard her shouting that she was better for Edward than Catherine was."

The old man turned his hands upward. "I don't know what she may have meant by that, or even if those were her exact words. I wasn't at the yacht club with my aunt and uncle and Edward. But what I remember about Violet is that she was a bit of a mother hen. She might have been trying to look out for Edward, just as she looked out for her brother, Frank, and for me."

It was obvious that Joseph had given the matter a lot of thought over the years. Had he been troubled by it? He suggested, "This is conjecture, but maybe she suspected that Catherine was only interested in the Hathaways' money. Violet might have voiced her concerns because she felt a sense of loyalty toward her employer. Perhaps when the Hathaways wouldn't listen to her, she became frustrated and reacted impulsively."

Throwing Catherine's camera into the water and destroying the Hathaways' gas ration book seems like extreme behavior for someone who hardly ever raised her voice. If Violet really did that just to protect the Hathaways from someone she thought was a gold digger, it's even more of an overreaction than if she'd done it out of jealousy.

Paige suggested, "People aren't usually that passionate about something unless it's personal."

"I understand your doubt. I wish I had more evidence to prove what I'm saying." Joseph held up a finger, as if an idea just struck him. "Was there a photo of her admirer in the locket? I could look at it to confirm it's not my cousin."

"No. There wasn't a photo of a man inside. There wasn't a photo of my great-aunt, either. I don't even know what she looked like," said Paige sadly.

"Ah, well, that's easy enough to remedy," suggested Joseph. "Just look in the mirror. You could be her twin—she was lovely inside and out."

For the first time, being compared to her great-aunt was a compliment and Paige could feel herself blushing. "Thank you."

"Can you believe I never got to say goodbye to her?" Joseph lamented. "After she destroyed my aunt and uncle's gasoline stamps, they forbade me to go anywhere near her or the cottage. They wouldn't give me a reason why and as a boy I could only imagine that she'd been stricken with a contagious illness. Not only was I worried about Violet, but I missed being in her care."

Aww, poor Joseph. He must have been so confused, thought Paige. *The Hathaways should have considered his feelings—he was only a child!*

He continued, "The following week, the Navy was scheduled to conduct an important practice drill. They were holding it beyond those cliffs, right over there." He pointed to the right of the cottage. "As usual, they'd informed the residents in advance, so they wouldn't create a panic. Violet had promised that I could help her serve cold beverages to the seamen, which I considered an honor. I'd been looking forward to it for weeks."

Paige smiled to imagine the young Joseph, in awe of the brave sailors and wanting to do his part by bringing them cool drinks. "Were you allowed to serve beverages with your relatives, instead?"

"No, they didn't get involved in that kind of thing. But the drill was abruptly canceled for some reason, so I wouldn't have been able to serve the men anyway. The following weekend, my eldest sister came and brought me back home to Canada. Over the years, I only saw my father's side of the family every now and then, when we went to Boston or they came to Montreal. So, as I've said, I didn't know the full story about Violet's emotional breakdown until I was much older and heard the stories."

Somehow, coming from Joseph, the term, "emotional breakdown," sounded empathetic instead of disparaging, the way it did when other people said it. He continued, "Many times over the years I've wanted to drop her a line to tell her how much her tenderness had meant to me as a child. But I was concerned that getting a note from me might stir up unpleasant memories of that summer."

"Mm," murmured Paige. "It's completely understandable why *you* didn't write, but I'm afraid my family should've tried harder to connect with her, considering that they always said how lonely and sad her life on Dune Island was."

"Most of her adult life probably *was* lonely and sad," Joseph agreed. "But it wasn't always that way. During the summer of 1943, she was in love with a young man and he was in love with her. I know because I witnessed it."

Paige didn't doubt Joseph's childhood account of spying on Violet, but she had to ask one more time, "And you're sure that young man wasn't Edward Hathaway?"

"I'm sure." He gave a definitive nod. "Even if I hadn't seen her smooching with that curly-haired fellow, I'd bet my life that Violet and Edward Hathaway were never a couple. She'd never go out with someone like him."

The irony surprised her, and Paige burst out laughing. "I'm sorry, it's just that's what people always said about Edward— that *he* wouldn't go out with someone like Violet."

"That may have been the popular opinion, but I believe it was the other way around." Joseph explained, "Edward wasn't a bad person—and I should emphasize that he wasn't a liar, either. When he said he'd never been romantically involved with Violet, he was telling the truth. But in hindsight, I think he may have felt like less of a man because he couldn't enlist in the armed services. He tried too hard to impress others and to fit in, even though he rarely succeeded. I think that Violet, on the other hand, must have been content with who she was. She had an inner strength and from what I saw, she didn't mind staying in the background, even before what happened at the yacht club."

Paige nodded slowly, acknowledging Joseph's remarks.

"When you grew up, did you ever share your opinion about Violet with your relatives?"

"I tried, but it was a touchy subject, something the older generation rarely discussed. Keep in mind that Edward passed away very young. So certain relatives felt I was speaking ill of the dead, when I was merely expressing how fond I'd been of Violet."

Paige tried not to sound critical when she asked a final question. "And you never told your aunt and uncle that they were wrong about her being infatuated with their son?"

"No. As I've said, I never told *anyone*," he emphasized. "On occasion, I've questioned whether I'd done the right thing by remaining silent. But I figured Violet had a very good reason for allowing people to believe what they believed about her—and it wasn't my right to set the record straight."

Paige reflexively lifted her hand to fiddle with the silver heart. She still wasn't sure what to make of Joseph's story, but she told him again, "Well, I'm glad you decided to confide everything you remembered about that summer and what Violet was like. It means a lot to me to hear it."

"It means a lot to *me* to express it." When Joseph looked at her, Paige noticed his eyes were tear-filled and she realized how burdened he must have felt carrying this secret all these years. She reached over and gave his hand a squeeze.

Then, to lighten the mood, she half joked, "Of course, now I have a mystery to solve... Figuring out who the 'other Edward' was."

"I wish I could help you with that." He abruptly stopped talking and twisted his head toward the driveway. A black convertible was approaching. "Aha, my ride to the airport has arrived."

"You're leaving Dune Island already?" Paige blurted out in dismay. "You've told me so much about my great-aunt, but I've hardly gotten to know *you* yet."

"Life is full of surprises," he said with an impish wink. "Maybe we'll both be back next summer and we can pick up where we left off."

If only, thought Paige sadly.

She walked Joseph to the car, where they spontaneously gave each other farewell embraces. Then Paige stood in the driveway waving until the convertible drove up the hill and out of sight.

THIRTEEN

Traffic on the way to Benjamin's Manor was the heaviest Paige had experienced so far in Hope Haven. It wasn't only vehicles contributing to the congestion, either: pedestrians, cyclists, skateboarders, and strollers crowded the roads and sidewalks, creating slowdowns at every intersection, curve, and corner. Paige didn't mind. Talking to Joseph had whetted her curiosity about Violet's love life, and as traffic crawled along, she reflected on what he'd told her.

I guess it's plausible that Violet knew more than one Ed, since it's a common name. And by all accounts, Edward Hathaway didn't sound like a good match for her, so I can believe she didn't have a crush on him after all, Paige reasoned. *But it's very hard to accept that she'd destroy the Hathaways' ration book just because they wouldn't listen to her about Catherine having ulterior motives for dating their son.*

Furthermore, if there really was a second Ed, why did his relationship with Violet end? Did he break up with her because he was ashamed of her public outburst? Or had Violet effectively ended their relationship by retreating into isolation?

Paige kind of doubted that's what happened. The inscrip-

tion in the locket—*Hold me in your heart always and forever*—
indicated their feelings for each other were strong enough to
withstand the fiasco at the yacht club. And now that Paige
thought more about that line, it sounded as if Ed had given the
locket to Violet as a parting gift. Perhaps it was meant to be a
reminder of his love, as well as a request for her to stay true to
him while he was gone. But why was he leaving?

Maybe he was only vacationing here for the summer? Or...
Mid-thought, Paige snapped her fingers. The answer was so
obvious: Ed could have been a local resident who'd given Violet
the locket before he "went off to war," as people used to say.
Maybe he was one of Violet's classmates she'd been dating in
secret because her brother and father were overly protective?

Almost instantly, she was struck by yet another possibility.
*Ed could have been a sailor or soldier who came to Hope Haven
for training! Maybe he was only here temporarily before shipping
out again.*

Paige recalled the docent, Marge, bragging that her own
mother had received several proposals from servicemen she'd
met at the local USO. Perhaps Violet had been involved with a
serviceman, too?

*If Ed had just been deployed overseas, that might explain
why she overreacted about Edward Hathaway photographing
Catherine. Maybe Violet was so distraught about her boyfriend's
departure that she couldn't bear to see a phony like Catherine
happily dating Edward Hathaway,* Paige surmised.

She didn't condone her great-aunt's destructive behavior at
the yacht club and she couldn't quite comprehend why she'd
lived the rest of her life in solitude, either. But from her own
experience of breakups and heartaches, Paige certainly understood why Violet might have been so emotional in the moment.

Her mind whirled with more questions. *If Ed really was
enlisted in the service, what happened to him after the war?* she
wondered. If he was local, had he returned to Hope Haven to

discover Violet had become a recluse? Or was his hometown somewhere else, and once he went back, they lost touch? An even more tragic possibility occurred to Paige. *I hope he didn't die in combat...*

She turned into the parking lot adjacent to the library to check her voice mail before continuing to the beach. *Too bad all the libraries are closed for the holiday weekend or else I'd pop in and research the local archives for a high school yearbook or some kind of public directory. It would be interesting to see how many Eds there were on the island when Violet lived here.*

Instead, she turned off the car ignition and checked her voice mail. She was surprised to find she didn't have any messages from Tara, and equally surprised that four real estate agents had returned her calls. Without exception, they wanted to know the address of the property she intended to list for sale.

I refuse to give that information unless they satisfactorily answer the questions I pose to them, first, Paige thought. *Which means I'll need to speak directly to them.*

She made another round of calls, but once again, no one picked up. She left messages, but since it was a holiday weekend, she didn't expect replies until Monday. She repeated her interest in discussing their qualifications, saying, "Rather than playing phone tag, please leave a message stating when you'll call next week—or when I can meet you at your office, if that's more convenient. You can also email or text me the times that work for you."

She was just about to start the car's engine when she received a text from Dustin.

Hey, Paige, you there?

Pleased because her brother rarely texted her, she dictated:

Hi, Dustin. What's up?

Dustin:

> That's what I was wondering. Any luck with a
> real estate agent yet?

Paige bristled. She should have realized he wasn't texting just because he wanted to touch base with his sister. She replied:

> I told you I'd let you know when there's
> something to report. So don't hassle me
> about it.

She deleted the second sentence and hit the send button. Dustin texted back:

> Okay, just checking. I didn't hear from you
> yesterday so I thought you might not be talking
> to me.

Paige clapped her hand against her forehead. July 4 wasn't only a national holiday; it was also the day Dustin was born. *I've got a lot of nerve to criticize Tara for being so self-absorbed, when I completely forgot all about my brother's birthday.* She quickly dictated:

> Happy belated birthday, Bro—so sorry I
> missed it.

Always the joker, he wrote back:

> No prob. What did you get me?

She had a flash of inspiration and texted him a photo of the imported cars in the Hathaways' driveway, saying:

> Choose one.

A second later, he wrote:

> Whoa. Where'd you take that photo—Geneva Int'l Motor Show?

She answered:

> Nope—the neighbors' house.

Dustin:

> Too bad I didn't know there were cars like that next door. I would've gone with you to Dune Island.

Half-annoyed, half-amused, Paige said into the mic:

> Yeah, that is too bad because I could've used some help getting the cottage ready to sell.

Dustin didn't miss a beat:

> But it IS ready, right?

Paige mumbled, "*It's* ready, but *I'm* not." It wasn't the first time she'd felt that way, but it was the first time she'd given voice to the emotion. When she realized she had pressed the mic icon and her phone had captured her sentiment, she quickly deleted the text and replied:

> Someone's coming to take down the beech tree next week and I've got a little more painting to finish. But otherwise, yes, it's ready.

> Great. Because the sooner we sell, the sooner I can have a luxury convertible in MY driveway.

> I thought you wanted a new boat?

BOTH.

Paige waited but apparently Dustin's one-word reply was the end of their brief conversation. Even though she'd felt justified ending the conference call early on Tuesday—and she still wasn't going to let Dustin or her cousins boss her around—Paige was glad her brother had reconnected with her. She didn't like being at odds with her family members and she felt more than a twinge of guilt for forgetting his birthday.

I suppose I should reach out to Tara. I won't talk about the estate, but I can at least ask her how the second phase of the party planning is going, she thought.

But after she tapped her cousin's name in her contacts list, Tara's voice mail immediately picked up, so Paige continued to the beach. The lot was full and parking was prohibited on the street nearby, so she tried another beach, and then another and another one after that. She finally found an open space in a lot at the fifth beach she visited.

She'd barely gotten out of her car when the woman who'd parked next to her said, "Remember to put your parking pass in your front window. I left mine in my purse last year and I had to pay a hundred-dollar fine, even though I'd already purchased the weekly pass. I just didn't have it displayed when the ranger came around to check. But, at least my car wasn't towed—I've seen that happen, too."

"I didn't know I needed a parking pass." Paige hadn't noticed an attendant or a ticket station when she drove in. "Where can I buy one?"

"Online. Or at the Town Hall, but it's closed for the holiday weekend."

Disgruntled, Paige muttered, "That's helpful." Then she quickly clarified, "I meant Town Hall, not you. I'm glad you told me I need a pass."

"No problem. And in case you're like me and you don't

have access to a printer, keep in mind you don't need a pass after four p.m. Or in the morning before nine. Just be sure to move your car before the rangers arrive. They're ruthless about parking violations." The woman shook her head in disgust. "Really makes me wish I could afford a waterfront rental, so I wouldn't have to deal with this kind of nonsense."

"Yes, it is annoying," Paige agreed.

As she relinquished her spot to an incoming car of beachgoers, she waved and thought, *Congratulations! You've won the parking lottery.*

Next, she tried several beaches in Lucinda's Hamlet, but the situation was the same there as it was in Benjamin's Manor. She finally gave up and decided to go for a hike in the bird sanctuary, where free parking was plentiful. Unfortunately, so were the mosquitoes. By the time she returned to the cottage, she was hot, hungry, and itchy.

She was also very cranky at her neighbors' guests. *Thanks for ruining my freedom to enjoy the beach that's right in my front yard*, she imagined herself saying to them. But even as the snide thought ran through her mind, Paige knew they weren't really to blame. She was the one who'd chosen to put up a barrier that she wasn't tall enough to climb over.

If only it had occurred to me to buy more tape when I was in town, I could've taken down the NO TRESPASSING sign, gone for a swim, and then constructed a lower barricade when I was done, she thought.

But since she had no inclination to face the traffic again, Paige frittered away the day in the cottage, which she'd come to appreciate was far preferable to the crowded beach—even if it meant she couldn't go swimming.

On Saturday morning, Paige took the beachgoer's advice from the previous day and arrived at the nearly deserted bayside parking lot by 7:00. The water had receded nearly a third of a mile and although the damp, flat expanse of sand was conducive to walking at a brisk pace, she kept stopping to explore the tidal pools.

Unlike the other side of the island, where the waves swept the shallows nearly clean, these puddles were teeming with scallop, periwinkle, oyster, and jingle shells. Paige also discovered hermit crabs, mussels, razor clams, and moon snails. As she bent to examine the marine life, the sun beat down on her back and a balmy breeze blew her hair across her face.

If it's this hot already, this afternoon should be blazing, she thought. *I really wish I had a parking pass. Then I could've stayed here all day.*

She dawdled on the flats as long as she dared before heading back down the beach toward her car. Halfway there, she paused in a deepening tidal pool to observe a horseshoe crab as it glided past her feet. It reminded her of Joseph's story about how Violet had helped him make a helmet from a horseshoe crab's shell.

"Ack—look what's coming our way and it has a very long stinger," exclaimed a woman who was wading with a small child several yards away from her.

"That's not a stinger. It's his tail," the boy told her. "You needn't be afraid, Mummy. He won't harm you."

Paige smiled at the child's adult-like phrasing, which sounded even more mature to her ear because of his calm composure and his accent. All of a sudden, she was staggered by an epiphany: the reason Violet's love interest had spelled *favorite* with a "u" was because he was British.

He must have been a member of the British military—maybe he was a sailor with the Royal Navy, she deduced.

She was so excited about the possibility that she may have figured out who Violet's boyfriend was that she forgot to stop at the hardware store for supplies to redesign the NO TRESPASSING sign. *I wish the museum were open today—I could ask if Marge has a list of the British servicemen who were assisting in Hope Haven during World War Two.*

But what would she say if the docent asked why she was interested? Paige couldn't very well tell her that searching for the truth about what Violet went through just felt like the right thing to do.

I don't want to lie, but I don't want to disclose any of Violet's private business, either, she fretted. *Maybe it's a good thing the museum is closed. It gives me time before Monday to come up with a plausible reason that won't involve telling Marge about Violet's locket...*

As she neared the driveway at the bottom of Spindrift Lane, she noticed Seth coming from the direction of the beach. Wearing a shorty wetsuit, he was carrying his surfboard beneath one arm and holding Blossom's leash in his other hand.

Just then the dog noticed her and broke free of Seth's grip. Paige crouched down and Blossom charged forward to give her a slobbery greeting.

"Well, hello," she said, laughing. She scratched behind his ears. Then she stood up, still petting him, and added, "Good morning, Seth."

"Hello." His greeting was noticeably less enthusiastic than Blossom's had been. He picked up the end of the leash, balanced his surfboard upright beside him and ordered the dog to sit.

"It's okay, he just wants affection," Paige said. "Or a treat. Is that what you want, Blossom? C'mon, let's go get one."

"No. Blossom, sit," Seth commanded again loudly. To Paige he said, "I don't want him getting used to going inside the cottage."

"Oh, right." She appreciated that Seth was trying to break Blossom of the habit, so she offered, "I can pop in and bring a treat out here to him, then."

"No, I don't want him getting used to treats, either. He needs to lose weight."

"So do I, but I still indulge now and then. Everything in moderation." When Paige's joke failed to elicit a smile from him, she figured Seth was miffed because she'd been so testy about Lexie offering to install a privacy fence on her property. But before she could address the subject directly, he told her he'd received a definite answer from the tree service company.

"They've confirmed their crew can come out here on Tuesday. It'll take all day and they'll probably be here for a few more hours on Wednesday. Does that work for you?"

"Yes, that's fine." She gave him her most amiable smile, but Seth narrowed his brows in return.

"You sure you want to go through with this? Because we need to draw up some paperwork, for legal purposes. So if you're going to change your mind about this, too, it's better if I know sooner rather than later."

Confused, Paige replied, "I'll sign whatever you need me to sign. But what do you mean by, if I'm 'going to change my mind about this, too'? What have I ever changed my mind about?"

Seth motioned toward the far dune. "You said I could use your stairs and then you blocked them off with a no trespassing sign."

"Ohh, right. I completely forgot about that—and I figured you'd be able to step over it anyway." After Paige explained why she'd constructed the barricade, Seth turned red-faced.

"I can't believe Grant's best man came down here after I explicitly told him this was private property and he couldn't trespass on it."

"To be fair, he *did* ask if they could use the stairs. Besides, his son really wanted to play on the beach and I got the feeling he was the one in charge," Paige remarked tongue-in-cheek.

"I don't know about that. It seems to me that *Princess*

Kayla's wish is her father's command," said Seth, obviously poking fun.

"Yeah, can you imagine how much more authority she'll wield once she learns how to talk?"

They both chuckled before Seth turned serious again. "Listen, most of my family's guests are leaving today, but I'll remind them again that your property is off-limits. I'm sorry I took the no trespassing sign as a personal offense. I've really been on edge about preparing the grounds and garden for Lexie's wedding. And as much as I love my extended family, well, let's just say that tensions run high when we all get together under the same roof. But that's no excuse for me to get bent out of shape so easily."

"Trust me, I understand how family dynamics can affect a person," Paige assured him. "On Tuesday night, I had a very unpleasant call with my brother and cousins. I think that's part of the reason I reacted so strongly when you suggested I allow Lexie to install a privacy fence near the cottage. I mean, I'm still not sure she had *my* best interests in mind, but in a way, it was a generous offer. So I'm sorry I wasn't more gracious about it."

"It's not a problem." Seth hesitated, toeing the sand before he looked up and met Paige's eyes. "But there's something I want to make very clear. I haven't been trying to butter you up so you'll agree to my cousin's requests. Lexie didn't even know I re-hung the shed door. And the only reason I brought you lobster was because it was my lunch break and I was hungry and... and I thought we'd both enjoy eating good food in good company."

Paige beamed. "I *did* enjoy it."

"Me, too. Maybe we can do it again sometime."

It didn't seem like the right time to mention she'd only be on Dune Island another week or two. So she suggested, "How about if I make us brunch after you're done surfing? Since you're going to remind your remaining guests that the stairs aren't safe for children, I'll get a pair of scissors to cut through the duct tape—I've been dying to go swimming, too."

The water was so cold compared to the air that by the time Paige was acclimated enough to immerse her head and shoulders, Seth was done surfing. But after setting his board on the beach, he returned to the water where she was floating in the gentle swells. They bobbed together for a little while until their small talk was interrupted by a series of large, oncoming waves and they had to duck beneath them. Paige shrieked with delight when she emerged, exhilarated from the nippy surge of water washing over her.

"This is *amazing*," she raved. "There aren't any waves like this at the lake I usually swim in."

"Does that mean you don't know how to bodysurf?" asked Seth.

"I tried once when I went to the Caribbean, but I wasn't very successful."

"Yeah, it can be tricky, but I'll teach you."

Seth demonstrated how to hold her arms, where to stand, and most importantly, when to plunge forward so the momentum of a cresting wave would propel her toward the shore. Despite his patient instruction, it took Paige at least a dozen attempts to figure out the timing. More often than not, she dived too late and the waves rolled on without her. A couple of times she dived too early and the water crashed right on top of her, pushing her down against the sand instead of carrying her forward.

But once she got the hang of it and torpedoed straight toward the beach, she was hooked. Although she was an avid swimmer and water skier, she'd had no idea that bodysurfing was so much fun.

After almost an hour, Seth asked, "You ready to get out? You're shivering."

"I just need to catch one more." But Paige took ten more rides before she reluctantly dragged herself onto the dry sand. Her equilibrium was out-of-whack, and she staggered sideways, ahead of Seth.

"You're walking like a drunken sailor," he teased, holding out his arm so she could grip it while she shook the water from her ears.

As they stood side-by-side drying their goose-bumped skin with towels that had been warmed by the sun, Paige remembered what Steve had said about how once she went in the ocean, she'd never want to come out again—and that she'd never want to leave Dune Island, either.

At this moment, I wholeheartedly agree with him about both of those statements, she thought. *Then again, I usually feel this way whenever I'm on vacation, so it's probably more of an indication of how stressed I am at work than anything else. But I'm still very glad I took down the barricade and went swimming.*

After changing into dry clothes, Paige made a simple lunch —it was too late to be called brunch any more—of sweet potato hash, eggs, and avocado. She set a bowl of water out for Blossom and Seth allowed her to give him a treat after all. The dog gobbled it down and then stretched out between the two chairs on the porch, as if he belonged there.

"I usually just hold my plate on my lap, but if you help me move the table out here—" Paige started to say, but Seth interrupted her.

"I'm too hungry to move furniture," he said. "Let's hold our plates."

They ate in silence, both devouring their food almost as quickly as Blossom had consumed his. Toward the end of the meal, Paige told Seth that she'd had an interesting conversation with Joseph the previous morning.

"I know. When I called him last evening to make sure he'd arrived home safely, he mentioned how thrilled he was that he'd gotten another chance to chat with you before he left. I could tell it really meant a lot to him."

"It meant a lot to me, too." Paige pressed her hand to her heart. "Did he tell you we talked about the past, and what he remembered about my great-aunt Violet?"

"No. He didn't tell me anything about your discussion at all —except how much he enjoyed it. So please don't feel pressured to share anything about it, either."

"I don't feel pressured, but there is something I want you to know." She had already decided that, just like Joseph, she'd never tell anyone else that he'd seen Violet kissing someone beneath the beech tree. It wasn't Paige's story to share. However, she felt comfortable confiding, "He was adamant that Edward Hathaway didn't give Violet this locket. And I think he's right."

"But the inscription is signed *Ed*."

"I know, but Joseph believes it must have been another guy named Ed. And now, I believe that, too. I think the Ed who gave my great-aunt this locket was British."

"Why?"

"Here. Let's see if you can find the clue." Paige opened the locket and leaned forward so he could read it. Seth inclined his chest toward her, their faces mere inches apart as he squinted at the pendant.

If our mouths were a little closer, we'd be kissing, she thought, catching her breath. The idea of their lips touching nearly made her lose her balance.

"Ah, I see it now," he exclaimed after a moment, his words warm on her cheek before he pulled back. "He used the Oxford English way of spelling *favorite*."

"Well spotted," she announced in her best BBC voice, using humor to deflect his attention from her face, which felt like it was on fire. "I think this Ed might have been serving here during the war, possibly as a member of the Royal Navy."

She told him about what she'd learned at the museum, and her plans to speak to the docent on Monday. "I hope she doesn't ask me why I want a list of British sailors' names, because I don't intend to share any details about my great-aunt's life with her. It's too private."

"I won't say anything about the locket or Violet to anyone, either," Seth promised. He set his utensils on his plate and looked into her eyes. "Listen, this is going to sound like I'm nagging, but I need to check with you one more time... Are you absolutely sure you're okay with cutting down the beech tree?"

"Yes. I am." She nodded. "I'm sure."

"Then what am I hearing in your tone that makes me nervous?"

Paige tried to brush off his concern by laughing, but she couldn't. "I know cutting down the tree is a good decision and I honestly *want* to do it, especially since Lexie's paying for it and it'll make your life easier. It's just that—this is going to sound sentimental—I feel like I can't bear to see it lying on the ground. Once the tree and the stump are completely gone, I'll be fine. But I don't intend to be here *while* they're chopping it down."

Seth looked concerned. "Where will you go?"

"Probably sightseeing. Or to one of the bayside beaches. I'll go to the library, too, since it's one of the few places I can consistently get a signal for my cell phone."

"But it's going to take the tree service a day and a half. They'll be here from dawn to dusk on Tuesday. What will you do that evening?"

Paige hadn't really thought this out. "Maybe I'll check out the nightlife in Port Newcomb. As long as I don't come back until after dark, I won't be able to see the remains, right?"

"You'll see them the next morning. Even if you try not to look, you won't be able to miss it." Seth rubbed his hand hard across his face. "Okay, so here's the thing. I didn't relay this message sooner because I didn't want to offend you again or for you to feel like this is charity or something. But Lexie knows how noisy it's going to be around here with chainsaws running all day and she's offered to pay for your accommodations at an inn from Monday evening through Wednesday afternoon."

"That really isn't necessary."

"Actually, it is—you shouldn't have to tolerate a disruption like that on your vacation. Honestly, she really wants to do this as a token of her gratitude, and it's the least you deserve," Seth insisted.

Paige briefly wondered if she should clarify that she wasn't technically on vacation, but then she decided it wouldn't have any bearing on Lexie's offer. "Okay, thank you. That would be lovely."

"Great. I'll confirm the details and get back to you," he said with a smile. "And since the tree service crew isn't from the island, I don't know what their clean-up process is. So I'll check in on them after 5:00 on Tuesday afternoon and midday on Wednesday to personally make sure every last twig is picked up and carted away before you return. As long as you're sure that you're okay with cutting down the beech tree?"

"Yes. I'm sure," she said and finally, her tone matched her words.

On Sunday morning, Paige had one voice mail message. To her disappointment, it was from Seth—she'd been hoping he'd deliver the message in person.

"Hi, Paige," he said. "Just wanted you to know that Lexie was delighted to make arrangements for you to stay at Serenity Inn and Spa in Benjamin's Manor. It's five-star accommodations."

When Paige heard that, she felt a little guilty. She would have been content to stay at one of the hotels on the Boardwalk.

Seth's message continued, "You can check in anytime after three on Monday and she requested a late checkout on Wednesday, in case the tree service crew hasn't finished by noon."

There was a long pause and she thought he'd forgotten to disconnect, but then he added, "I, uh, hope you enjoy yourself and that you don't worry about anything going on at the cottage or with the tree. I've got it covered."

He's got it covered, Paige repeated, grateful for Seth's willingness to go above and beyond his duties as a landscaper. *I'm going to tell Tara about the inn and spa—she loves to talk about stuff like that.*

"Hi, Tara," Paige said cheerfully when her cousin answered the phone a moment later. "How are you doing?"

"How do you *think* I'm doing?"

Paige was taken aback by her tone, but she didn't want to get into a tiff, so she sympathized, "Uh-oh, have you been ill again?"

"Ill? Ill? Yes, I'm *ill*. I'm sick to my stomach. And I have been for two days. I can't eat a thing!"

Paige started to say, "I'm sorry to hear that."

As usual, Tara didn't let her finish. "You *should* be sorry. It's your fault. What gives you the right?"

Paige was confused. Was Tara angry because she had cut their conference call short the last time they spoke? Or because Paige had declared that she'd contact a real estate agent when she was good and ready to contact one? "The right to do what?" she asked.

"The right to tell my daughter that we should cancel the engagement party," shrieked Tara, and burst out crying. "How *dare* you? After all the money Glenn and I have invested and after all the work I've done, how could you tell her to call it off?"

"That's not what I told her," Paige said quietly. Her cousin

sounded on the brink of hyperventilating and Paige knew she
needed to calm down. "I only suggested she speak openly with
you about how she feels about the party and how worried she is
about your health. Honestly, Tara, I'm worried, too."

"Oh, don't give me that. If you were truly worried about my
health, you wouldn't be dragging your feet about contacting a
real estate agent and coming home to help me." Tara was both
shouting and sobbing simultaneously. "And you *certainly*
wouldn't have tried to persuade my daughter to cancel the
engagement party! I've been so sick to my stomach over it that
Glenn almost took me into the ER last night because he thought
I was dehydrated!"

"Checking in with your doc might not be such a bad idea."
Paige was growing more and more concerned about Tara's physical and emotional well-being.

"Oh, save it. I know you think you're so smart, but I don't
need your medical advice. I don't need *any* advice from you at
all. And neither does my daughter," Tara shouted.

Glenn must have come into the room because Paige could
hear him talking in the background before her cousin continued
in a slightly quieter voice, "You know, Paige, I can understand
why you're so interested in Violet's life and why you'd prefer to
stay alone in her cottage—it's because you're just like her. And
if you don't want to help me plan Cami's party, you don't have
to. You don't even have to attend it, for all I care. But I will *not*
allow you to ruin it for us, simply because *you're* not marriage
material! So I'd appreciate it if you didn't talk to me or my
daughter until it's over!"

Oddly, after Tara hung up, Paige's first thought was, *I hope
Glenn stays with her until she calms down.* Tara's behavior and
remarks may have been completely unfounded and unfair, but
her emotional response seemed extreme, even for her. Knowing
that insomnia could wreak havoc on a person, Paige was
worried.

She was also *livid*.

But mostly, she was sad.

She rested her head against her steering wheel, trying not to cry. Paige knew the miscommunication between Cami and her and Tara could be discussed and resolved. And she was sure that with rest and stress alleviation—and maybe some medical guidance—her cousin's mood would improve. Tara would realize how out of line she'd been and she'd apologize. But right now, Paige felt as if she'd been attacked. Verbally accosted.

Ironically, she didn't mind her cousin comparing her to their great-aunt. Now that she'd learned more about Violet's character, Paige considered the comparison to be a compliment. It was Tara's remark about her not being "marriage material" that made Paige's eyes well.

It wasn't because she felt that way about herself. She knew she'd make an excellent spouse. But sometimes she had to wonder why none of the men she'd dated had ever felt that way about her. After all, Trevor wasn't the first man who'd gotten engaged to the very next woman he'd met after he'd dated her; he was the *third*.

To be fair, Paige was relieved that she hadn't married any of her former boyfriends. Especially those she'd dated in her twenties—she'd never wanted to get married as young as the other women in her family did. But the more years that passed, the more she questioned whether she'd ever meet a man that *she* thought would make a good husband for *her*. And the truth was, she really wanted to.

I still don't think I'm envious, she reflected. Definitely not envious enough to ruin Cami's party or to refuse to let Lexie cut down the dead beech tree. Not even envious enough to hope—although she *had* imagined it—that Trevor's fiancée would ditch him for the smarter, younger, wittier literature department chair at his college.

But if Paige wasn't jealous, then what was that gnawing

ache in her stomach whenever she received a wedding invitation or heard news about an acquaintance getting married? Was it competition? Loneliness? Despair? Whatever it was, sometimes she felt as if it were going to consume her from the inside out.

After a little cry, Paige wiped her cheeks with the back of her hand. *I've got to look on the bright side*, she told herself, lifting her head. *In a few days, this will blow over. Tara will come to her senses, and when she does she'll want my help again. But meanwhile, at least I won't have to listen to her harping on about which stamps to choose for the engagement party invitations, or complaining that the guests haven't RSVP'd yet...*

FOURTEEN

On Monday morning, the museum was teeming with children from a local camp and the docent was so flustered that she didn't question why Paige wanted a list of names of British military members who served on Dune Island during the war.

"Yes, I have that information," she said, rummaging through her desk. "I can print it out for you but right now I need to find a bandage. There's a boy upstairs who cut his finger on a blade of beach grass from the children's coastal ecosystem display."

"I'm a nurse. I'll help him," offered Paige. She pointed to the wall behind the docent. "Could you hand me that first aid kit, please?"

Marge glanced over her shoulder and then clapped her hands against her cheeks. "Ack! Where's my head today?"

"It's hard to think straight with so much noise," Paige empathized as the docent handed her the white metal box. "Don't worry, I'll take care of it."

Although the boy was sobbing big alligator tears, his injury barely amounted to a papercut. "It really stings, doesn't it?" she empathized, and he nodded, crying harder. "Sometimes, it's the little nicks and toe stubs that hurt us the most. But I promise, you'll live."

After she'd cleaned and bandaged his thumb—and after she'd given him lots of attention—the boy gave her a huge hug and then trotted off to join his peers. The camp counselor also thanked Paige profusely. It made her remember how much she'd enjoyed being a part-time substitute nurse at the local school the year she'd been caring for her dying grandmother.

When she returned to Marge's desk, she reported, "The boy's all set. He wasn't even bleeding by the time I got there."

"Thank you for taking care of that for me." Marge lifted a piece of paper from the printer tray. "Here's the list you wanted. It contains the name, rank, and military branch of each British man who came here to help train the US troops. Ordinarily, I wouldn't have this information at my fingertips. But a few years ago, I was part of a group that worked on a special project for the government. It was to commemorate the seventy-fifth anniversary of D-Day, with a special emphasis on the collaboration between the US and the UK on here on Dune Island," she boasted.

Paige sincerely replied, "The government was fortunate to have your help, especially because you have so much personal knowledge about the island."

"I considered it an honor to contribute to the project." Marge beamed for a moment, but lines etched her forehead again when she looked at the paper in her hand. "Unfortunately, you'll see not all these men made it back to the UK. See these asterisks? They denote sailors who died in accidents while training."

Paige noticed that there were about half a dozen names with asterisks after them. That seemed like a high number of accidental deaths and she hoped the men hadn't lost their lives to an ordnance explosion. "What kind of accidents?"

"You'll have to read the fine print—it's very tiny so I can't see it. But if memory serves me right, I believe one of them drowned. Another man died after he fell scaling a cliff. But the biggest loss occurred in the summer of 1943. Two boats with sailors who were stationed on Dune Island collided in bad weather during a drill off the Cape Cod coast. There weren't any survivors. In total, eighteen men died, including four from England."

"That's tragic," Paige said somberly.

"It really is. My mother told me it was a very dark time in the island's history. When residents heard the news the following day, they—" The docent stopped short because a young girl was approaching the desk, walking with her knees pressed together. "Yes, dear, may I help you?"

"I can't find the bathroom," she breathlessly explained.

"It's around the back, to the left of the stairs."

The girl started to leave but she abruptly stopped. "Which way is *left*?"

"Here, I'll show you." Over her shoulder, Marge told Paige, "I'm happy to help you if you need more assistance, but tomorrow or the next day might be a better time to chat."

"Thank you—and thanks for the list—I really appreciate it," she called as the docent and the child slipped from the room.

Paige decided to steal a quick peek at the World War Two exhibit, homing in on the photo she'd seen previously of the man wearing a Royal Navy uniform. Could he be Violet's Ed? She doubted it. Although the photo was black and white, she could see the short, stocky man pictured here had blondish hair. Joseph had said the man Violet was kissing was tall and thin and his hair was dark and curly. Paige quickly circled the room, but she didn't see anyone in the other photos matching Joseph's description, either.

She read through the list of names as she was walking to her car: there wasn't a single Ed among them. There wasn't an Edward, Edwin, Edmund, Eduardo or Edgar, either. When she reached her car, she read the list again, touching each name with her finger to be sure she didn't skip anyone. There was a Theodore and a Frederick. Usually, they'd be abbreviated as Ted and Fred, but maybe "Ed" was short for one of those names?

Disappointed, she drove home to take a quick jaunt down the beach before she ate lunch and packed for her stay at the inn. As she walked, Paige contemplated whether her hunch about Violet's boyfriend being British was wrong after all. Or was she right about him being British, but wrong about him being in the military? Was there another Ed out there somewhere that Paige had yet to discover? She supposed she could solicit Marge's help, but Paige was still hesitant to involve the docent in personal research about her great-aunt.

This is so frustrating. I have even more questions now than I did when I first found the locket. It reminds me of helping Tara decide which stationery to use for the party invitations, she thought, stamping the sand from her feet on the top landing of the staircase. *Maybe it's a good thing I'm going away for a few days... Being in a new location will keep me from obsessing about this.*

Yet as she pulled out of the driveway later that afternoon, Paige was unexpectedly overcome by homesickness for the cottage. She didn't have that much time left on Dune Island and she regretted that she was going to miss even a morning of front-row seating to the sunrise, not to mention the constant cadence of the surf.

It's only for two days and I'd better get used to it because pretty soon I'll be leaving Hope Haven for good, she sternly reminded herself. Halfway up Spindrift Lane, Paige stopped to take one last sideways look at the heathland, where the beech tree appeared to be waving its limbs at her.

Her eyes brimming, she lifted her hand and whispered, "Bye-bye, Violet's tree."

. . .

Paige's suite at the Serenity Inn and Spa was the perfect blend of grandiose sophistication and homey coziness. Adorned in classic coastal décor, its living room featured a gas fireplace and sitting area opening to a balcony, which provided a panoramic view of the bay and harbor. A second set of French doors in the bedroom led to the balcony, as well. Paige ran her hand across the luxurious bedding, pleased to note the mattress was king-sized.

I'll sleep well tonight, she thought as she made her way to the bathroom and peeked at the marble vanity, the deep soaking tub, and the glass steam shower. *This will be a nice change from dashing outside in my bathrobe.*

Paige set her suitcase on the luggage rack and as she began unpacking, the room phone rang.

"Hello, Paige," said Lexie. "I'm so glad you picked up. I've been wanting to speak to you in person, to tell you how much I appreciate your willingness to cut down the beech tree. But Seth wouldn't give me your number, if you can believe it."

Paige actually *could* believe Seth had refused to give Lexie her number, but she didn't admit it. "You're very welcome about the tree. As you know, the arborist confirmed it was dead, so this works out best for both of us," she said. "And I'm glad you called because I wanted to thank *you* for treating me to a stay at such an extravagant inn. It's very generous of you."

"Oh, good, I'm delighted you like it!" squealed Lexie. "Did the concierge explain the services? I requested the all-inclusive package, so feel free to schedule a massage and facial, and to visit the salon, too."

"Oh, you really didn't have to do that." Paige was uncomfortable that Lexie was lavishing her with such expensive provisions. She didn't want to feel indebted.

"Don't be silly. It's the least I can do for someone who's

helping me have my dream wedding. Besides, all my brides-maids and Grant's groomsmen, as well as my future in-laws, will be staying there for an entire week. I'm giving the inn so much business that they provided your room *gratis*. So don't worry about the expense."

In that case, I won't, thought Paige. "Thank you—I feel very spoiled."

"I forgot to mention meals for two are included with your room. I told the manager I wasn't sure if you'd be staying alone or with a friend." Lexie giggled. "So if you want to invite Seth to dine with you, feel free."

"Seth?" Paige repeated, stunned by her bold suggestion.

"Or someone else, it doesn't have to be him. It's just that he's been working such long hours and I'm sure by the time he gets home in the evening, he's too tired to cook a good meal for himself. Since you two have seemed to hit it off so well, I figured you'd both enjoy it."

No wonder he didn't want to give his cousin my phone number, thought Paige. *Clearly, she's one of those brides who's so giddy about getting married that she's trying to matchmake everyone in her path who's single.* Her response to Lexie was a noncommittal, "Thank you for the suggestion."

"You're most welcome. Enjoy!"

After she'd finished unpacking, Paige consulted the brochure of spa services, which was so extensive she couldn't decide which one to schedule. Overwhelmed, she perused the dinner menu instead, but there were even more choices and her head began to spin. She set the menu aside and picked up the list Marge had given her. Another scan of it proved what she already knew: it didn't include anyone named *Edward*.

Paige lifted the pendant around her neck, pried it open with her thumbnail and turned it upside down. Even though she'd memorized the inscription, she scrutinized it again, to be sure she wasn't overlooking anything:

> *Violet, my love*
> *My favourite flower—*
> *Hold me in your heart*
> *always and forever.*

Ed, Ed, Ed, who are you? she silently asked the tiny signature squeezed into the point at the bottom of the heart. *If only I knew your last name, or even your last initial, that might help me expand my search…*

She'd read the inscription dozens of times, but only now did it strike Paige that both letters of Ed's name were capitalized. What if *Ed* wasn't an abbreviation or a nickname? What if his full name was too long to fit in the small space and he'd used his initials, E.D., instead?

For a third time, Paige perused the alphabetical listing from Marge. There were only two surnames starting with the letter D. The first was Dalton, Henry. The other one read: Danforth, Ernest.

"That *must* be him," she exclaimed aloud, noting that he was a lieutenant in the Royal Navy. But her elation quickly turned to despair when she noticed there were three asterisks following his name. She ran her finger to the corresponding notation at the bottom of the page. Even though she already knew what the triple asterisks indicated, she read it again:

****Died in two-boat collision off the coast of Cape Cod, August 21, 1943*

Because she'd been so focused on finding a sailor named Ed, Paige hadn't paid attention to the dates of the fatal accident. But now that she noticed the year, 1943, a shiver rippled down her spine. *That was the summer that Violet suffered a breakdown.*

Had Paige stumbled upon another contributing factor to what had caused her great-aunt to retreat from society? Or, had Ernest's death *triggered* her outburst at Edward Hathaway? Could it have been that she was so sad about losing her secret love that she'd taken it out on her neighbor when she'd seen him and Catherine together?

The possibilities seemed endless and Paige had no way of proving them. She didn't even know how to confirm whether the man who'd given her great-aunt the locket was Ernest Danforth. The more she thought about it, the farther Paige felt like she was from figuring out what had really happened between Violet and her love interest. Suddenly she felt as if her brain weighed a hundred pounds.

Although it seemed like a waste not to enjoy the view and the spa services while she was at the inn, all Paige felt like doing was lying down until her headache lifted. She didn't even have the energy to change into one of the plush white robes and matching slippers she'd seen in the closet. She kicked off her sandals, folded back the duvet and slid in between the silky sheets.

Paige slumbered until almost five o'clock and she woke up feeling completely reinvigorated.

Nothing like a good nap, she thought. *I hope Tara's getting more rest. Sleep deprivation can really affect a person's perspective.*

Paige wished she could check in to see how she was doing, but she doubted her cousin would answer her call. She tried her aunt instead.

"I can hear you much clearer today. Where are you?" asked

Sherry, so Paige told her about the tree, Lexie, and the inn and spa.

"I wish you and Tara were here to enjoy it with me. It'd be a good stress reliever." Since she didn't know whether her cousin had told Sherry about their argument, Paige was trying to be discreet. She didn't want to talk about Tara behind her back or get Sherry involved in their conflict; she only wanted to find out how her cousin was.

But Sherry seemed to understand the purpose for her call, and she cut to the chase. "Stress relief is exactly what Tara needs right now. She told me about your phone conversation and how she yelled at you the other day. She feels terrible about her behavior— she's going to call you after she's had more rest." Paige's aunt sighed heavily. "I'm confident you two will work out your differences on your own, so you don't need me to interfere. But knowing how thoughtful you are, I figure you're calling to check up on her and I wanted you to know she's... in a better frame of mind now."

Paige was touched to hear her aunt refer to her as caring; Sherry rarely complimented her like that. "Thank you for letting me know. You're right, I have been concerned about Tara. I'm glad she's feeling better and getting more rest. It seems like she's been overdoing it lately."

Sherry clicked her tongue. "Well, she's a lot like you."

"Like *me*?"

"Yes. You're always so busy taking care of everyone else, sometimes you neglect to take care of yourself." She chuckled. "Between you stressing out about work and Tara stressing out over the engagement party, I've been so worried about you both my hair is turning gray. *Grayer*, I should say. I admire your ambition, but sometimes you girls both need to lighten up and take a step back. Have a little fun. Otherwise, you'll wind up sick or unhappy."

Tara and Paige's personalities were so different that it

hadn't occurred to Paige that she and her cousin were alike in that way. "You're right. I *have* been awfully tense ever since I took the job at the hospital. But this is the perfect occasion for me to exercise better self-care. Listen to what the spa here offers."

After reading the list of services to her aunt, who suggested she get a warm shell massage and seaweed facial, as well as a pedicure, Paige read her the dinner menu.

"It all sounds delicious. I'm sure whatever you choose will be scrumptious," Sherry said. "It really is a shame that Tara or your friend Mia weren't there with you. Then you wouldn't have to dine alone."

"It's okay. I'm used to it," Paige replied. But in the back of her mind, she'd already decided she was going to ask Seth to join her the following evening.

It rained intermittently on Tuesday, so Paige stayed at the inn. To her amusement she found she couldn't get used to walking on carpeting again. *I never would have thought I'd prefer the grittiness of sand on a hardwood floor to the softness of a thick carpet like this.*

However, she did really appreciate having uninterrupted internet access again. She spent most of the morning researching people named Danforth who lived in the UK during the 1940s, but it was a futile pursuit. Regardless of how many Danforths she found, she had no real way of knowing if they were related to Ernest, or even how she'd use that information to determine whether he was Violet's fiancé.

With a sigh, Paige closed her laptop.

She knew she should take advantage of the strong cell phone signal to talk to real estate agents, but she didn't make any attempts to reach out to them. And when they returned her calls from the previous week, she found an excuse not to answer. She did, however, chat with Seth, inviting him to dinner, and he accepted.

"Whatever you do, please don't give me any updates about the tree, though, okay?" she requested. The last thing she wanted to do was embarrass herself or ruin their evening by becoming sentimental and weepy like she'd felt yesterday when she was leaving the cottage.

"Not a problem," he agreed. "I'm sure we'll think of a lot more interesting things to talk about."

Ten minutes before Paige was supposed to meet Seth in the lobby, she received a video call from her cousin.

"Hi, Paige. How've you—" Tara started to say, but before she completed her greeting, she interrupted *herself*, for once. "Did you get your hair cut?"

"No." She touched her sideswept bangs. She'd wanted them trimmed but the stylist had suggested she let them grow out instead. "I had it done."

"Well, that style makes your eyes look huge." Her effusive praise was so rare that Paige assumed she was only saying it to make amends, but then Tara added, "And I can hardly see any dark circles—did you have your makeup done, too?"

Paige laughed in spite of herself. "Nope. I mean, I'm wearing lipstick and mascara, but I applied that myself. I think my undereye shadows aren't as noticeable any more because I'm tanned and I've finally caught up on my sleep. I've been taking a lot of naps lately... How about *you*? Are you feeling more rested?"

"Yes, although obviously I'm not quite as relaxed as you are." Tara's voice quavered, a sign she was on the brink of tears. "I'm sorry I lost it on the phone the other day. I said a lot of things I didn't mean, especially about not wanting you to talk to me or not to bother coming to Cami's party. After she heard me going off on you like that, she told me I'd misinterpreted what she'd said that *you'd* said. I'm sorry I blamed you for trying to ruin her party. I know you'd never do that. I don't know what came over me..."

"That's okay. I forgive you. I understand how severely sleep deprivation and stress can affect a person's—" Paige stopped mid-sentence. "Sorry. I realize you don't like it when I give you unsolicited medical advice. But it's only because I'm concerned and because I know that our moods are affected by our physical health, and vice versa. Not because I'm trying to prove I'm smart."

"You don't have to prove it. Not to me, anyway. I already know how smart you are. I mean, yeah, sometimes you can be a little overbearing with medical advice. But I'm very proud of your nursing career. I admire all you've achieved—I realize it's taken a ton of hard work."

Maybe it was because she was so surprised by all the compliments Tara was paying her, or maybe it was because on some level, she still felt stung by the remark, but Paige retorted, "Thanks, but what else am I going to do with my time, since I'm not 'marriage material'?"

"What's marriage material?" Tara genuinely didn't seem to understand the reference.

"Who knows? You're the one who said it." Regretting that she'd mentioned it, Paige tried to shrug it off. "Never mind. You've apologized, and you were really tired, so it doesn't matter any more."

"I don't remember saying that, but if I did, what I meant was that, you know, you're different from the rest of the women in the family," Tara explained, which didn't make Paige feel better. She elaborated, "You're more focused on your career than on getting married. And you're more independent. I'd never want to live alone, but you don't seem to mind—in that way, you're kind of like Violet."

"It's true, my career means a lot to me and you're right, I don't mind living alone, necessarily." Paige felt very vulnerable admitting it to her cousin, but she took a deep breath and said, "But you're wrong if you think I don't want to be married and have children some day."

Tara was quiet a moment and then she stuck her chin in the air and said, "Yeah, well *you're* wrong if you think *I* don't want to go back to college and have a career. Now that my babies are starting to leave the nest, I've been thinking a lot about picking up where I left off when I dropped out of school to marry Glenn. Although I'll probably be the oldest person in all my classes."

"Not necessarily." Paige encouraged her, "I think you'd fit right in. The average age of college and university students is a lot higher than it used to be."

"Yeah, and women are getting married a lot later in life now, so there's still time for you, too," said Tara. "Although we might want to start planning your wedding now, so you can have a short engagement once you actually meet The One."

Paige laughed. "Let's finish planning Cami's engagement party and her wedding, first."

"You're still willing to help me?"

"Of course." Paige hesitated. It wasn't her place to tell her cousin what to do, but she gently prompted, "Wouldn't it be helpful—and a lot more fun—if Cami pitched in, too?"

"Oh, believe me, she'll be helping from now on." Tara chuckled. "You weren't the only one I yelled at the other day. Glenn, Cami, and the boys all got an earful about how they needed to start giving me a hand around the house. And I agreed to take things down a notch in regard to the party."

Aha, she's finally starting to delegate, thought Paige. "How's that working out for everyone?"

"I don't know how the rest of my family feels about it, but

it's working out great for me. Right now, they're all in the kitchen, making dinner."

"Oh, no!" exclaimed Paige. "I forgot about the time—I'm meeting someone for dinner. I've gotta go or he'll wonder if I've stood him up."

"No, wait, I want to hear about him," pleaded Tara. "Who is he? How'd you meet? What does he do for a living?"

"I'll tell you tomorrow, but right now I've really got to go," Paige repeated.

"Just tell me his name so we could track him down if it turns out he's dangerous or something."

"His name is Seth, but he's not dangerous."

Tara wasn't satisfied. "Don't you know his last name?"

"It's... Hathaway."

"He's a *Hathaway*?"

"Yes," she admitted. "But I'm not holding it against him."

When Paige sailed into the lobby a few moments later, Seth was gazing out the window, back turned and hands in pockets. He was wearing chinos and a tight-fitting, short-sleeve shirt with a geometric pattern that made her slightly dizzy the closer she got to him. Or was there another reason for that whirling feeling?

She gently touched her hand to his back. "Hello, Seth."

When he turned to face her, he did a noticeable doubletake, which might have been flattering, except that he said, "Hi, Paige. You look really... different."

Unsure how he meant it, she didn't thank him. "I went to the salon—Lexie insisted I pamper myself," she awkwardly explained.

"Right. Good idea." His smile didn't reach his eyes.

What's wrong? Does he think I'm taking advantage of Lexie's generosity? Or is he annoyed that I'm late? She apologized for her tardiness.

"No problem. I was running behind, too." He frowned. "I stopped by the cottage to check on—"

Paige covered her ears. "You promised you wouldn't give me any updates about the tree, remember?"

"None at all?"

She dropped her hands. "What?"

"You don't want any updates at all?"

"Not unless you're going to tell me that at the last second, the tree sprouted leaves, so the crew left it standing." She was trying to make Seth laugh, but he looked even more uptight.

"Sorry, that's not what happened."

"I never expected it to," she assured him and then motioned toward the hall leading to the dining area. "C'mon. I've been looking forward to having lobster thermidor ever since I got up this morning."

"I've been looking forward to this meal all day, too." Again, it wasn't necessarily a compliment, but at least this time the skin around Seth's eyes crinkled when he grinned at her.

Despite the threat of rain, they decided to eat on the dining terrace overlooking the harbor. Because they were the only diners outside, the atmosphere struck Paige as both casual and romantic.

After the server took their order, Seth asked if Marge had given her any helpful information about "English Ed," as he called Violet's admirer. Paige told him her hunch about the signature being Ernest Danforth's initials instead of his name.

"That makes sense," he said. "Are you going to track him down?"

"Unfortunately, I can't—he was one of a group of sailors who died in a training accident."

Seth tipped his head and asked. "The boat collision off the Cape Cod coast?"

"You know about that?"

"Sure. It was part of our local history curriculum in school.

We're very proud of the role that Dune Island, as well as the Cape, the Vineyard, and Nantucket, played in the war."

"You should be—it's impressive. I love learning things I never knew about US history." She sighed. "I'm also glad I've discovered things I never knew about my family's history while I've been here. Unfortunately, the more I learn, the more questions I seem to have..."

Paige confided that maybe it was time to accept that certain parts of her great-aunt's life—especially her love life—would remain a mystery.

Seth raised an eyebrow. "You'd be content to do that?"

"I might not have any other choice. I mean, I could keep trying to research Ernest Danforth and maybe I'd eventually be able to get in touch with his descendants, but what are the chances they'd know whether he had a girlfriend while he was on Dune Island? Besides, as my cousin pointed out to me the other day, Violet's past doesn't really affect the present, so maybe I should let it rest. It's not really my business anyway."

"I hear you saying the words, but somehow, I don't quite believe you're giving up on your search for answers."

Paige giggled. "You're right. I'm probably not giving up altogether, but I'm going to back off a little. Besides, I have other things to focus on, like..." She almost slipped and said, *Like selling the cottage*, but she didn't want to ruin this special evening by mentioning that soon she'd have to leave Hope Haven.

"Like what?" Seth asked.

"Like helping my cousin Tara plan an engagement party—long distance—for her daughter, Cami."

"Are they as over-the-top about it as Lexie is about her wedding?"

"Almost, but not quite. They haven't chopped down any trees yet," joked Paige.

"Then I assume they're not requiring their family and

wedding party members who don't know how to dance to take lessons so they can waltz at the reception, the way my cousin is?"

"Seriously? Lexie's doing *that*?"

"Yep. My class starts next week." Seth rolled his eyes in disgust. "As if that's how I want to spend every Monday evening until the wedding."

"Pfft. It shouldn't take you *that* long to learn. The waltz is easy. Stand up, I'll teach you." Paige rose and tugged his hand. "C'mon, no one's out here. This music is perfect and we have the entire dance floor to ourselves."

"But there's also an entire dining room full of people inside who can see us." Seth didn't pull his hand free, yet he didn't budge from his chair, either.

"That's okay. We don't know them," she coaxed.

"*I* might. Besides, it's starting to rain."

He was right. The umbrella above their table caught the fat droplets, but the dance floor was unsheltered and they might slip on it. Paige released his hand and sat back down. But Seth took her fingers in his again and asked. "Can I take a rain check... for a private lesson?"

Paige breathed the question, "When?"

"Saturday evening?"

"Sure." She found her voice again and gave him a saucy grin. "Does Blossom need a lesson, too?"

"Nah," said Seth. "He's not invited to the wedding."

FIFTEEN

"How was dinner?" asked Tara when she called at 8:00 on Wednesday morning.

Because it was drizzling again, Paige was sipping her coffee in bed instead of on the balcony. She had opened the door and windows, hoping to hear the surf against the shore the way she could at the cottage, but the bayside waves were too small and faint. She didn't hear any birds, either, although she enjoyed watching the boats come in and out of the harbor.

"It was fabulous. I had lobster thermidor." Yet as delicious as it was, it hadn't compared to the lobster roll that Seth had brought to her at Violet's cottage.

"I was asking about the company, not about the food," said Tara. Proving that she hadn't completely changed overnight, she didn't wait for Paige's response before shifting the conversation to her favorite topic. "What did you have for appetizers? Cami, my mom, and I are trying to choose the menu for her party."

Paige spent the next forty minutes discussing hors d'oeuvres and appetizers, as well as table centerpieces. She didn't mind since it was rainy and she still had several hours to kill before returning to the cottage. She could have made another appointment for a massage or facial, but the treatments had lost their appeal. Paige didn't mean to be ungrateful, but after two days she felt that nothing the inn and spa offered was nearly as relaxing as walking on the beach—or even as relaxing as sitting in a straight-backed wooden chair on the porch, eating a tuna sandwich and staring at the view.

Before ending the call, Tara hinted, "So, everything else is progressing all right?"

"Yes. I've heard back from several real estate agents, but I haven't chosen one yet." Of course, Paige couldn't do that unless she actually spoke to one of them, first, but she didn't mention that part. When she was done talking to Tara, she intended to set up appointments to interview her top choices. "Now that the tree is down, I can invite the best candidates to see the property. Things should move quickly after that—and from then on, we can work together remotely."

"Great. So that means you'll be coming home this weekend?"

"Mmm, maybe. I might stay here a little longer."

"Why? Because you're seeing the Hathaway guy again?"

Paige denied it. "No. Because it's almost impossible to get a ferry reservation on the weekend. That's when the vacationers leave."

Tara let her off the hook with a warning. "Just be careful. You know what happened to Violet..."

Actually, I don't know. Not for certain, anyway, thought Paige after she disconnected. She fell back against the pillows. Seth had been right: it was easier said than done for her to accept the possibility she might never find out who Violet's secret love was or what happened between them. Not knowing was very dissatisfying and it made her antsy.

She was also glum that soon she'd have to leave Dune Island, but she knew she couldn't procrastinate hiring a real estate agent any longer. She had narrowed down her options to two. The first, a man named Mark Howe, had a very impressive sales record. The second one's name was Marianne Doty, and Paige appreciated it that she consistently returned messages, but she didn't seem pushy.

Before providing her address, Paige made sure each of them understood she hadn't selected a real estate agent yet, and that she wouldn't until she'd had a more thorough conversation about their experience, skills, and availability. She invited Mark to meet her at the cottage on Thursday at 2:00, and Marianne was invited on Friday at 4:00.

Paige realized that as a courtesy, she really should let Seth know about her plan to sell the cottage. *I'll tell him on Saturday —but not until* after *I've taught him how to waltz*, she decided.

Even though Lexie had arranged for a late checkout, Paige left the inn immediately after eating breakfast. She spent several hours pretending to be a tourist. She shopped for souvenirs, strolled along the boardwalk, and visited several must-see attractions including the cranberry farm and the most iconic ice cream shop on the island, Bleeckers.

By 2:00, she was growing impatient. Seth had said he'd call when every last trace of the tree had been removed and the crew had left. *What's taking so long?* she wondered.

At 3:00, she checked her phone again, only to realize she must have had her notifications turned off because he'd sent a text at 12:30, giving her the all-clear to return. Paige's eagerness to get away from the crowds in town overshadowed her dread at seeing the landscape without the beech tree for the first time and she raced toward Highland Hills.

As she approached the Hathaways' house, she avoided glancing toward the heathland from the main road. But halfway down Spindrift Lane, she came to a full stop and gathered her nerve to take a long, hard look at the heathland now that the beech tree was gone.

Stark was the first adjective that popped into her head,

followed by *desolate* and *bleak*. Her mind couldn't adjust to the tree's absence, and for a moment, she felt like she'd made a terrible mistake by allowing it to be taken down.

Then her focus shifted to the immense blue ocean just beyond the cliffs. And it occurred to her that if she'd never known the beech tree had been on the heathland and she'd happened upon this view, she'd consider it striking. While there was no denying how different the seascape looked, it was still absolutely arresting.

When she neared the end of the dirt road, she spotted Seth sitting on her porch steps. Had he been waiting for her ever since he texted at 12:30? He got to his feet and strode toward her, gingerly balancing what looked to be a tin the size of a dinner plate in front of him. Had he brought lunch for them again? *It must be spoiled by now. No wonder he's frowning.*

"Hi, Seth. Sorry it took me so long to get here," she immediately apologized. "I didn't see your text until a few minutes ago. I feel bad you waited for me. I know you've got a full schedule with all your other clients, but I appreciate it that you made sure the crew completely cleaned up everything here."

He tipped his head at her quizzically. "You're not upset?"

"Not nearly as upset as I thought I'd be. I mean, it'll take a while to get used to it, but the heathland is still beautiful, even without the beech tree."

"What about the shed?" He pointed over her shoulder.

Paige turned to see it. She'd been so focused on how the landscape looked without the beech tree, that she didn't realize the shed was missing, too. She didn't care about the rickety little hut; her only concern was that Violet's sewing machine had been inside it. She tried not to panic. Maybe the crew had to move it so they could navigate their large equipment closer to the tree. It was possible that they had used a forklift to transport the shed—and Violet's sewing machine—up the hill for safe-keeping.

"Where is it?" she asked, facing Seth again.

"The tree service crew hauled it away, along with the other debris."

She felt sick to her stomach. "What? *Why?*"

"A huge section of the tree landed on it—totally crushed it to smithereens. It was unsalvageable."

"I don't care if all that was left of it was a single splinter," she cried. "They should have left it where it was. They had no right to remove anything from the property except the tree."

"Actually, *I* gave them permission to haul away what was left of the shed. The rubble inside it, too."

Paige's cheeks smarted with heat. "Why would you do that?"

"Like I said, the shed and its contents were utterly demolished. Besides, you'd said there was nothing in it but empty bottles and cans," explained Seth. "So I made a judgment call."

"It wasn't *your* call to make," she countered, her lower jaw trembling. "You should have let *me* decide what I wanted to do with *my* property."

"You're the one who asked me to be sure everything was cleaned up before you returned," he reminded her. "I tried to tell you what happened to the shed at dinner yesterday, but you didn't want to hear a word about it."

Paige couldn't believe he was being so dense. "I didn't want to hear about the *tree*, but you should have told me what had happened to the *shed*. If the tree had landed on the cottage, would you have allowed the crew to haul that away without consulting me, too?"

Seth's nostrils flared but he kept his voice low. "Listen, I know you're upset right now, but that's a ridiculous comparison."

"No, what's ridiculous is that I trusted you and..." Paige's throat tightened and she blinked back tears, unable to finish her sentence.

While she struggled to regain her composure, a sleek silver sports car came zooming down the hill and pulled to a stop a few feet from where Seth and Paige were standing. The man who got out of the car was wearing a slim-fit linen blazer and dark sunglasses.

"Hi there. You must be Paige? I'm Mark Howe." He bared his teeth in a too-bright grin and held out his hand. When she didn't shake it, he reminded her, "We spoke on the phone this morning—I'm the man who's going to sell your property for twenty percent more than any other real estate agent on this island could ever get for you."

Paige's tearfulness was quickly replaced with annoyance. "Our appointment isn't until tomorrow at 2:00."

"Right, but I was passing by, so I thought I'd take a sneak peek," he glibly replied.

She stared daggers at him. "You'll have to come back tomorrow at 2:00, as we agreed. I'm right in the middle of something."

"No prob, keep doing what you're doing. I'll take a self-guided tour of the property and then pop my head into the cottage. Don't worry if it's messy. I've seen every—"

Fed up, Paige interrupted. "No, you *won't* take a tour," she stated firmly. "Not today and not tomorrow, either. I don't like doing business with people who break our agreements. I've just decided to hire another real estate agent, so please leave."

"I get it, point taken." He winked at Seth, as if the two men were sharing a private joke. "She doesn't pull any punches, does she?"

"I asked you to leave." Leaning forward, Paige looked in his eyes and loudly emphasized, "*Now.*"

He shook his head but strode toward his car, muttering, "All the women in that family must be lunatics."

As Mark sped up the hill, Seth narrowed his brows at Paige,

whose heart was still racing from her interaction with the real estate agent. "You're selling the cottage?"

"I don't want to discuss my family's property with you," she snapped. Then she turned and started toward the porch, but he caught up and stepped in front of her, walking backward.

"I'm sorry the shed was destroyed, but Lexie will pay to have it replaced."

Paige came to a halt. "You think that every problem can be eliminated by Lexie throwing money at it, don't you?" she accused him. "I don't care about the shed. I cared about what I found in it—my great-aunt's sewing machine. And please don't tell me your cousin will pay to replace that, too, because frankly, there isn't enough money in the world."

She pushed past him but again he hopped in front of her, extending the rusty tin he'd been holding. "One of the guys found this embedded in the roots when they were taking out the stump, so they cut it loose. It must have belonged to someone who lived here."

"Gee, thanks." Paige's voice dripped with sarcasm as she snatched it from his hand. "This really makes up for the loss of Violet's sewing machine. I can't say how indebted I am to you and your family for cutting down the beech tree."

She stormed into the porch, letting the door bang shut behind her. She flew down the hallway to her bedroom, where she climbed on top of the air mattress. As she hugged the tin to her chest, it clinked against the locket and Paige burst out sobbing.

She didn't know if she was more upset that her great-aunt's sewing machine had been demolished or that Seth had disappointed her so deeply.

I know it wasn't his fault that the tree fell on the shed, she thought. *But he really should have asked me if I wanted to get rid of it. Yes, I shut down the conversation at dinner, but how was I supposed to know he wasn't trying to give me an update on the tree itself? He should've tried harder to talk to me about what had happened.*

In the end, Paige would have had to get rid of the shed anyway. But not before she had sifted through the wreckage. *Even if Violet's sewing machine had been bent or crushed, I would have kept it for sentimental value,* she cried to herself.

As much as she cherished her great-aunt's pendant, the sewing machine was a reminder that there was more to Violet's history than her broken romantic relationship. She was also a talented, professional woman, who had literally worked her fingers to the bone supporting herself as a seamstress.

Violet's sewing machine was the one thing from her past that I could have kept as a symbol of her independence and determination... and now it's gone, Paige lamented.

After a few minutes, she sat up and reached for a tissue. She blew her nose and wiped her eyes, and then she gave the tin a little shake. Whatever was inside it shifted, making a dull clattering sound. Paige was almost afraid to open it; she didn't think she could handle another unpleasant surprise today.

The lid was rusted shut, so she scuffed into the kitchen for a knife. It took a bit of patience, but eventually, she managed to wedge the tin open. Inside was a square of gauzy fabric that appeared to have been partially eaten by insects.

Uh-oh, I hope I'm not going to find the remains of a tenant's childhood pet under here, Paige thought. But when she gingerly lifted a corner of the dingy material, the first thing she saw were two wooden spools. The thread must have decayed because both spools were bare, and the bottom of the tin was littered with bits and scraps. She also found what appeared to be a long, flat ribbon but when she unwound it, she recognized it was a measuring tape, although its numbers and markings were missing. Paige realized, *This tin must have belonged to Violet.*

Peeling back the dirty fabric square completely, she discovered a second, smaller, rectangular tin about the size of a flask. It wasn't nearly as rusted as the outer circular container and Paige could easily read some of the words printed across one side: "Smooth Cut." Something else was written beneath that, but she could only make out the letters O-B-A-C.

"OBAC," she repeated aloud several times, sounding out the syllables until the full word dawned on her. "Tobacco. Smooth Cut Tobacco." She didn't think her great-aunt had been a smoker, so she assumed the smaller tin stored additional sewing supplies.

Indeed, when she popped open the lid, Paige slid out a small, tightly folded bundle of fabric. It was pale blue and there were over a dozen needles slid lengthwise into it in a tidy row. Clearly the fabric had served as a makeshift pin cushion, and the tobacco tin was a way of protecting Violet's sewing needles.

Knowing how poor her great-aunt had been as a child who'd lived through the Great Depression, Paige admired her in creating this sewing basket. She pictured Violet as a youngster, sitting beneath the beech tree and sewing to the background music of the birds and waves, with the perfume of wild roses and honeysuckle permeating the air. She imagined that every now and again, Violet would glance up, to appreciate the sheen of the ocean and the cottony texture of the clouds.

She probably left this little homemade sewing kit beneath the tree one day and later she thought she'd lost it. As Paige placed the items back inside the tin, she grew tearful again, thinking, *It must have become covered with sand and dirt, until eventually, it was completely forgotten...*

SIXTEEN

Paige woke to a steady rain pattering the rooftop on Thursday morning. Her head ached and she didn't need a mirror—or her cousin Tara—to know that her eyes were puffy from crying and her nose was pink from blowing it so often.

The previous evening, her initial disappointment in Seth had given way to anger at herself. *I had a bad feeling about cutting down the tree,* she'd brooded. *I shouldn't have let them do it. Or at least, I should have been here. Maybe if the crew had known the owner was watching them, they would've been more careful and the shed wouldn't have been flattened...*

But today was a new day and she wasn't going to spend any more time ruminating about what she should have done or what she wished would have happened. Paige had a goal to accomplish: tidying the cottage a final time for her appointment with the real estate agent, Marianne, on Friday. She also wanted to gather her belongings, so she'd be ready to leave as soon as possible. *The last thing I'll need to do is talk to Steve before I go, like he requested. I wonder if it's too late to make an appointment for Monday?*

Paige suddenly remembered she'd also promised Seth she'd teach him to dance on Saturday evening, but she couldn't imagine he'd want to keep their date. *Right now, the only dancing I want to do is to waltz right out of his life and I'm sure the feeling is mutual.*

By 2:00, the rain had subsided into a fine mist and the cottage was gleaming. Paige had just begun making a salad for a late lunch when she heard the soft crunch of tires against the dirt driveway. Because she wasn't expecting anyone, she assumed Mark Howe had arrived for the appointment she had canceled.

I can't believe he has the nerve to show up here again, she thought, racing to the porch. But it was Emily, the artist from the beach, who was parked in her driveway. Paige hurried outside as Emily got out of her car.

"It's nice to see you again. Have you come to paint the seascape?"

"No, not today. I'm on my way to pick up my husband from work, but I thought I'd stop to chat for a minute. I drove by on Tuesday and I noticed the crew taking down the beech tree..." She paused and twisted to look behind her. Then she met Paige's eyes and asked, "How are you adjusting to the new view?"

"It seems strange that it's gone, but I'm already starting to get used to it," said Paige. "It's probably a bigger adjustment for you, since you've been driving past it for years?"

"Yeah. I have to admit, even though I figured it was going to be cut down, when I saw the barren heathland for the first time on Tuesday, I gasped and pulled over to the shoulder of the road. My poor husband thought I was having an asthma attack or something."

Paige chuckled. "It's probably the first place his mind goes because of his profession—I'm the same way."

"Maybe, although he should be used to my melodramatic temperament by now," Emily replied with a smile. "When I stopped again yesterday, the landscape took my breath away for another reason. I noticed details about the vegetation and the dunes I hadn't noticed before because my eye was always drawn to the tree. Even the sky seems different now. I can't wait to paint it from a new perspective. I mean, I still wish the beech tree was there, but since it's not, I'll try to embrace the change for the new opportunities it offers."

"That's a good way to look at it," said Paige. *It's a good way to look at a lot of things...*

"It's probably also easier said than done, especially for you, since it's your family's property. Anyway, I'm rambling when what I really came to do was give you a gift..." Emily reached into the back seat of her car and produced a long, rectangular canvas. "I painted this over the course of a year shortly after I moved to Highland Hills."

She angled the painting sideways so Paige could see that Emily had depicted the tree four times—once in each season— in a row across the canvas. As she beheld the third tree, the summer rendition, Paige could picture Joseph climbing the copious, leafy branches. And she could imagine her great-aunt meeting Ernest on the northeastern side of the trunk, which would have afforded them privacy from anyone in the mansion or the cottage.

"It's beautiful," she uttered. "It must have taken you forever to paint. I'd love to keep it, but only if I can pay you for your work."

"No way. This is my gift to you," Emily vehemently insisted. "I wanted to show you it to be sure you liked it before I frame it. See, when I pulled over on Tuesday, I came down here to ask you if I could have some of the wood, but you weren't home. The arborist said he had explicit instructions to haul everything away, so he thought it would be all right to let me have a few pieces. I only took enough wood to frame this painting and another one that's hanging in my house. It didn't seem right not to save something to remember the tree by. I hope you don't mind?"

"Of course, I don't mind. What a lovely idea." Paige was so moved by Emily's thoughtfulness that she got a little choked up.

"The wood needs to dry thoroughly before I start carving it. But if you're willing to wait, I can bring you the finished product when you return next summer."

Two tears bounded down Paige's face and she quickly whisked them away with her fingertips. "I'm sorry. It's just that I'm..." she started to explain, but she had to stop and try again to get the words out. "I'm—I'm not coming back next summer. I'm selling the cottage."

"Oh? That's okay. I can ship the painting to you." Emily bit her lower lip, before asking, "Have you already found a buyer?"

Several more tears moistened her face and Paige pushed her palms against her eyelids. Ordinarily, she wouldn't allow herself to become weepy in front of a stranger but somehow Emily seemed like a friend she'd known for years. She cleared her throat and answered, "Not yet. I'm meeting with the real estate agent tomorrow."

"Then there's still time to change your mind," suggested Emily, making Paige laugh in spite of herself. "No, I'm serious. I was in a similar position a few years ago. At the last minute, I decided to stay on Dune Island and live in my family's cottage year-round. Best decision I ever made."

"If it were up to me, I might be tempted to reconsider selling. Unfortunately, my family is involved, so..." Paige turned her hands up, letting her voice trail off.

"I understand," said Emily. "But if anything changes, just remember, Hope Haven Hospital has a severe nursing shortage. When I told my husband about you, he said with your background, you'd be a shoo-in for any department at the hospital. Or at any medical office."

After they'd exchanged contact info and Emily had left, Paige returned to the kitchen to finish preparing her meal. As she chopped a cucumber, she reflected on her sudden tearfulness about selling the estate and leaving Dune Island.

What am I so sad about? It's not as if I've been coming here since I was a child and this is our beloved family cottage, she told herself. *Sure, it's a gorgeous setting, and overall it's been very relaxing, but that's only because I'm here on vacation. I wouldn't feel the same way if I lived here permanently. And since I'm not on friendly terms with one of the Hathaways, it would be like history was repeating itself...*

She removed a plate from the cupboard, intending to serve herself a heaping portion of salad, but suddenly, she felt too melancholy to eat anything at all.

By evening, Paige had packed most of her things, except what she'd need to use or wear for the next couple days. Standing in her bedroom, she considered what to do with Violet's "sewing basket." Although she'd wanted a memento of her great-aunt's profession, she didn't see the point in keeping the outer tin. It was in such bad shape and she didn't know how she'd clean it or remove the rust. The wooden spools were rather generic, but Paige decided to save them anyway; maybe she could craft them into something useful later. She also wanted the old tobacco tin and the fabric inside it.

Paige pulled the material out and studied the neatly arranged needles. *Violet must have liked everything to be as organized as I do*, she thought. Then it occurred to her that the fabric was a very pale shade of blue. She knew Cami wouldn't want it, but Paige decided, *If I ever get married, I could make*

something out of this and use it for something old, something
borrowed, or something blue. I wonder how much material is in
here...

She removed the pins and began to unwind the bundle of
fabric. To her amazement, she discovered it had been raveled
around a wad of yellowed paper. As delicately as she could,
Paige unfolded the pages and saw they were covered, front and
back, with neat, small cursive that was just dark enough to see.

"It's a letter!" she exclaimed breathlessly and brought it to
the living room, where the light was better.

Dated August 21, 1943, it was addressed, *Dear Ernest.*

"Oh!" Paige caught her breath. She felt both shocked and
delighted to discover that she'd been right; *ED* stood for Ernest
Danforth's name.

Her jubilation was short lived. She reread the date at the
top of the page: August 21, 1943. That was the day that the
paperwork from the museum indicated Ernest Danforth had
perished in the boat collision. Paige wondered, *Did Violet write*
this as a kind of elegy, upon hearing he had died?

With a heavy heart, she took a deep breath and read the first
paragraph:

I didn't find a note from you, so I assume you weren't able to
come by last evening. It's just as well since I couldn't steal
away from the house. But I was very sad I didn't get to see you
before you left for Cape Cod for your weekend of drills and
training. My father is doing quite poorly, so I don't know if I'll
be able to meet you here after you return to the island on
Sunday, either. But I'm desperate to tell you something. It's so
important that it can't wait until we speak in person.

"So Ernest *hadn't* died yet when Violet wrote this—or at
least, if he did, she hadn't found out about it yet," Paige
reasoned aloud. Either way, it was clear that Ernest hadn't seen

the letter Violet had left for him beneath the beech tree. It didn't seem fair that Paige should read it now, since the intended recipient had never had the opportunity, but she soberly continued:

> By the time you read this, I'm sure you will have already heard that I caused quite a commotion yesterday afternoon at the docks in Port Newcomb. Frankie told me some of the things people have been saying about me—I can only imagine the rest of it! I know you trust me far too much to believe anything unless you've heard it directly from me. The next time we speak in person, I'll tell you more, but until then, I'm confident you'll be able to read between the lines of what I'm writing.
>
> As you know, I have a sisterly affection for Edward Hathaway, even though he's two years older than I am. It's my observation that he's absolutely innocent about women's motives and the games they play. And I admit, I felt protective of him when C. arrived on the island and started flirting with him.

Paige stopped reading. *C. must be an abbreviation for Catherine. Catherine Brown—the one whose camera Violet threw in the water. The girl that Joseph said he'd thought was insincere and only interested in the Hathaways' money*, she thought. *But why wouldn't Violet write out her full name?*

She continued to peruse the missive:

> I tried very hard to withhold judgment and give her the benefit of the doubt. I didn't breathe a word against her to anyone, not even to you because I didn't want to damage her reputation if I was wrong. But it seemed to me she was using him, probably because his family has such a high standing on the island. Anyway, she didn't seem like a good match for him at all.

Paige flipped the page over and read a list of her great-aunt's grievances against Catherine:

> *Firstly, unlike most people around here, C. didn't have good manners. One time after our sewing circle, Mrs. Williams invited all us girls to stay for supper. She served fresh fish, which as you know, isn't rationed, and native butter-and-sugar corn-on-the-cob her husband grows in the backyard. But C. turned her nose up at the corn. She called it "livestock feed," which I thought was very insulting to our generous host and hostess.*

Paige chuckled. At first glance, Violet's reason for not thinking Catherine was a suitable match for Edward seemed almost petty. But there was more:

> *It also bothered me that she wouldn't admit to making a mistake. One afternoon, Barbara was admiring C.'s shoes (I think Barbara wanted to borrow them) and she asked, "What size do you wear?"*
>
> *C. distinctly said, "Size thirty-seven."*
>
> *Barbara repeated, "Thirty-seven? Even my brother doesn't wear size thirty-seven and his feet are huge!"*
>
> *Everybody squealed with laughter, but C. turned red-faced and insisted she'd said "seven," not "thirty-seven."*
>
> *It seemed silly to me that she'd be so embarrassed by a slip-of-the-tongue that she'd lie about it. Why not just admit it?*

Now Paige wasn't sure what to think. She could see Violet's point, but since Catherine hadn't lived on Dune Island year-round, like the other girls in the sewing circle, maybe she'd wanted to fit in. Maybe when they'd laughed at her, she'd felt ridiculed by them?

However, when she read what her great-aunt wrote next, Paige didn't feel so sympathetic toward Catherine:

What troubled me most was that C. was boy-crazy. All she ever wanted to talk about were the recruits bunking on Pinnacle Point. When the other girls told stories about sneaking up the hill to meet the soldiers near the barracks, she'd question them about what paths they used to avoid being caught by the sergeants. If she was as interested in Edward as she pretended she was, why would she want to risk creeping up the hill at night, especially since she could have gotten in trouble for it?

I probably should have expressed my concerns earlier to Edward, but he's so naïve and I didn't want to hurt his feelings by suggesting she wasn't truly interested in him. What if I was wrong? It's one thing to report an odd-shaped boat or an unusual nighttime noise to the authorities. But it didn't seem fair to point a finger at C. just because she's a little different.

Paige was struck by her great-aunt's compassion, which was probably the result of Violet's own experience of being ridiculed for being different. She sighed, and kept reading:

Besides, C. was supposed to go home to Connecticut as soon as the dock was repaired, and the ferryboat was running again. Since it didn't seem that her relationship with Edward had come to any harm, I thought it best to keep my opinions to myself.

"That sounds reasonable—and mature," mumbled Paige. She flipped to the next sheet of paper, anticipating that she'd find out why her aunt had had such a drastic change of heart that she'd ended up throwing Catherine's camera into the water.

However, yesterday afternoon when I returned from the market, my father told me he thought he'd seen a young couple on our staircase to the beach. Because of his limited vision, he couldn't be sure, but he said it looked like Edward had been photographing a girl in her swimsuit. You understand why I couldn't allow them to trespass like that without confronting them, can't you?

"Why not?" uttered Paige. All she could guess was that Catherine was wearing a swimsuit for the photograph that Violet deemed immodest. *It seems kind of intrusive for her to try to police Catherine's wardrobe, even if technically they were on her family's property.*

The letter continued:

I ran up the hill to the Hathaways' house and asked to speak with Edward, but Norma, the maid, told me that Edward and his parents had gone to Port Newcomb with C. Apparently, she wanted to leave the island ahead of the big storm that's coming this evening. The Hathaway family intended to take her to Hyannis in their motorboat.

However, Norma said they'd just phoned because they'd forgotten their ration book of gasoline stamps that they needed in order to buy fuel for their boat, so she was going to bicycle to the yacht club to give it to them. I volunteered to deliver it instead, since I needed to talk to Edward anyway. Norma hadn't finished scrubbing the floors yet, so she was grateful for my help.

When I caught up with them in Port Newcomb, Edward and C. were eating ice-cream cones, and Mr. and Mrs. Hathaway were talking to some yachtsmen a little further down the dock. I noticed C. was wearing her fancy camera case around her neck and I was so upset I was shaking.

I marched up to her and questioned, "Did you ask Edward to take photos of you on my family's staircase?"

She shrugged and answered, "Yes. After I have them developed, I'm going to send him the prettiest one, so he can take it to college with him."

I told her I couldn't let her do that and I said I wanted her to hand the camera over to me right that instant.

Edward didn't have a clue what was happening. "What's the big deal?" he asked. "Why are you so steamed, Violet?"

"The big deal is that you and C. were trespassing on my family's property, so technically those photos don't belong to you," I said. Then I turned to C. and repeated, "I'd like you to give me the camera, please."

"Why are you acting so strange?" Edward questioned me again.

"She can't help it. She *is* strange," said C. "Ignore her and she'll go away."

She went right on licking her ice-cream cone and looking out over the water as if I were invisible, but I could see her hand trembling. Edward gave me a funny look and he shook his head, so I pretended to leave. But at the last second, I twirled around and pulled the camera case strap over C.'s head and I chucked her camera into the water.

Edward shouted, "Hey! Why would you do a stupid thing like that?"

"Why would *you* take a photo of her on my family's staircase? You should know better!" I shouted back at him, but he wasn't listening. He was crouching down and leaning so far over the edge of the dock that I thought he'd fall in—which would've been tragic, since he doesn't know how to swim. But the camera was beyond his reach and it had already begun sinking.

Mr. and Mrs. Hathaway came rushing toward us and all the other boaters were looking our way. Some of Frankie's classmates who worked at the yacht club were gathering on the dock, too.

"Violet, what in the world has gotten into you?" Mrs. Hathaway asked.

Before I could defend myself, C. lied and said, "She's crazy. She's been telling everyone that Edward likes her, but obviously, he likes *me*, and now she's lashing out because she's jealous."

Right away Mr. Hathaway lectured Edward, who'd given up trying to fish the camera from the water. "What have we always told you about not getting involved with the hired help, Edward?"

Of course, he denied it. "I'm *not* involved with Violet, Father, I swear—and I never have been," he said. "I don't know what gave her that idea but it wasn't from anything I've ever said or done!"

So then Mr. Hathaway turned and lectured me instead. "That was a very expensive camera, Violet. You realize you're going to have to replace it."

"The water won't be as deep when the tide goes out," said Mrs. Hathaway. (I could tell she felt sorry for me.) "Maybe someone could dive in and get the camera then?"

But C. insisted, "No, that's too dangerous. With all these boats coming and going, a diver might get hurt. Besides, the camera's already wet, so it won't work anyway. I just hope this chocolate stain comes out of my clothes."

She said that because when I'd pulled her camera strap over her head, I'd knocked her cone from her hand. There was ice cream dripping down her blouse and skirt. So Mrs. Hathaway gave her a handkerchief to wipe it off.

Meanwhile, Mr. Hathaway wasn't finished lecturing me yet. "I really am surprised at you, Violet Atkins," he said. "Your behavior was rash and destructive. I'm afraid we can't employ you to look after our nephew any longer."

I pleaded with him not to fire me, because I knew it would devastate little Joseph, but Mr. Hathaway insisted, "I can't have someone like you influencing my family."

"You don't understand," I told him, but I couldn't very well give him a public explanation. Even if I took Mr. and Mrs. Hathaway aside and whispered my concern to them, I doubted they'd believe me. I needed to involve the authorities, but I was afraid if I went to get them, the family and C. would have left by the time I got back.

Mr. Hathaway kept harping on me. "You've destroyed C.'s property, you've upset my family and you've humiliated yourself. Young lady, you need to turn around and leave before I ask those Coast Guardsmen to escort you home." He gestured behind me and when I turned and looked I saw three officers at the other end of the dock.

Little did he know, he'd pointed out my solution. I removed the ration book from my handbag and I held it out to him, saying, "Norma asked me to give you this."

When he reached for it, I pulled my arm back and shredded the book of stamps into a dozen pieces and then threw them into the water like confetti. "If anyone's a bad influence on your family, it's C. She's a terrible match for your son and he shouldn't be hanging out with a girl like her!"

It worked: Mr. Hathaway became so angry he summoned the Guardsmen and told them what I'd done. He said, "We aren't interested in filing a report against her, but please take Violet home and tell her father about this. He'll need to give me his ration of gasoline and reimburse C. for her camera."

It was humiliating to be paraded past all the people gawking at me on the dock, and I admit, I was so nervous I could barely hold my head up. But as soon as we were out of earshot from the crowd, I told the Guardsmen, "You can't let C. leave the island. I threw her camera into the water and destroyed the ration book because she's a trespasser. She was

taking photos on my family's staircase leading to the beach this
afternoon. I live in Highland Hills, on Spindrift Lane, a dozen
dunes south of the inlet."

They understood immediately, and one of them went back
to bring C. and the Hathaway family into their headquarters
for questioning, too.

"They understood *what* immediately?" Paige exclaimed in frustration. *She* didn't know what Violet had meant. Why was it such a crime for Catherine to "trespass" on the Atkinses' property, especially if all she was doing there was letting Edward snap a few swimsuit pics of her?

Paige was so exasperated she refused to read any further until she'd figured out what her great-aunt had meant. She reviewed what Violet had said to the Guardsmen that had made them decide to bring the Hathaways in for questioning:

"You can't let C. leave the island. I threw her camera into the
water and destroyed the ration book because she's a trespasser.
She was taking photos on my family's staircase leading to the
beach this afternoon. I live in Highland Hills, on Spindrift
Lane, a dozen dunes south of the inlet."

As she read her great-aunt's words a second time, something stood out to Paige. Violet had emphasized the exact location of her family's property—and that's what seemed to alarm the Guardsmen.

Was there a naval ship in the distant background that day? Paige wondered, recalling that the docent had told her that photos of the military were censored from publication during the war. *C. didn't work for a newspaper, did she?*

Paige reviewed the first few pages of the letter, scanning them for the paragraphs Violet had written about Catherine to make sure she hadn't missed an important clue. But there was no mention of Catherine's occupation.

All Violet said was that Catherine had rude manners, she couldn't laugh off a slip of the tongue, and she was more interested in the soldiers than in Edward...

"Oh, wow," groaned Paige, clasping the top of her head. "Wow, wow, wow, wow, wow! I can't *believe* it."

She'd neglected to read between the lines, as Violet had urged Ernest to do. But when she considered the text again, Paige realized there was no missing the hints: Catherine had thought an American summer staple, corn-on-the-cob, wasn't suitable for human consumption. She'd misspoken by referencing a European shoe size. And she was unduly preoccupied with learning the best path to use when sneaking up to the barracks on Pinnacle Point.

Her voice a whisper, Paige said, "Violet thought Catherine Brown was a *spy*."

Other parts of the letter caught her eye now, too. Violet had said that Catherine was using Edward because of his family's "high standing" on Dune Island. Paige initially had thought her great-aunt had meant the Hathaways' wealth. But now she understood that Violet had actually been referring to the vantage point of their property overlooking the water and the cliffs.

Paige snapped her fingers. It occurred to her that Catherine wanted her photo taken on the staircase because it was so close to where the big military drill was going to be held—the one Joseph had said was canceled abruptly. *Was she going to show the photos to someone who would have sabotaged the sailors?*

She also remembered what Seth had said about people accusing Edward of being a draft dodger and a spy. *I doubt he was*, thought Paige. Otherwise, why would he have risked falling into the harbor to retrieve the camera from the water? Clearly, when Violet had written that Edward was "absolutely

innocent," she'd been indicating he didn't have a clue about
Catherine's espionage.

*But just because Violet suspected she was a spy doesn't mean
she actually was one,* Paige reminded herself before picking up
where she left off:

> *I spent a long time at their headquarters, talking to the
> Guardsmen. For national security reasons, they asked me to
> swear I wouldn't tell anyone—including my father, my
> brother, and even the Hathaway family—about my suspicions.
> (They also indicated that Edward and Mr. and Mrs. Hath-
> away would be cautioned against ever discussing the subject.)
> Because so many people had already thought I'd acted in a fit
> of jealousy because Edward liked C., instead of me, the officials
> requested that I continue the charade.*
>
> *I agreed not to tell another soul what had truly happened,
> with one exception: you. I said I intended to confide in my
> fiancé, who was trustworthy beyond compare.*

Paige stopped reading and gasped. "Violet and Ernest were
engaged?"

She simultaneously felt ecstatic to discover that the young
couple had intended to get married and crushed that they
hadn't made it to the altar. Paige swallowed the lump in her
throat and read the last few paragraphs:

> *At first, they pressured me to change my mind. When I
> wouldn't, one of the officers pointed out, "She's probably
> worried if her fiancé hears she was jealous over another guy,
> he'll dump her."*
>
> *Of course, that wasn't the reason. I know you'd never
> believe I'd ever love anyone but you. The real reason was that
> you and I couldn't keep a secret like that from each other.
> Eventually they must have accepted that I wasn't going to*

change my mind, because they thanked me for doing my part to protect our shores, and they let me go home.

Once I got there, I burst into tears, mostly from relief. But when I told my father the story that I'd promised the Guardsmen I'd tell him, he thought I was crying because I was brokenhearted that Edward didn't like me. He seemed quite worried and I'm afraid it's affecting his health. (On a selfish note, now that I've talked to him about my wish to have a boyfriend, he might be more accepting when I eventually tell him about _you_!)

Frankie wasn't home yet, but when he returned later, he said everyone in town was talking about how hysterical I'd been and what a fool I'd made of myself. He was spitting mad. He claimed he hates living on Dune Island and he can't wait to leave. I think he's ashamed of being associated with me and I can't blame him. He's at such a difficult age; on the brink of manhood but still so juvenile.

He said he was going to give Edward two black eyes for hurting my feelings, but I told him it was all a misunderstanding. I said that I'd mistaken Edward's small talk for flirtation —that I had believed what I wanted to believe because I liked him so much—but that now I realized he was only being polite because his parents employed me to babysit Joseph. I felt guilty about lying to Frank like that, but I would've felt worse if he had gotten into a fight with Edward on my account. There's already so much fighting in the world...

For Frankie's sake, I hope he _does_ leave Hope Haven after he finishes school. I'll miss him dearly, but because of the vicious way people gossip around here, I know he'll never live down what I did. I don't want him to lose his temper and then get a reputation for being a hotheaded thug. I want him to live his adulthood somewhere else, if that's what will make him happy.

Paige's eyes welled. In the back of her mind, she had alternately blamed Violet for shutting out Grandpa Frank, and Grandpa Frank for not caring enough to visit his sister more often. But now that she understood what happened, she realized they'd both loved each other in their own way, despite their estrangement.

Blinking, Paige read on:

It's very painful to know that by swearing to secrecy, I've caused my father and brother deep grief and embarrassment and I've damaged our family's good name. But those difficulties are teeny-tiny compared to the sacrifices that you and all the other servicemen and women across the world are making. So I'm going to bear the disgrace as a privilege, knowing it was the right thing to do—and knowing how proud you'll be that I did it.

A loud sob escaped Paige's throat, but she covered her mouth with her hand and finished reading the letter:

The sky is rumbling and it's supposed to rain straight through until late tomorrow afternoon, so I'd better run out and bury this letter in its hiding place. I'm slipping it into an additional tin to keep it dry, since last time it stormed like this, my words were washed away and it's vital that you can read this.

If I'm not here on Sunday evening, you'll know why. But I'll meet you as soon as I can. Until then, I'll be thinking of you, as I know you are of me...

With love,

Violet

The tears she'd been holding back flowed freely down

Paige's cheeks. The mystery about Violet and the young man who'd given her the locket was solved. Now she knew her great-aunt's version of what had happened during the summer of 1943. But the real story was so heartachingly tragic, she almost wished the past had stayed buried beneath the grand old beech tree.

SEVENTEEN

The plastic inflatable air mattress squeaked when Paige rolled over. She lifted her phone from where it was resting on the windowsill. It was 2:18 a.m. and she still couldn't stop thinking about what she'd discovered in her great-aunt's letter to Ernest.

Even before the incident at the dock, everyone underestimated her, reflected Paige. *She may have been overly protected by her father and content to stay in the background socially, but she was no shrinking violet. She was brave and smart and observant. She did whatever she had to do, to protect Dune Island and her country.*

There was something delightfully ironic about her great-aunt using her own "invisibility" to spy on a spy. And yet, Violet herself hadn't seemed to take any pleasure in reporting Catherine to the authorities, nor had she rushed to judgment. In her letter to Ernest, she'd sounded reluctant to confirm her suspicions. She'd given Catherine the benefit of the doubt until it became clear that she had to speak up.

It took a lot of courage to do what Violet did, thought Paige. *I can't imagine myself or my peers being that brave when we were teenagers.*

There was no denying that Violet had become reclusive after the summer of 1943—but not because of an unrequited teenage crush, or because she'd been publicly humiliated. It wasn't even necessarily because she was burdened with caring for her father or saddened by her brother's departure, although those circumstances must have been overwhelming, too.

Now Paige was convinced that what had triggered her aunt's *real* breakdown was the death of her fiancé. Ernest Danforth, her one and only love. The man she had kept in her heart always and forever, just as he'd asked her to do.

How terrible it must have been to bear her grief—and her secret—alone, thought Paige.

For the rest of Violet's life, she'd remained loyal to her promise to her country. She'd abided by the story that Edward Hathaway had broken her heart by liking another girl. The only person Violet had ever tried to confide in was Ernest—except he'd died before learning the truth.

The boat collision must have been big news across the island. Paige guessed that Violet had heard about it from her brother, Frank, some time after she'd concealed the letter in its hiding place for Ernest to find it.

She could only speculate why, after learning of Ernest's death, her great-aunt had never reclaimed the tin from the earth. *Maybe she was so traumatized, she forgot all about it. Or maybe once he'd died, she couldn't bear to see her final love letter to him again.* It was even possible that Violet had deliberately kept the tin buried in its symbolic grave as a way of mourning Ernest's death and the loss of the life they'd hoped to share together.

Regardless of why she'd left the tin beneath the beech tree, it was clear that Violet had intended the letter for Ernest's eyes only. So now that Paige *had* discovered the letter, she didn't know what to do with it. She was aware that it was historically significant, and she supposed it contained information the government might be interested in protecting.

Yet she couldn't allow her great-aunt's love letter to wind up on display in a museum or for her name to become a footnote in a World War Two documentary some day. Paige rationalized that as far as she knew, it had never been *proved* that Catherine was a spy. *So if I keep the letter, it's not as if I'm withholding evidence of a crime,* she thought. *Besides, there's nothing in it that Violet hadn't already told the authorities.*

Paige felt such a strong responsibility to keep her great-aunt's letter confidential that she couldn't imagine even sharing its contents with her family members.

I don't want to upset Aunt Sherry by saying something about Grandpa Frank that contradicts her beliefs about him, she thought. *And I don't want the guys to crack jokes or Tara to be dismissive about what I've discovered. Besides, it's like Joseph said. Violet had a good reason for not telling anyone what really happened. For eighty years she chose to endure the public's scorn and her private grief in silence—so who am I to set the record straight now, when that's not what she wanted?*

If her family questioned why Paige seemed to suddenly lose interest in Violet's history—especially in regard to her romance with Edward—she could say she'd learned as much as she could about their great-aunt. She'd tell them that she realized some things would always remain a mystery, and she finally agreed with them that it was time to leave the past in the past, and to focus on the present.

Although she had a small worry that someone might find Violet's letter among her own possessions, Paige couldn't bring herself to destroy it. She decided she'd take it home to Illinois until she could come up with an idea about how to safeguard her great-aunt's secret.

I'm just glad I learned about it before I sold the cottage, she thought. *Who knows what would've happened if the new owners had removed the tree and found the tin?*

All at once, Paige's sarcastic parting words to Seth on Wednesday came back to her: "Gee, thanks. This really makes up for the loss of Violet's sewing machine. I can't say how indebted I am to you and your family for cutting down the beech tree."

She felt her cheeks flush with shame as she realized the accuracy of her statement. If it hadn't been for Lexie paying to cut down the beech tree—and for Seth overseeing the clean-up process so carefully—Violet's love letter to Ernest might have been exposed for all the world to read. Paige couldn't imagine a more upsetting violation of her great-aunt's privacy.

Before she fell into a fitful sleep, she resolved to call Seth to apologize and to express her *sincere* gratitude. *I only hope he's open to hearing it...*

Paige pulled into the Highland Hills Library parking lot by 7:00 on Friday morning. She'd thought if she called early enough, she'd reach Seth before he started work, but she only got his voice mail. Rather than leaving a message, she hung up and strolled down Main Street to a café. After buying a scone and coffee, she strolled back and called Seth again.

When she reached his voice mail a second time, she said, "Hi, Seth. It's Paige." Her mouth was dry, and her voice sounded growly. She cleared her throat. "I'd really like to talk to you about something important. Could you please stop by if you go to Lexie's tonight? Or if you get this message before 9:00 this morning, you can call me back. I'll be in range for another hour. After that, we'll probably end up playing phone tag, so it might be better if we speak in person. There's something important I really need to say to you." Aware she was repeating herself, Paige abruptly disconnected.

For the next hour, she sat in her car, sipping her coffee and nibbling her scone as slowly as she could. By 9:00, he still hadn't called her back. She surfed the internet for fifteen minutes. Then for half an hour after that. Finally, she gave up and went to the fish market for cod. *I'll buy extra, just in case Seth shows up at suppertime...*

As Paige walked to the inlet, she couldn't get Violet and Ernest out of her mind. She'd discovered so much about her great-aunt since coming to Dune Island, but she was curious to learn more about Violet's curly-haired fiancé. *Maybe I should ask Marge to help me research Ernest after all?* she thought. *I could give her some vague reason for being interested in him, like that I think he might have become acquainted with my family while he was on Dune Island...*

But what additional information would the docent be able to uncover, other than perhaps his hometown, and a few facts about his relatives? Most of Ernest's immediate family had probably passed away, too. And even if they were still alive, it wasn't as if Paige would get in touch with them, so what would be the purpose?

And now that she thought about it more, she realized she already knew quite a bit about Ernest Danforth. Such as that he must have been very diligent and highly skilled to have been sent to Hope Haven to aid in training US soldiers and sailors. He'd died serving his country—and indirectly, serving the US, too—which meant that he was honorable, dutiful, and self-sacrificing. In her letter, Violet had called him trustworthy beyond compare. His tree engraving and locket inscription showed he had a romantic side, too. And clearly, unlike so many other people, he had recognized and cherished Violet for who she was.

No wonder she loved him—in many ways, they were a lot

alike. When Paige considered how young her great-aunt was when Ernest had died, she thought, *I'd rather be almost thirty-eight and still waiting to meet my soulmate, than to meet him at eighteen but spend the rest of my life without him...*

After circling back and climbing the staircase to Violet's property, Paige turned to peer across the blue, undulating expanse. It occurred to her that Ernest had perished somewhere in the waters between here and Cape Cod.

If my fiancé had died near where I lived, I'd probably move as far away as I could, so I wouldn't be reminded of him every day, she thought. *But maybe Violet wanted to be reminded of Ernest. Maybe seeing the ocean—and the beech tree—brought her comfort.*

That might explain why, despite her hardships and grief—and although she could have made a fortune from selling the property—Violet had never wanted to move. Hadn't Steve suggested that even in her dotage and ill health, she'd still yearned to return to the cottage?

Not only is this where Violet found true love and where she lost it, but it's also where she and her brother were born, and where her parents died. It's where she established herself as a seamstress and continued to run her own business, well into her seventies, Paige reflected. *This is where Violet lived her life—and she lived it on her own terms, regardless of what anyone, including her own family, thought of her.*

Suddenly, the prospect of putting the estate on the market made Paige's stomach turn. *Violet entrusted her home to me. Knowing what it meant to her, how can I sell it?* she asked herself. *And why should I? I love it here, too!*

Paige allowed herself to entertain the possibility she'd been suppressing for almost a week: she could sell her condo and use the money to repair the cottage roof and windows, and replace the furnace, and then *she'd* live in it year-round. Emily had said there was a nursing shortage on the island, so she shouldn't have any problem finding a job.

The solution seemed so simple in theory. In reality, keeping the cottage would put Paige in an untenable position. Her brother and cousins would be furious at her for not selling the estate and splitting the profit with them. To be honest, Paige couldn't really blame them; she agreed that it seemed like a selfish thing to do. She didn't want to create friction within their family. And if she kept the cottage, she'd also have to deal with a lifetime of her brother and cousins making cracks about how she was becoming too much like their eccentric, old-maid great-aunt.

Yet on the other hand, she thought, *Who cares what they say or think? People said a lot worse about Violet. Besides, fair is fair. She left the cottage to the eldest unmarried female in the family, and that's me. I've had to endure the knocks that come with being single, so why shouldn't I reap this benefit?*

Paige made it to the center of Highland Hills within seven minutes and she didn't wait until she was parked to call Mia.

When her best friend answered, Paige didn't even ask how she was before announcing, "There's something really important I need to run by you and I want you to be dead honest about it, okay?"

"Okayyyy..." Mia agreed slowly, sounding nervous.

"I want a divorce."

"*What?* When did you get married?"

"I didn't. Not to a man, anyway. But my brother and cousins have been teasing me about how I'm married to my job. And if they're right, well, then, I want a divorce."

"For a minute there, you had me going," Mia said through her laughter.

But Paige was serious and she explained in a rush, "I mean,

I've tried really, really hard to make it work. I even moved closer to the city and bought a condo I can't afford just so I wouldn't be stressed about the commute. Which did help a little, but not enough. Then I came here to Dune Island and I've been eating and sleeping better, and getting lots of exercise. And the best part is, it seems to happen so effortlessly. I can't tell you how much more relaxed I am—it's amazing. Anyway, I've been making all these plans about how I can continue these good habits and recreate this feeling back in Chicago. But the truth is, I don't think I want to. I'm done."

"With nursing, or...?"

"No, I still love being a nurse. I just want to work in a different setting. Like in a private practice, or even in a school."

"Then that's what you should do. Your health and happiness are too important to sacrifice."

"Yeah, but I don't just mean I want to work in a different clinical setting... I mean I want to work in a different geographical setting, too," Pagie clarified. "I want to work *here*, on Dune Island."

"Then that's what you should do," repeated Mia. "I'll miss you, of course, but I'll visit all the time. Honestly, we'll probably get together more often than we do in Chicago, since you've been too wiped out to socialize..."

"You'd be welcome to visit anytime you want. But the question is, can I really go through with this?"

"What's holding you back?"

"It seems so selfish of me to keep the cottage when my brother and cousins are counting on the money," Paige said.

"Hang on. They *want* the money but that's not the same as needing it," Mia pointed out. "And if they did need it, I know you'd give it to them. I've seen you make one sacrifice after another for your family, including taking a huge pay cut so you could care for your grandmother when she was dying. If anything, your brother and cousins would be selfish for expecting you to give up a cottage where you really want to live. A cottage that's rightfully yours. It's not as if you're *taking* anything from them, Paige. It was never theirs in the first place. It would be different if you sold it and kept all the money—"

Paige cut in, "That can't happen. If I ever sell, I'm required to share the proceeds. It was part of my great-aunt's will."

"Then that cinches it. And actually, they should be happy because the more renovations you make and the longer you keep it, the more it'll go up in value."

Paige was quiet a moment. "I can't believe I'm saying this, but I think I'm going to do it. I think I'm really going to keep the cottage."

"Great!" exclaimed Mia. "When can I visit?"

"Like I said, whenever you want—and I really mean that." Paige looked at her phone. It was nearly 4:00. She was almost late for her appointment, so she'd have to forfeit her chance to call Seth again. "Uh-oh. Sorry, but I've got to go meet the real estate agent and break the bad news to her."

When Paige arrived at the cottage, the real estate agent, a gray-haired woman wearing a khaki linen dress and a colorful silk scarf, was leaning against the hood of her car, facing the water.

She greeted Paige with a warm smile. "Hello, I'm Marianne."

"I'm Paige. It's so nice to meet you. I'm sorry to keep you waiting."

"I'm glad you did. I've been enjoying the view and the air. Even though rosa rugosa are all over the island, I can't ever seem to get enough of the fragrance."

"Mmm." Paige inhaled and exhaled slowly, partly to appreciate the scent and partly to stall. She didn't quite know how to break her news to the woman.

But then Marianne asked, "Are you sure you want to sell this property?"

Paige's mouth dropped open. "N-no," she stammered. "I'm not. I mean, I *don't* want to sell it. I just decided a few minutes ago... How did you know?"

"You'd be surprised how many potential clients change their minds at the last minute. It's as if once they contact me, it suddenly becomes a reality. That's when they know what they *truly* want."

"That's sort of what happened with me. I'm so sorry," Paige apologized. "It must be awfully frustrating for you to have this kind of thing happen repeatedly."

"I'd rather it happens now than further along in the process." Marianne readjusted her scarf, which was blowing in the breeze. "To be honest, it always makes me sad when a client doesn't have any option *except* to sell their beloved Dune Island home, especially one that's been in the family for generations, as yours has. If you don't have to sell, I'm glad you've decided not to."

"Still, I feel awful for bringing you all the way out here for nothing."

"It wasn't for nothing. As I said, I got to enjoy the view... And I got to meet the woman who chased Mark Howe off her property."

Paige cringed. "You've already heard about that?"

"Small island. Word travels fast." She winked. "Good for you."

"You're right," said Paige with a laugh. What did she care if people gossiped about her? "Good for me."

It hardly took Paige any time at all to unpack. As she slid her clothes into the drawers, she made a mental plan for telling

Dustin, Tara, Christopher, and Rick that she wasn't selling the estate after all.

I'll just have to rip the bandage off all at once, she said to herself. *It's like the real estate agent said, better to change my mind now than further along in the process. Like when they've already put down payments on cars or boats or more extravagant weddings than they can afford.*

She expected there would be hurt feelings and anger, and maybe she'd get the cold shoulder for a while. But what Mia had said made sense. Yes, Paige was inheriting the estate because she was single, which might not seem fair. But she was also inheriting the repairs and the high property taxes. If she ever sold the property—and maybe she would, if all her half-formed plans for a life here didn't work out after all—they'd all benefit from the investments she'd made in it. And ultimately, the decision was Paige's to make, regardless of what they thought about it or wanted for themselves.

I'll call them this weekend, she thought. *Once I make sure I can get a job here, I need to hand in my resignation at the hospital in Illinois. I also should let Tara know my availability will be limited for the rest of the summer. I'll still do what I can to help her prepare for the engagement party, but she'll be getting more help from Cami now anyway...*

But the most important thing on Paige's to-do list was talking to Seth. Even though she'd just returned from town, she raced back so she could check her voice mail, but no one had called. She tapped his number, but once again, he didn't answer, so she left another message.

Maybe he just hasn't had time to listen to his voice mail yet. Or maybe he's going to stop by to talk in person after work, Paige tried to convince herself. Yet as she drove back to the cottage, a tiny part of her was worried that Seth might *never* want to speak to her again.

When she passed the Hathaways' mansion, she noticed

several more cars than usual parked in the driveway. *Lexie must be in town again. I suppose that means tomorrow a plane will fly past with a countdown banner,* she mused, feeling less annoyed by the idea than she'd felt last week. *Will only the number of days change or will Grant add a new note this time?*

For supper she made cod and fresh asparagus and brought it to the porch, where an unexpected rain shower was gently drumming the rooftop. Balancing her plate on her knees, Paige picked at her meal, but she was too distracted to eat. She could hardly wait to apologize to Seth for her outburst and to thank him for taking such good care of the tin that held her great-aunt's letters.

Maybe I should go check my messages again, she dithered. *But if Seth comes by while I'm gone, I'll miss him.*

She turned to face the mansion. Nearly the entire lower left wing was illuminated, and so were several of the upper-level rooms. Although it was too dark on the cottage porch for anyone at the house to see her, Paige had a clear view into the Hathaways' large windows and sliding doors. This was as close as she'd come to watching TV since she'd arrived on Dune Island, and despite feeling a little nosy for eyeballing them, she was riveted.

It appeared that most of the people were seated around a very large dining table, but every now and then, Paige caught a glimpse of someone entering or exiting the room. It was difficult to tell from this distance, but the guests appeared to be wearing formal attire—or at least, the women were dressed in long gowns.

I wonder if Seth's up there tonight. Maybe that's why he didn't return my calls—he had to get ready for his family's dinner party, Paige thought, picturing him in a tuxedo. *I wouldn't be surprised if Lexie's trying to set him up with one of her bridesmaids at this very moment.*

The possibility clawed at Paige's imagination and made her

stomach hurt. She hurried inside, changed into her nightgown, and climbed into bed. As she waited for the bilious feeling to pass, she decided that if Seth didn't show up to surf tomorrow, she'd drop in on *him* at *his* house.

"Where's a good 'carrier seagull' when you need one?" Paige grumbled aloud on Saturday morning.

She'd been sitting—and pacing—on the porch since sunrise in eager anticipation of seeing Seth and Blossom heading down to the beach. But it was now 11:00 a.m. and there still wasn't any sign of them. Once again, she didn't want to leave her post to call or look for Seth just in case he came while she was gone.

I've got to install a landline, she thought, mentally adding it to the list of necessities she'd need now that she'd be living in the cottage year-round.

By noon the tide and waves were no longer conducive to surfing and Paige gave up hope that Seth was coming. She was going to have to go to him.

If Violet could be intrepid, I can be intrepid, too, she resolved and drove the short distance up the hill to the Hathaways' circular driveway. She parked behind a convertible that would've made her brother, Dustin, drool with envy.

As she tiptoed past the fountain toward the front entrance, it belatedly occurred to Paige that the Hathaways might not answer the bell, since they weren't expecting her. However, before she reached the portico, the door swung open and a young woman wearing a Harvard sweatshirt and cutoffs stepped out. She had a cap pulled down to her eyes and she was humming.

"Hello," said Paige and the woman flinched visibly. "Sorry, I didn't mean to startle you."

"It's fine. I just didn't hear you—earbuds," she explained, removing them with a smile. "Can I help you?"

"I'm Paige from the cottage down the hill," she said.

"Oh, yeah. Uncle Seth has told me about you. I'm Amelia."

Paige's mouth went dry, imagining what he might have said to his family about her, but then she remembered. "Oh—you must be his niece who named Blossom."

"Guilty." She wrinkled her nose and hunched her shoulders in an exaggerated cringe.

"Blossom's a great name for him," Paige insisted. "And Blossom's a great dog. Usually, he visits me at the cottage on Saturday mornings, but I haven't seen him today. I haven't seen your uncle, either, and I... wanted to discuss something important with him, so I popped over to ask Lexie for his address."

"Trust me, you don't want to talk to her right now. She's got pre-pre-wedding jitters and I swear it's contagious because the entire household is acting strange. That's why I'm escaping." Amelia's candor reminded Paige of Joseph; the Hathaway family was really starting to grow on her. The young woman added, "But I can tell you where Uncle Seth lives."

Fifteen minutes later, when Paige turned into Seth's driveway, he was rounding the corner of his house in her direction, dragging a blue tarp of twigs and shrubbery trimmings. Blossom loped forward to greet her and as she petted him, Paige gathered her nerve to look Seth in the eye.

"I'm glad you're home," she said. "I've been trying to reach you."

He rubbed his chin with his work glove. "I've been busy."

"That's what I figured. When you didn't come to surf this morning, I thought I'd better stop by to make sure we're still on for dancing lessons tonight."

"Sorry, can't. Change of plans."

Paige felt hurt by his terse reply, but considering how she'd acted the last time she'd seen him, she couldn't blame him for shutting her down now. "That's disappointing, but I understand."

"In fact, I'm kinda busy now, too, so..."

Obviously, he was dismissing her, but Paige wasn't going anywhere until she'd tried her best to make amends. "This will only take a few minutes. I wanted to talk to you about the sewing mach—"

Seth interrupted, "I've tried to track it down at the local refuse and recycling centers, if that's what you're going to suggest. But apparently, all the debris has already been transferred to an off-island center. Unfortunately, it's as good as gone."

"Wow, you did that? What a great idea. Too bad it didn't pan out, but thanks for trying anyway." Paige was touched by his thoughtfulness and effort, especially in light of her attitude toward him on Wednesday. "But what I was going to say is that I need to apologize for overreacting when I found out you'd given the crew permission to haul away the shed. I know it was unsalvageable and you were just doing what I'd asked you to do —you were making sure everything was completely cleaned up before I returned."

Seth shrugged. "You had a right to be angry. I should have double-checked with you. Like you said, you trusted me—and I blew it. So I'm the one who's sorry."

He sounded sincere, yet his rigid stance and the way he avoided looking at her directly made it seem as if he was still angry about something. Paige realized if she wanted him to open up to her, she'd have to be vulnerable with him, first. She took a deep breath and said, "Thanks for apologizing, but like I said, I overreacted. I, um, I come from a family who doesn't really value a woman's professional achievements as much as they value her marital status or how many children she has. And since I'm not married and I don't have children, Violet's sewing machine was a very important symbol to me. It was meaningful for different reasons than her locket is."

Seth nodded, but he still didn't meet her eyes or make a verbal reply.

Paige continued. "Anyway, as disappointed as I was to lose the sewing machine, I shouldn't have taken out my frustration on you. I really appreciated it that you were there to oversee the tree removal. You've been so considerate and responsible and there's no one I would have trusted more to take good care of the property."

He removed his work gloves and clapped the dirt off them before stuffing them into his back pocket. When he finally looked directly at her, she could see the hurt in his steel-blue eyes. "Yet you didn't trust me enough to tell me you're selling it."

Paige was stunned. Was that why he was acting so standoff-ish? Because she hadn't told him about selling the estate? Or could it be that he was upset because he thought she wasn't coming back next year?

"The reason I didn't tell you I was selling the property had nothing to do with not trusting you, Seth. I mean, okay, maybe initially I was a little concerned that if Lexie found out the estate was on the market, she'd buy it so she could bulldoze the cottage before her wedding." Paige giggled nervously, but Seth's lips were pinched into a tight line. "Mostly, I didn't tell *anyone* what my plans were because I was concerned if the word got out I'd have real estate agents turning up unannounced—like Mark Howe did the other day. I wanted to get the cottage ready for showings, first."

"Yeah, makes sense," said Seth, but he sounded skeptical. Indifferent. As if he'd just said it to end the conversation. Paige couldn't let that happen.

"And after a while I didn't tell you because... I guess because I was in denial about giving up the cottage. Maybe deep down, I wasn't ready to sell it," she said, but that was only part of the reason. Should she risk telling him the rest of it? After a momentary wavering, Paige added, "I also wanted to hold on to the illusion that a romance was developing between us." Her heart pounded as she admitted it out loud.

"That was no illusion." When Seth looked into her eyes, hope ballooned deep within her chest. Then he said, "But it doesn't matter now, does it?"

He turned to walk away and Paige grabbed his arm. "I'm not leaving, Seth."

"Your choice, but I've got work to do." He pulled free of her grasp and started walking again.

"No. I mean I'm not leaving the island," she said, stopping him with her voice. He pivoted and faced her. "I'm not selling Violet's cottage. I'm moving into it permanently, year-round, not just in the summertime. I plan to work in a medical clinic here." The words were tumbling out so fast that she was stuttering. "I-I-I love Dune Island. I can see why my great-aunt never wanted to leave, no matter how alone she may have been or how many unkind or ridiculous things people said about her." Veering off topic, Paige told him, "You know that tin you gave me? It contained a letter that proved she was in love with the British sailor I told you about, just like I suspected."

"English Ed?" Seth asked, causing her to laugh.

"English *Ernest*," Paige reminded him. Although she'd never share Violet's secret, later she might explain a little more if Seth gave her the chance, but right now she had something else to express. "Anyway, my point is that I'm moving into the cottage permanently and I'd be crushed if you didn't still feel..." She didn't know what word to use that wouldn't sound presumptuous. "If you didn't still feel *neighborly* toward me."

"Neighborly?" A look of wry amusement crossed Seth's features. He motioned to her. "Come here, I want to show you something."

With Blossom tagging behind them, Paige followed Seth into the backyard, through a patchwork of crooked pitch pines and stubby scrub oaks and down a slight decline. About thirty yards behind the house, they came to a stop in front of a single flower emerging from a bed of brown leaves and pine needles.

Standing a little over a foot high, the flower's stalk had two bright green leaves at its base. Its tip was adorned with maroon ribbony sepals that showcased a hanging magenta pouch-like bloom.

"We know that Ernest's favorite flower was a violet. That one's mine." Seth pointed to the bright-pink blossom. "Do you know what it's called?"

"No, what?"

"It's a lady slipper, a rare wildflower that only grows in a certain kind of soil. Specifically, it thrives in fungus. So it's extremely difficult—almost impossible—to propagate them commercially," he explained. "It reminds me a lot of you."

She was taken aback. "You associate me with something that thrives in fungus?"

Chuckling, Seth shook his head. "That didn't come out right. See, it's in the orchid family, and it's considered a symbol of capricious beauty. It's unique and delicate, but it's also a very hardy perennial. Which is why it can survive our harsh New England winters."

It reminds him of me! The comparison was heart-melting.

Seth wasn't finished explaining yet. "When I met you on the ferry, I had just come from a super intense meeting with Lexie and Grant. We'd been arguing about the gazebo and Lexie was in a foul mood, which is why she was absolutely horrible about helping you get your keys from under the car. I was so embarrassed by her behavior I could hardly look at you, but you handled the situation graciously. Most people would have told her off."

"I *felt* like telling her off," admitted Paige.

"Yeah, but my point is, you *didn't*. Instead, you expressed concern about me getting my clothes dirty," Seth reminded her. "You didn't act angry when Blossom trotted across your freshly scrubbed floor, either. And when I mistook you for being the housecleaner you didn't seem insulted."

"Why would I be insulted? I cleaned houses to put myself through college. It might not be the most glamorous way to earn money, but it's a perfectly respectable occupation."

"I agree. But a lot of women I know wouldn't. You're different. You're so unpretentious and sincere and kind. Not to mention, you agreed to have the beech tree removed, which saved me a *huge* amount of time and aggravation."

"Allowing Lexie to cut down the tree benefitted me, too," Paige pointed out.

"Arg. Stop arguing with me about how wonderful you are." Seth's frustration struck Paige as both comical and sweet.

"I just don't want you to think I'm nicer than I am. Or that I'm a pushover or something..."

"Believe me, I don't—I was there when you sent that real estate agent packing, remember? I know you stand your ground when you need to," Seth assured her. "What I'm trying to say is that during a very stressful, contentious time for my family and me, you were like this rare, beautiful wildflower springing up out of nowhere."

Paige was nearly speechless, but she managed to utter, "So, in other words, *neighborly* isn't how you'd describe your feelings for me?"

"No. *This* is how I feel about you." Seth put his hands on her shoulders and drew her to her tiptoes, their mouths blending for a prolonged, delicious moment. Then Paige sank to her heels but he didn't release her.

With embraces like this, who needs waltzing? she thought, and nestled even closer against his chest.

EPILOGUE
LATE SEPTEMBER

"What a summer," Paige remarked to Seth, who was seated beside her on the porch. She still couldn't quite believe all that had happened during the past two months. Not only had she put her condo in Chicago on the market, handed in her resignation, officially moved to Hope Haven, and secured a new job at a local pediatrician's office, but she'd also helped Tara and Cami finish planning the engagement party from afar and she'd hosted what had seemed like a never-ending stream of visitors.

As expected, her brother and cousins initially had been peeved to learn that Paige had decided to live in Violet's cottage permanently, and they'd tried in vain to talk her out of it. Then, for about two weeks, they'd stopped talking to her altogether. However, when she'd texted them a reminder that her Hope Haven residency meant they'd have free accommodations in one of the most desirable vacation spots in the country, they'd realized they'd rather visit Dune Island than hold a grudge against her.

Dustin, Rick, and Christopher had spontaneously arranged a "guys' road trip" to Hope Haven in August, so they could try their luck at deep-sea fishing. They'd hauled a small trailer of

Paige's belongings with them, and they'd even promised to return the following spring to install a few panels of a fence near the shower, which she decided she wanted after all for extra privacy.

She'd traveled back to Illinois with them to attend Cami and Dylan's engagement party, which was preceded by a thunderstorm that nearly sent Tara into an emotional tailspin. But an hour before the event began, the rain let up and a vivid rainbow arced over the lake, ending right above the venue with a more dramatic flourish than Tara ever could have planned. Cami and Dylan were delighted with the festivities, and their guests had a terrific time celebrating the announcement of their upcoming marriage.

Likewise, Seth had reported that Lexie and Grant's wedding was an elegant, memorable, and exceedingly lavish occasion. After seeing the gorgeous photos he'd shown her, Paige had to admit that the beech tree would have altered the flawless effect of the bride and groom posing against the backdrop of unbroken sky and sea. And she was genuinely glad that Lexie had the dream wedding she'd always desired.

A few days after the engagement party, Tara accompanied Paige back to the cottage, planning to stay for a week. But she felt so relaxed, she wound up staying for two. She spoke so highly of her time there that Sherry was already planning a trip the following spring.

Mia had flown to Dune Island twice, each time for extended weekends. She'd barely met Seth when she'd pulled Paige aside and gloated, "Didn't I tell you the next guy you got involved with would be for keeps?"

"We've hardly been seeing each other for a month. It's way too early to say where our relationship is going," she'd objected but she hadn't meant it and Mia hadn't believed her anyway.

"You're going to be married to him within eighteen

months," she'd insisted. "I'll say it again now to save myself the time when you get engaged. *I told you so.*"

Because Steve, the estate attorney, was too professional to gloat or say *I told you so*, Paige had said it for him. "I came to tell you that you were right," she'd announced when she'd stopped in at his office. "I don't want to leave Highland Hills, so I'm keeping the estate and moving into the cottage."

He'd just nodded and grinned. "I'm so pleased you're staying. If you love summer here, just wait until you experience autumn—in some ways, it's even better."

Thinking about his comment now, Paige smiled. She absently twiddled her fingers against Seth's kneecap. "It was wonderful having my family and Mia visit—otherwise I might have felt homesick because I moved so abruptly. But I'm glad it's officially the first day of autumn and now things will quiet down while I'm getting used to my new job."

"You already sound like a true-blue Dune Islander," he replied. "As much as we love summer, we love the fall even more. The tourists are gone, the roads, restaurants, and beaches aren't crowded any longer, but the weather's still warm enough for surfing and swimming."

"Are you kidding me? The weather's *sweltering*," griped Paige.

"Yeah, summer was slow to get here this year and it seems like it's going to be slow to leave. But you're from the Midwest, so I thought you'd be used to weather extremes."

"I thought so, too, but the first week I was here, I had to keep moving all the time to keep warm. Now, it's the opposite. All I want to do is laze around here on the porch where there's a nice breeze." She chuckled. "Little did I know that the best room in the cottage isn't even *in* the cottage—especially now that I've got this comfy love seat and lounge chairs."

"And you can't beat the view," remarked Seth, making a sweeping gesture. "Although I can hardly see the ocean any more. When are we going to do whatever it is that you have planned?"

"In a few minutes. We have to wait until it's completely dark."

"Hmm." Seth wrapped his arm around her and nuzzled her ear. "I like the sound of that."

"That's not what I mean." She playfully elbowed his ribs. "C'mon, get up. We might as well go now."

Seth groaned but he rose to his feet as she darted into the kitchen. She retrieved the tin from the counter and hugged it to her chest.

"What have you got there?" he asked when she returned.

"You'll find out in a minute. Don't forget your shovel," she whispered as they stepped outside, so he grabbed it from where it was propped against the cottage. "Are you absolutely positive no one can see us from your family's house?"

"Yes. The house is closed until they come back for Thanksgiving. If anyone's in the house right now, they're an intruder and we'd hear alarms going off." When they came to a stop where the beech tree used to stand, Seth exclaimed in a hushed tone, "Oh, I know what we're doing. We're digging up something else you think Violet might have left behind, aren't we?"

"No. We're going to *bury* her tin again. I've been pondering how I could protect it without destroying it, and it dawned on me that I should put it back." Paige said softly.

"Aha, I see where I fit into your scheme. You invited me here because I own a shovel, right?"

"Yes, and you have the muscles to use it," she teased before turning serious. "But mostly it's because I wanted you to know how much I trust you, Seth. I'm confident you'll never try to read Violet's letter or tell anyone else where it's hidden."

"You're right, I won't. And tomorrow when I can see better, I'll patch up the ground around it, so no one suspects a thing.

Including Blossom. Last thing we need is that dog getting curious."

When Seth had carved out a space about three feet deep, Paige handed him the tin. He lowered himself flat on his stomach and carefully set it in the ground. Then he stood again and suggested in a reverential tone, "Do you want to say anything before I cover it up?"

Paige hadn't expected to feel this emotional, so she kept her comments brief and general, whispering, "Thank you for being the kind of woman you were, Aunt Violet. I'm glad I got to know you a little bit through your letter to Ernest, but I'm putting it back now because, well, because it's nobody else's business." Paige tried to giggle but it twisted into a sob in her throat. She quickly ended by saying, "And thank you for the cottage. I really love it and it's a privilege to follow in your footsteps by living here. I'm... I'm very proud of your legacy."

With tears in her eyes, she bent down and sprinkled a handful of sandy soil on top of the tin. Seth refilled the hole, neither of them speaking until he'd finished. It was sweaty work, and she could smell his musky odor, now as familiar and appealing to her as the scent of salty sea air and wild roses. He smoothed the ground over a final time and then set his shovel aside and drew her to his chest, asking, "You okay?"

She tilted her chin so she could peer up at him. "Never better. Thanks for helping me to do this, Seth."

He paused to brush aside her bangs, which were nearly long enough now to tuck behind her ears, before he leaned forward.

"My pleasure," he mumbled, his mouth meeting hers.

The vibration of his words on her lips set all her nerve endings on fire and she no longer felt like weeping. Paige kissed him back, slowly at first, but then more urgently, their arms a tangle as they slid their hands over each other's dewy skin.

"Wow. And I thought the *weather* was steamy," she said breathlessly when she finally pulled away. Seth laughed and moved in for another kiss, but she shook her head. "Someone's going to see us."

He persisted. "I've already told you, no one is at home up the hill."

"Right, but you never know who might be watching from the ocean. I think that's a ship out there." She turned her back to him, pointing to a blinking light on the horizon. "It could be the Coast Guard."

Seth wrapped his arms around her from behind, interlacing his fingers over her abdomen. Into her ear he whispered, "Or it could be the Royal Navy."

Leaning back against his chest, Paige imagined her great-aunt standing there, in that very spot, being embraced by Ernest. The beech tree was gone but the moon still shone over-head, the waves continued to crest and tumble, and true love endured, always and forever.

A LETTER FROM KRISTIN

Dear reader,

Thanks so much for choosing to read *Aunt Violet's Locket*. I always keep my readers' enjoyment in mind when I'm writing, so I hope you were thoroughly engaged in this story!

If you did enjoy it, and want to keep up to date with all my latest releases, just sign up at the following link. Your email address will never be shared and you can unsubscribe at any time.

www.bookouture.com/kristin-harper

It's incredibly rewarding to receive reader feedback and I can't tell you how happy it makes me when readers feel as if they've been transported to Dune Island!

If you'd like to share what you liked most about *Aunt Violet's Locket*, I'd be so very grateful if you could write a short review. I value hearing what you think, and your feedback is crucial to helping new readers discover one of my books for the first time.

In addition to sharing a review, you can also get in touch through social media, or my website, where you'll find my email address. I always try to reply as soon as possible.

I truly appreciate your feedback and reviews. And thanks again for reading *Aunt Violet's Locket*!

Best wishes,

Kristin

www.kristinharperauthor.com

 x.com/KHarperAuthor

ACKNOWLEDGMENTS

Heaps of thanks to my family, for always encouraging and supporting me, with an extra measure of gratitude for my sisters and nieces for helping me plot this story—on vacation, no less! (G., you were a *fantastic* research assistant.)

My deep appreciation also goes to the lovely and amazing Ellen Gleeson, my editor, as well as to every single other person at Bookouture who pours their talent into publishing my books. Not only are they the best and brightest in the business, but they're also the kindest.

Finally, thank you to my smart, thoughtful reviewers, and to my generous and wonderful readers—it's an honor to write for you!

PUBLISHING TEAM

Turning a manuscript into a book requires the efforts of many people. The publishing team at Bookouture would like to acknowledge everyone who contributed to this publication.

Commercial
Lauren Morrissette
Jil Thielen
Imogen Allport

Data and analysis
Mark Alder
Mohamed Bussuri

Cover design
Emma Rogers

Editorial
Ellen Gleeson
Nadia Michael

Copyeditor
Sally Partington

Proofreader
Elaini Caruso

Marketing
Alex Crow
Melanie Price
Occy Carr
Ciara Rosney

Operations and distribution
Marina Valles
Stephanie Straub

Production
Hannah Snetsinger
Mandy Kullar
Jen Shannon

Publicity
Kim Nash
Noelle Holten
Myrto Kalavrezou
Jess Readett
Sarah Hardy

Rights and contracts
Peta Nightingale
Richard King
Saidah Graham

Made in the USA
Las Vegas, NV
26 March 2024

87716313R10163